SAM,
THE *HOT DOG* MAN

SAM,

THE *HOT DOG* MAN

Based on the Story of a Legend

CAROL DURACKA

with **William Polacheck**

WESTBOW
PRESS
A DIVISION OF THOMAS NELSON
& ZONDERVAN

WestBow Press books may be ordered through booksellers or by contacting:

WestBow Press
A Division of Thomas Nelson & Zondervan
1663 Liberty Drive
Bloomington, IN 47403
www.westbowpress.com
1 (866) 928-1240

Scripture taken from the King James Version of the Bible.

ISBN: 978-1-4908-6931-5 (sc)
ISBN: 978-1-4908-6932-2 (hc)
ISBN: 978-1-4908-6930-8 (e)

Library of Congress Control Number: 2015901935

Print information available on the last page.

WestBow Press rev. date: 2/26/2015

Dedicated to:
My family—past, present, and future;
the hard-working people of,
"The Back of the Yards;"
And God because,
"You never know what God is going
to do."

CONTENTS

PROLOGUE:
MIND-BOGGLING REIGN

How *much* would I pay? How much would *anyone* pay to travel back in time? If I could spend just one more twenty-four-hour period of time in Chicago's "Back of the Yards," the neighborhood due west of the famous stockyards, I'm not certain how much I would pay to explore those streets of swirling paper-strewn tornadoes, wandering the cracked sidewalks and stained curbs yet again with my dear mother, my brother Lee, and our dad, Sam, "Sam, the Hot Dog Man." How much would I pay in order to inhale the stark aroma of those swimming scorched red hots and spicy tamales Sam habitually dressed and genuinely adored, selling them by the hundreds each and every night? How much would I pay to breathe in the choking vehicle exhaust clogging our throats, ears attuned to the jagged rumble of dark green city buses and wood-slatted cattle trucks, my forehead encompassed by the halo of Sam's ever-present, dimly-lit heady cigar? And how much would I pay to truly understand any one of Sam's countless exasperating secrets?

Hardworking; flag-waving; respectful of old and young alike, fond of drink yet God-fearing, the Back of the Yards' residents of the 1960's faithfully fed the world with their meaty goods, supplying and manning butcher shops galore with choice pork and prime beef. Opening on Christmas Day of 1865, by the turn of the twentieth century the stockyards had grown to 475 acres, at its peak processing 82% of all meat consumed in the United States. Scores of businesses were staunchly etched on every bend of the Back of the Yards, decorating each curve of 51st Street, 48th, Wolcott Avenue, Marshfield, Ashland, and Racine. Its ethnically built churches: the grand-pillared St. Basil's (Irish and German), St. John of God (Polish), Sacred Heart (also Polish), Holy Cross (Lithuanian), St. Rose of Lima, SS. Cyril and Methodius (Bohemian), St. Michael (Slovak) and St. Joseph (Polish mix), along with one lonely Methodist Church where Mother, Lee and I attended, were customarily filled to the brim. These churches' teachings were wholly evidenced by the fact our doors were never locked, the paint behind the skeleton key remaining white against telltale yellowed walls. Heavily scented with cigar, cigarette, and Crisco cooking residue, our apartment was like most others, rented out flats set within towering wood frame structures reaching for the sky. The majority of these lofty buildings had smiled proudly since the early 1900's, the heyday of Chicago's Union Stockyards. Bounded on the west and south by the old meat packing plants, the huge Drover's Bank on the corner of 47th and Ashland watched over the neighborhood like a fat brick king. Depositing their earnings from the animal stock they once so faithfully delivered, cattle drovers negotiated their livelihoods on the same exact spot Mother, Lee, and I also eagerly stood, forever awaiting yet another green CTA bus to haul us home after a Saturday of shopping on 47th Street.

"We've got to hurry," Mother would gently caution, warning Lee and I to make our final selection of cars, paper dolls, plastic barrettes, or a colorful spinning top from the Discount Department Store on Ashland Avenue. "Hurry kids, all the stores close at six." And before we knew it, assorted church bells would sing their heavenly choruses, tolling six times as the sun vanished somewhere beneath the eternal maze of grey concrete. Appearing with a large jangle of metal keys, the small-boned Jewish storeowners bid

Mother a pleasant goodnight, acquainted with her kind words and friendly smile. Along the main shopping district of 47th Street, men in the Back of the Yards would bow and remove their hats whenever approaching women shoppers, politely querying the neighborhood's many nuns. "Good Evening, Sisters. How are all of you doing?" Their polished greeting promptly forced habit-clad nuns to blush, their cheery spirits carried away by the bustle of the passing crowd. Though some groups of Chicagoans disparagingly recall the blood-drenched odor permeating the streets and sidewalks of the Back of the Yards, (particularly on hot humid, July days), to those of us who lived there it announced the familiar tang of home. In fact, this lone characteristic proved to be the quaint reminder, the sheer fact life here resembled no other place in the whole world. No, not in the whole wide world.

Shifting five miles east toward pretty Lake Michigan, her creamy whiffs love to prickle your skin, tickling like Sam's spry fingers. Odds are, my initial glimpse of Lake Michigan's crumpled waves began along Chicago's Rainbow Beach near 79th Street, its lathered currents slapping crudely against the park's rutted, uneven shore. The twirling whitecaps softly soaked the mind, drenched by a mosaic of people, and Sam. Funny how it seems as if certain human beings duplicate nature, their ripple effect echoing long after they have struck land. For Lee and I, our father, Sam, the hot dog man, proved to be such a human being, his peculiar life racing in undefined waves. Yes, millions of undulations snaking and bending, neither of us ever certain whether they be bone-chillingly explosive or distantly calm. Should we bite our lips hard until they bleed, or chew our nails down to the quick in raw fear of the words Sam might say or the deeds he might possibly do?

The salesman of the finest Chicago-style hot dogs this city has ever known, Sam was routinely sheathed with absurdly darkened and unnaturally tough, sun-burnt skin. His body nearly petrified from the thousands of hours he spent in Chicago's harsh elements, concealed within his once lean, six-foot-three-inch frame a host of spirit wars battled, ravaging a mind as quick as the Loop's bounding Lake Street El. Beginning his outdoor catering career the same year Sugar Ray Robinson won the world boxing championship, 1955 was a year of progress, hope, and wonder, particularly for the hustling entrepreneur. Before settling down on Chicago's working-class South Side with his wife, Virginia Mae, Sam had meticulously toured the city's vast unique neighborhoods, fifty wards in all. Muddled memories of numerous other American cities paraded through his senses in contrast, rattling like the coins Sam daily clanged in his silver changer for a quarter of a century. In the end, nothing measured up to Chicago.

But why *would* a man, any man, opt to mount an open-air, three-wheeled Cushman scooter, expertly converted into a hot dog wagon? As this question forever threaded through the recesses of my young mind, Sam's addictive fare routinely satisfied the proud laborers of the South Side's offices and factories during the busy lunch hour, feeding first and second-generation immigrant families, (children and grandchildren of the legendary stockyards) in the afternoons and at night.

Awed by Sam's uncommon profession beginning the day my own five-year-old body also willingly climbed, I curiously hoisted my narrow feet onto a shiny chrome kitchen chair to help my mother, Virginia Mae. Her unlined face beaming like a lit match, Mother's hands never grew tired as she playfully hummed. Watching her slice velvety bricks of the new-fangled, three-flavored ice cream dubbed, "Neapolitan," Mother smacked golden-baked, waffled wafers atop an extensive line of the trimly squared ice cream as tenderly as she swathed my little brother, baby Lee. Carefully enveloping each Neapolitan sandwich inside crunchy wax paper, Virginia's signature smile sealed every package with her own brand of love, a devotion too wrenching for most to understand.

Responsible for a family and escalating bills, the hot dog man soon needed a site of permanence, a base location where he could call his business home. Sam found that home on the gritty corner of 47th Street and Seeley Avenue, directly in the heart of the city's rough and tumble Back of the Yards. In the Back of the Yards, a tavern calls from nearly every corner and the houses are so close you can touch your neighbor's dwelling with a mere extended hand. Here was a site where Sam could be his own boss, be his own man, ascending to the kingship that flowed like a river coursing heavily through his veins. Conveniently positioned across the street from a popular tavern, Sam sold hot dogs for ten cents a piece, juicy tamales for a nickel, and cherry, tangy orange, and grape Popsicles sticking to your hands as well as your lips, for a mere two pennies. Divinely assigned to this extraordinary corner of city pavement, it is here where our existences would be forged, transformed into the maddening lifestyle Sam's loyal customers would never see. No, not in a million years; not in the quarter century of his mind-boggling reign.

Blessed with piercing, golden green eyes, Sam was tough as nails one minute, charming as a schoolboy the next. Lost in acute alcoholism and anger-coated guilt, he cunningly enchanted all manner of men. Becoming fast friends with powerful city officials, Sam was ready to discuss the affairs of state with any politician, from precinct captain to infamous Back of the Yards' community organizers. But along with Chicago's unpredictable weather, above all Sam wrestled himself. Trying to understand Sam's countless enigmas seemed futile. But then came the day when I was *determined* to understand, bringing much sought-after peace, refreshing as a silky Lake Michigan breeze.

Perhaps you have heard people around the world smugly boast, "There is nothing like a Chicago hot dog." I, however, would like to amend this famous adage by saying, "There is nothing like 'Sam, The Hot Dog Man,'" known to my brother and I as our father, our dad. Incidentally, why *would* a man, any man, choose to mount that clumsy, gas-spitting Cushman scooter? And how *does* one understand such a man as Sam? The answers to these questions require understanding, resolved only when one's life is unraveled—ripped apart piece by precious piece.

Here's how I have come to understand, forgive, love, and unravel the mystery of our father, "Sam, The Hot Dog Man."

PART ONE
Early Tremblings

LYNN - (Present Day)

My name means: "Dwelling by the torrents"

CHAPTER 1

Some Good

Even in the hardest times, there always seemed to be *some good* while living with my dad, Sam. Good can be unearthed like a buried treasure, akin to golden coins of hope. So when Sam, the hot dog man, did something good, it gave me hope. At three years old, I had witnessed Sam drunk and roaring through our apartment doorway like a lion; a few months later, he brought me home a special toy. That act of love somehow brought me hope. Then, Sam took me for an outing to one of the city's largest parks, as well as to the bowling alley where he often worked. When he lugged home our first real Christmas tree, it again gave me hope. It gave Mother hope as well. Sam often brought home all kinds of treats he and his Greek partner, Nick, eagerly sold, and whenever Sam haggled deals with the Dressler's cake man, Mother, my brother, Lee, and I thought we were in heaven, as we feasted on mushy chocolate, chewy strawberry, and creamy vanilla cake. Sam rode the bus downtown with us to see the new Montgomery Ward's store on State Street, and later he brought home a puppy for Lee and me, a crazed, shaggy-haired mutt named Candy. Although Sam had often squandered his profits on gambling and drink, there were always hot dogs stashed in the freezer, ready to eat in a pinch. And when it came time to playing with Lee and me, Sam stretched out his sturdy legs, giving us rides as if we were on a seesaw in the park. And boy, did we ever have some heart-throbbing games of checkers. Sometimes, I would even beat Sam.

When school began in the fall, Sam had carefully saved up enough money to buy new clothing and school supplies as we began our new grades in elementary school. And on many Saturday nights, Sam, Lee, and I watched the bowling tournaments, Sam expertly commenting on all the bowling tricks and the great men who performed them. *Yet more good.*

And then came the night Sam brought home a black-and-white television set he had won in a game. My dad gave that television to me! *More good.*

When I was in eighth grade, my friends wanted to go to a "charm school" at a huge department store downtown. Sam readily furnished the money, saying, "That would be a good thing for Lynn." When it came time to move (just as I was just preparing to attend high school) Sam heartily refused to live in a particular area rampant with racial strife, fearful of the potential violence that might have affected me. "Always carry at least a dime in case you need to make a telephone call, Lynn," Sam had often warned. "And carry your bills in your shoes; always watch your billfold in Chicago," he thoughtfully suggested. And when it came time to meet my fiancé's parents at a dinner in their home, Sam made it a point to get to know my new family. As he gave me away at my wedding, with a hundred emotions rolling around my soul, Sam was there.

At the time my first child was born, Sam visited me in the suburban hospital where I had given birth, "She sure looks healthy," Sam remarked with a tight smile.

While my heart began to soften concerning my relationship with Sam, one day I put my arms around his waist and said, "Hi, Dad." Shocked, neither of us knew what else to say. *Good again.*

Some years before he had left Chicago for good, Sam had gone to the store to buy a fingernail polish dryer and some chocolates for my birthday. The hot dog man had selected those gifts especially for me. I have never used that fingernail dryer, and don't ever plan to. And when Sam lay on his deathbed and I placed a telephone call to him hundreds of miles away, as we talked, an ever so tiny tear dripped from his failing eyes. *Extra special good.*

All that good could never be forgotten, even in the face of what seemed to be so much bad. My name, Lynn, means "dwelling by the torrents." Since God has changed my identity from dwelling *in* the torrents to dwelling *by* the torrents, I continue to see my father Sam's bad altered into *more and more and more good.*

But then there was the not so good.

RALPH

My name means: "Wise and strong"

CHAPTER 2

If I Catch You

Each distinctive nerve inside Albert's body soared with the force of the loudest blast known to man. Hushed secrets were guarded like costly diamonds, tumbling within the ready-to-explode man. His chest pounded like a workman's sledgehammer, and his gait sped as fast as a military cannon. His plump cheeks had grown tomato red, and his skin roasted like an open fire. Panting to a skidding stop, Albert realized there was no place to hide, no country to turn but the Promised Land. Yanking the young nobleman from his native country with an invisible cord, America's scent pulled him as powerful as a team of oxen.

Playfully circling the bobbing steamship, swooping seagulls wailed around Albert's throbbing head. *They are crying like the fools I left behind.* Only the Atlantic's billowing waves, lobbing its ocean-salted bits upon his bristling skin, eased the former nobleman's nightmarish flight. In the distance lay, The United States of America. It was in *that* nation where every man, woman, and child possessed "liberty and justice for all." But when evening came, Albert found it impossible to shake off the old life; he just couldn't do it. In the old life of the royal Bavarian court, night was day and day was night. Eating, drinking, gambling, and dancing while the moon brightly shone, and afterward sleeping until midday, was the rule rather than the exception.

"Get up! It's time for morning Mass," Albert's mother coarsely snapped. Shaking her dapper son from the comfort of his ornate bed, Mass was held every day of the year. Unless illness prevented the nation's elector from attending Mass, he then heard it within his private quarters. Yet, when the carnival season graced the palace, the exquisite balls and lush banquets lasted from dusk until dawn. But all that was *before* the fall of the monarchy, before their shimmering world had suddenly collapsed.

So when the midwife's cotton apron grew spattered and crinkly on election Tuesday in 1924, I have often speculated how my father's life altered at the announcement of "Albert, you *gut* a boy." I was plump as a holiday goose and jolly as a flittering chipmunk, but after the delivery of their two pie-faced little girls, the news of my birth wobbled my parents' senses. My radiant eyes, and thick cheeks haunted my father something fierce, heavenly sights blasting uneasy spirits within.

"Ralph," Mother had revealed some weeks earlier. "If it is a boy, his name will be Ralph."

All dolled up in pressed pants and a starched shirt as was his normal custom, Albert muttered my full name aloud. "Ralph William Polaieck. *Rolf Wilhelm*," he dryly tested, he and Mother floating in and out of their guttural tongue. Words buzzed throughout the Victorian-styled rooms like lighthearted bees, mulling through pungent smoke as Father flicked the ash of his lit cigar into a gold-edged porcelain bowl. Carefully adding to the slimy, sour-smelling chewing tobacco spat out several minutes earlier, with the flair of a grand king Father pranced around the creaky floors of our modest Minnesota frame house, thinking he was the "cat's miaow," God's gift to America. My two sisters, wide-eyed Katrina and timid, gaunt-faced Mary, took a quick peek at their new baby brother, a nearly bald Ralph. "Ralph Polaieck," uttered Albert once again, his slender nose pointy and scrunched. Firmly clenching his fists of pencil-long fingers until a purple vein nearly popped from the side of his bucket-wide neck: *They boasted the streets of America were made of gold—gleaming silver and piles of gold. I could strangle those double-crossing dummies.*

Soon enough, my sunny, milk-fresh face constantly reminded Father of the awful American hoax. To Father, my radiating gleam proved shimmery as mocking ghosts. His smallish eyes grew locked and surging, the twin balls remote as the nation he had so unwillingly escaped. "I used to *give* orders now I do nothing but receive them," Father groaned, filling the small room with billowing smoke. "Trudging three miles each night to the mill in the rock-hard, frosty snow, I do," he constantly complained with a misshapen scowl. Gone were the servants, the silk, the paintings, the rich tapestries, and all the gold. It had all evaporated like the swiftness of Father's dwindling cigar, the rolled tobacco too tiny to hold. Smashing the cinder-like remains deep within his pipe, Father crushed the sweet-scented bits roughly into a small cake so not even one ounce went to waste. A night watchman at Mankato's mill, the giant building was a multi-storied flourmill, shipping wheat north to the Twin cities of Minneapolis and St. Paul.

"You live on the other side of the tracks," was how our uncle with slick, parted in the middle hair described our small house. But not far from our house was Sibley Park Zoo. There, the curious zoo animals silently beckoned all the neighborhood kids to stop and enjoy their charm. Her cloth coat scraping against sturdy bare ankles, my Mother, Louise, often hauled the three of us to the park's zoo opposite the winding Minnesota River. Marble-eyed goats, pillow-fat, tongue-pink sows, and pole-necked geese gawked at the four of us with pebble-shaped glassy eyes. But one day a fearsome flood stole these beloved animals. Suddenly, our enchanting zoo slid into the dreary deluge as the Minnesota River rose high like Mother's bread, our pretty play park callously rinsed away. It gave us all the heebie-jeebies as Father spit into the porcelain bowl and spouted out,

"New address, new address," Father yapped, ordering the three of us to repeat our new address a few months following the devastating flood. "Say your new address," he barked. "Repeat it until you have it learned, ... perfectly." Moving into the big cucumber green house built in 1908, our three-bedroom, two-story frame was lodged on the corner of a slight North Mankato hill. "It looks like your prayers have been answered, Louise," Father reveled in his purchase. Tilting his head cockily toward Mother, her wiry hair was tied loosely behind her neck, wrapped in an unruly knot. "Holy smoke. Your daily visits to Divine Rosary Church have not been wasted," he smirked. Albert's familiar sharp-angled smile dipped down deep, his bottom lip diving like a graceful white heron seeking his prey.

Mother *never* missed a single Mass, faithfully attending Divine Rosary Church every morning. Founded by two priests only weeks before I was born, Divine Rosary was Mother's anchor, Mother's visible rock weighting her through all manner of terrifying storms. Driving in their open car, the two priests carefully noted how the land surrounding Divine Rosary had once consisted of only twin wagon tracks meshed within a tangled mass of high weeds. At their initial viewing of the coarse Minnesota ground, the faith-filled priests boldly declared that it didn't look like much, but God willing, that would all change. And that was exactly what happened. An enormous success with North Mankato's, (*Mahkato,* an original Dakota Sioux word meaning "Blue Earth") large German population, how happy Mother became when I was made an altar boy at Divine Rosary.

Raised on a Heron Lake homestead in western Minnesota by her Austrian parents, my grandparents, Carl and Alice Leipold, Louise was the youngest of five sisters. Because of a near deadly Dakota Sioux raid on the family's cabin, Mother became friends with God at a tender age; the homestead's farthest border was dotted with Sioux teepees.

"I vas alone in de cabin one damp afternoon," Mother often recalled, remembering the event with a wrinkly brow. "I dare not breathe as vone of several braves riding horses burst through the cabin's wooden front door."

Tumbling beneath the low rope bed, Mother's legs shuddered uncontrollably, quivering like tree branches in a Minnesota blizzard. Silent as a gathering basket, oh how young Louise begged God for her life. Rummaging through the family's belongings, one of the braves snatched whatever he pleased. The whole tribe then sprinted away on horseback, fleeing into the far brush. And ever since that fateful day, Mother's faith was planted staunchly in God. Not halfway, but staunch.

Hiking the long distance to work each night then trekking around the flour-dusted grounds of the mill, as the company's night watchman Father's back and bones were constantly aching and stiff. "Euw," he moaned, rubbing his lower back. But all the hair on my body instantly stood at attention whenever I thought of Father down there in the basement, asleep. Yes, Father slept in the basement instead of on the second floor with the rest of us.

"Your *Fader* must sleep on dat old kitchen door in *da* bas-e-ment," Mother tersely explained. Her eyes dull as the braised beef she stirred for our supper, one night after he had left for the mill I promptly beat it downstairs for a look see. Positioned on heavy, whitish grey cinder blocks, the old wooden door Father used as his bed had a thin blanket covering it. A small, matted-down pillow was situated neatly at the top. Peering about the dimness, the basement walls slunk in like a cave. Its musty odor desperately tried to speak, attempting to warn me something was wrong. Something with Father was terribly wrong. It became more noticeable when his peculiar bursts of laughter started to unexpectedly explode. Chewing his snuff Father would bitterly exude:

"Big dummies," he blurted into the feverish air. "Big, giant dummies."

"We got the eleven clams! We got the money," I rattled on one day to a few of my pals. Tufts of my butter-colored hair flapped like a flag below a crisp, blue Mankato sky. At nine years of age, I had just finished the fourth grade at the golden brick Divine Rosary School. In 1933, the state of Minnesota had no such thing as a driver's license. So piling into the sturdy Model A truck we had just bought with our own hard-earned dough, my pals and I took turns driving the choking vehicle. Off we clattered over roads leading from Mankato proper, then back to North Mankato where we all lived. The curved bend of the Minnesota River separated the two towns, the silver-green waterway waiting for us to dip our fishing poles into its steady flow. Summer's breeze lured like fizzy soda, tempting us to cast our lines. On the hottest of those July days the iceman felt sorry for us kids, chipping off frozen sections of ice to cool our tongues, wetting our panting throats.

"Thanks, mister," we yelled, waving to the iceman as the fresh liquid gushed down our dry throats, then bathing our broad chests. In five minutes flat I forgot Father's snarled glare as he ripped open the small check he received each month from the bank. After the crash of '29, all the money Father had carefully saved was suddenly gone. The same thing had happened to all my pals' folks so everyone winced through town with the same piercing knot strangling them. Although the Depression never seemed to end, I still had my paper route. Hustling *The Mankato News* in the early morning hours before school for some years, that was how I got enough clams to chip in to buy the Model A.

"Give us a couple bottles of nip, Bub," Father would direct the store clerk every Saturday morning, a sharpness knifing his strict tone. Recognized mainly by his familiar crooked grin, with time, Father's eyes had grown increasingly hard and cold like the iceman's glistening pieces of chipped ice. Slapping down enough coins to pay for our brew, his shoes were shiny as the noonday sun. Father always dressed as nifty as the president. Jeepers, what great suits he wore! Handsome as any moving picture star or high horse government official, not a single spot spoiled the most expensive garments Father's paycheck could afford. Gurgling down the amber alcohol, we swallowed together just like in the "old country." Feeling as turned-out as Albert himself, I enviously watched Father puff on his fragrant cigar; mumbling a few curse words in the old country dialect, he then expertly spit. "Heeeh," he exhaled, allowing the alcohol to loosen his frazzled nerves.

Beneath North Mankato's dusky streetlamps, the lazy summer turned speedily into fall, the leaf-scented days disappearing into the sullenness of another frozen Mankato winter. Slogging through a sleeting rain, I sure hoped the nuns would be happy in class. Whenever Divine Rosary's nuns were smiling, the whole school seemed to smile. But when they were in a sour mood, I could hardly wait to go home where Mother's oniony beef soup simmered on the kitchen stove. I would even welcome the staggered strains of *Wagner* Father often tuned in on the radio. Eerily penetrating the tight air, Father's stinging cigar fumes fused with vinegary, steamed *kraut*.

"Honor thy Father and thy Mother, this is the commandment with a promise." I had heard God's order from the nuns for so many years I often envisioned Moses' stone tablets inside my sleep. Yet I also pictured Father's sneering stare, his voice brassy as a steam engine's screech, and his face resembling dark, thickened clouds. Stomping the floors without reason, he clomped through the house roaring like a lion, uttering creepy, mixed-up words. Rigid as the door he rested upon, whenever Father disliked his food, his eyes enflamed as coal fire.

"This food is no good!" He shouted in stabbing rage. "I want real food, not some scratch." Scaring the living daylights out of us, Father hurled his whole platter onto the wooden floor, causing the four of us to scatter and hide. At age fourteen I was muscled and trim, playing football for my high school team. But then, on one mad day everything shriveled up as tiny as the jagged gravel along the Minnesota River. The pleasant rustle of the tree branches outdoors, the din of the slight river breeze, even the traffic's daily drone abruptly stopped. My heart began to pound, pulse, and beat; I felt its rumble inside my bones. Father's skin-tingling footsteps sprinted ever so close, closer, and closer ...

"If I catch you I will kill you!" Father's threat blasted the house with the force of a flying mortar. Our quarrelsome clash had blanketed my soul like the cruelest north wind, and all my senses became frozen as Canadian ice. My clear vision blurred. My sharp ears rang. My broad mouth was parched, and my sturdy fingers were taut as a fishing line. Kill? *Kill!* Stuffed with the medley of death was my long titled nose. *I know he could do it. I've got to high tail it out of here.* Chasing me like some scoundrel around the first floor of our sparsely furnished home, that day Father was a rabid bulldog and I was his hunted prey. Racing around and around our claw-footed oak table like a trotting pheasant under the gun, Father's stick-long fingertips nibbled at the collar of my shirt, obsessed with starving hate. Certain death awaited me—I just knew it! An inch within nabbing my collar inside his ogre-like grip, I would have been dead if he had caught me. Bounding around and around the oak table like furious beasts, my sides burned as if they were about to split open. *Do it now!* I heard the warning as plain as day. Darting straight as an arrow, I contorted like a man on fire, right out the front door.

"Oh dear Godt!" Mother shouted, her brain thrashing as fiercely as my frazzled chase with Father. Fearing her whole heart would drop onto the quaking floor, "He's lost hez mind," moaned Mother. Sputtering her own brand of chopped English into the air, "And now my son, my only son, haz run avay," she exclaimed, relaying the whole scene to me some months later. Raking her chaffed fingers over the bark-hued strands of her coarse hair, with a flat frown Mother nervously added, "And I didn't know iv you, Ralph, vere ever koming back." Attending Mass the following day, Mother's legs quivered like the sputtering candles set before the altar of her beloved Divine Rosary Church. *Help me, God. I didn't know my husband—I didn't know he would crack.*

Alone. Alone! Alone? Rifling through my pockets, our green house on the low hill dwindled to a mere dot. I didn't look back as the setting sun flickered inside my dazed eyes. Though a few inches of snow crunched lightly beneath my feet, a Boy Scout knife soothingly cooled my burning right hand. I had that, some Bull Durham, and the clothes on my back. My soul was dead with fear, and my skin crawled as I prayed. Plastering on a spongy grin I exhaled and wondered: *What could I do next?* Ever since I was a young boy I'd been enamored by the huffing trains skittering along the tracks of Union Depot. So that night I judged their blunt pull, my only chance of getting away. *I'd never let him catch me, never.* Watching the squeaking train cars cough then slow, I sucked in air and bent my legs, leaping high and strong as a bullfrog. Tumbling into the boxcar like a battered container of squashed fruit, the train slowly picked up speed. *CLANG! WHOOSH!* Tart sulfur fumes filtered into the drafty boxcar where my brains were still rattling. My paws and pants had become slimy from matted grime and shivering sweat.

"Where ya goin' son?" a greasy-haired farmer asked, his half-dozen family members huddled around the old coot like wide-eyed cattle. Their bodies stunk like overripe trash and their overalls were badly torn, randomly speckled with black oil and smashed bits of food.

"West, out West," came my rapid reply. Tossing the family a rickety smile and a shrug, my chest tightened as thoughts floated through my aching temples. "Far west," I smartly added.

"We's headin' to Californie," a younger fellow piped up, tipping a small jug of water through limp saggy lips. "We's don't hav anyting left, kid. Not a ting."

Salvaging dark brown tobacco bits from my Bull Durham sack, though a tiny section of the bag was ripped because of my awkward plunge, I extracted a small white paper to prepare a smoke. My hands were pasty, colorless as the dusky twilight. Known as "The Cheapest Luxury in the World," the pressed tobacco was crammed tightly inside my muslin drawstring sack, the natty bag fitting neatly within any one of my pockets.

"Hey kid," the cloudy-haired granddaddy lifted his chin to speak. "See ya got ciggies. We'll trade ya some grub for one or two of 'em tobackee ciggies."

"Good enough for me," I answered, my stomach rumbling in time to the shifting boxcars. As the shadowy miles bumped warily by, I jammed salt jerky and corn pong far into the back of my mouth. It was nothing compared to Mother's old-fashioned cooking—juicy sides of beef and succulent fruit pies placed regularly upon our big oak dining table, the very same table …

"Butt me, will ya?" The farmer nudged the puffing granddaddy. Closing my eyes, a picture of our two-story house rushed into my mind. Mother's homemade dinners angrily pierced my heart, stabbing like the sharpest pine needle in the countless passing forests. My bedroom, however, stood empty.

Father's routine had been forever broken, but so had mine. Yet, it seemed as if the trip ahead allowed me to arrange the uneven pieces of my life, *the best a fourteen-year-old boy possibly could.*

CHAPTER 3

Making Camp

"Hey, why's the train stopping?" My question spewed out in a sputtering cough. Tipping my body toward the thrashing ruckus outside the rocking boxcar, my eyes were still groggy with aged dust. The commotion tensed my limbs; my dusty pants and shirt were wedged awkwardly against my sticky, reeking skin. Wanting to upchuck more than anything in the whole world, I closed my left eyelid, peeking through a slim gap of the halted car. Bitter coal exhaust painted my parched throat with its sooty brush, our makeshift toilet in the far corner was urgently filled to overflowing.

"See anythin' out there kid?" questioned the wandering farmer. "Ya know, could be this here engine is needin' water," he guessed. "Or, could be stray cattle on the tracks. Or maybe they be switchin' cars agin," the unshaven man idly muttered with a yawn. Stretching his bony legs with a faint whimper, the holes in his denim overalls had ripped even further. Meeting my gaze, the farmer whispered a solemn warning through his dense beard. "Don't make a sound, kid, this ain't no game. Shh, someone's comin'."

GONG! BANG! BONNNGG! I got a load of the clatter hanging in the boxcar as the metal bar twanged against the cars' bottom steel rims. The continuous shrill chimed like a thousand church bells inside our ears, echoing against the solid steel and wood.

"Train dick, Ralphie boy," the sullen farmer sniffed the dank air, his eyes worn and muddy. Unbolting the groaning door a precious inch, a hard-eyed railroad detective evenly scanned the contents of each of the resting hoppers. "He's a real live wire this one is. That meat sure got one filthy mug. Yeah, train dick, kid."

"I'm takin' off, pal," I said in a whisper. Pivoting on my toes like an engine on a roundabout, my keen sight was fixed toward the fire-lit hobo camp I noticed a few minutes earlier. "See ya," I gulped, considering the railroad car's high slope. With a single breath, I jumped down feet first. Sliding smugly into the moist earth, my legs raced like they did on the football field.

"Hey kid, you git back here," hollered the train dick. "I'm gonna break yur arms, boy!" Tearing off like greased lightning, the hobo camp's restful aromas drew me like a housefly into their musty wonderland. *Run to the camp; gotta keep running. Take that you huckleberry.* I was wheezy and winded when a motley crew of men muttered behind some brush, slowly coming into plain sight. Along the stumpy banks of the Platte River, I was finally out of reach of the screwy detective. Sniffing Nebraska's main river, the Platte was long, leisurely and shallow, much of it nothing more than a braided stream, slapped with a swampy bottom. Puffing so hard I could barely stand, my mind buzzed like a disturbed beehive. Finally making eye contact, the hobos were unfazed.

"Where ya all from, boy?" Someone yelled. Although I could barely make out his form through the tangled brush, my soul shifted to full awareness.

"Minn-esssota," I stuttered, the scent of my state's crystal clear lakes snaking through my battered nostrils. The acrid stench of seared beans, stale alcohol, smashed butts, and putrid body odor permeated several wooden crates encircling the crackling bonfire, beating away the faint Minnesota scent. A few feet away, scores of bean cans were amassed into soaring piles, mounted as tall as the smokestack of Father's mill. A handful of roustabouts were shuffling around the smoky site, the river's fusty reek quietly mingling with the roasting beans, soggy soil, and dirty sweat. "I was ridin' the cars," my teenage voice jiggled, retreating instantly to my altar boy faith. *Dear Jesus, Mary, and Joseph.* "Been ridin' for awhile."

"Gotta smoke, kid?" A lanky man questioned, his forehead and left cheek smeared with rubbings of Platte River mud.

"Yeah, and some jerky. I'll trade ya for a squat," I answered, trying to sound loose as a goose yet trembling like a bundle of wheat dumped in an open field. Wrapping up inside a scratchy feedbag for warmth, on my first night at the camp I was enveloped as a dead man so no one could get at me—no one. For the first time I thought: Could Mother, *or Father,* have believed how I was swathed in smutty old rags and tatters of oil-scented cloth, trying to fall asleep in a "squat," a tiny section in the squatters' shack made from scrapped beer boxes and mildewed board? After wiggling like a worm night after night on stinking boxcars, I had grown alert to the slightest rustle. W*ere the hobos helping themselves to my jerk and dried up corn pong crumbs, the only food I had left in my sack?* The high-pitched, erratic tones of a harmonica disturbed my sleep, awakening me well past midnight. The muffled swish of fishing lines expertly met the sparkle of the flickering fire's pungent sizzle. "Sure am hungry," I gaped at the frying grub. Eagerly following its' smoky trail, my eyes were on the verge of watering. An ogre-eyed chap squinted through the blackness, our sight divinely linked through the gooey smoke.

"Here kid, I'll fire you up some of that 'ole fish we just nabbed." Grabbing a handful of coffee grounds from a large burlap bag, the dwarf-high man dipped a dented gallon tin can deep into the lazy Platte. Tossing in the grounds then expertly placing it on a flattened sheet of steel, he plopped down on a crate waiting for the coffee to boil. Watching the fish hunks hiss and shrink over the crackling fire, the ogre-eyed dwarf's hand suddenly produced a rusty serrated knife. Clutching a couple of the sizzling fish hunks with the knife's spiky point, ogre eye whacked a hole clear through its charred underbelly. Its juices trickled like water, bathing the weedy dirt beneath our feet. Snatching a nearby stick, the hobo politely handed me the twig of cooked meat. "Here kid. I'm only bein' kind to ya 'cause I was just like you once, right before the century-markin' war. I don't wanna see ya get a bum rap, okay?"

Furrowing my brow, "What century-markin' war?" I naively posed.

"You sure dense, kid. The Spanish-American War, what else? Almost killed me, it did. But I taint 'bout to fight no other silly war, got a war right here jest tryin' to survive." Munching on some charred fish bits, the hobo's nearly hairless head shone like a miniature moon in the twisting shadows. Scores of small hollows were punched into his skull, imitating the craters of the full moon overhead. Swiveling his head directly toward me, "Ya know, kid, we can't stay in this here camp too much longer. Naw, the weather she's a changin' and I ain't 'bout ready to freeze any more of these toes the good Lord gave me."

"What's your name?" I asked, the only question I could think of making me look a might better than a stupid sap. "I'm Ralph."

"Names Al."

Al! Albert! My mouth fell ajar with thoughts of Father, hearing his name once again.

"Say Ralph, you okay? Hey, ya sure talks funny. Where you from?"

"Up north, ... Minnesota."

"Cold up there, eh? I come from Oklahome but been 'round all these states pert near fifty years. Yeah, jest ridin' the cars. No worries 'bout water though, there always be plenty o' that." His bare feet were brushed black as a beer barrel with grunge and his paper-thin lips coiled in a funny way. "Take a good look at these here toes, Ralph from Minnesota."

Each one of Al's ten toes resembled the blackened ends of the scattered twig stubs strewn all over the riverbank. The sight nearly caused me to gag. "Eh, what happened to your toes, Al?"

Giggling like a dame, Al hacked for several seconds. "One night snow come up out of the north and froze 'em toes solid as ice. Ain't nothin' kid. They do hurt now and agin," his eyes narrowed, bowing gently toward the ground. "But we make our own medicine, kid. Pass me that dere big medicine jug. And say, take a swaler if ya like."

Swigging the liquid for a taste, my throat instantly smoldered like the hobos' campfire as it traveled to my belly, the brew reeking like paint thinner. "Heh, heh. See ya ain't used to the good stuff. Still wet behind the ears, is ya kid? Taint's got no time to break in any new kid, specially when I got my own speculation to do," Al's mouth broadened, his wrinkled expression drinking in the river's mellow breeze. "Why don't ya get in that hole over dere and go to sleep, eh? Be better for ya in the mornin'. Yeah Minnesota Ralph, jest git in your hole."

Unlocking my eyes in the dawn's hazy light, I blinked several times, trying to erase the stench. Someone had stolen my Bull Durham sack along with all the papers. *Was it the lanky fellow, those two dumb mute brothers, or maybe even Al?* Taking pity on my desperate search, another of the hobos looked sideways then divulged, "We share alls we got here till it's gone. But don't worry, kid," the hunched-back man added. "Jack'll be back here after breakfast with some good tobackee." Chomping down all I could on a makeshift table made from nothing more than a collection of large splintered crates and a plywood top, the fellow named Jack finally showed up. His pockets were loaded to the gills with butts; he was also carrying a whole fruit pie and some orange-colored preserves. After a few minutes, Al returned to the table, giving me the low down on Jack's doings.

"See, kid," Al leaned in, his deadened toes covered by a mismatched pair of washed-out boots. "Jack goes into town, headin' straight for the city bank smack in the downtown square. Gettin' all the leftover butts outta the sand tray, he then looks for the painted "X" mark on any fence post where kind folks are willin' to help us hobo fellers out. That's how we gets all kinda goodies—pies, potaters, jams, few days' old bread, anythin' else no one wants. We sure can use it all, yeah." Licking his lips smeared with the peach preserves, "We take turns, kid, see. Tomorrow be yer turn, Ralphie boy. But remember this," burped Al. "To be a bum you don't need much. Just need somethin' called Entrance Fee. Once you got *that*, kid, someone will always trade you up for somethin' you need. This here weather she is changin' like I said, and weez all soon be goin' south," he pointed downward. And by the way, kid, don't take any wooden nickels!" In less than a week I hopped a boxcar heading further west, the train pulling out as the hobos broke camp.

A cold chill ran through my blood when I noticed the rattling boxcar I'd careened into was jammed with ice cold, blue steel pipes. My stomach became squishy, jiggling like a mud puddle near the Platte. During one of my railroad adventures near Mankato, I had seen one of my best pals standing in front of these same sort of blue steel pipes, the two of us ridin' the rails around town. When the train unexpectedly jerked, one of those steel pipes killed my dear friend. Yeah, the poor kid's body suddenly lay motionless as a stone, causing me nightmares for days on end. Now that I was back in the boxcars traveling west, other memories leaped through my mind like grasshoppers in the prairie.

Since everyone knew me in my small hometown, I seemed to get into more than my share of scrapes. Knife-toothed dogs gnawed at my ankles as I rode my bike on the newspaper route I had hustled for years. When I finally got home, Father had sharpened the blades on our steel push mower until the edges were razor-sharp, sharp enough to slice the strand of hair he had yanked from his wavy, bean brown head. Standing in our front yard I wondered: *Why is he sharpening those blades like some hog butcher in a meat market?*

One afternoon I saw the man down the street, a guy who was building a new home. The fellow was using a huge, thick-haired workhorse to plow and dig out his basement. No machines for that character. And not long afterward I got my first real job working in a local bowling alley, beginning my long trade as a pinsetter. And I would never forget the day (while working in a nearby tavern) I was tapping wooden barrels of beer down in the basement below. Without any warning whatsoever, the barrel pipe slipped from my bare hands. The pipe was so pressurized it flew like a bullet straight up the basement floor, missing the bartender by a scant inch. Returning my gaze through the boxcar's wobbling cargo door, I thought of Al and the other hobo bums.

"But I am a hard worker and I ain't no bum," I said aloud. I had set pins, tended bar, delivered papers, and even shoveled rocks. Springing down from that roving boxcar of mixed memories, I headed toward the town's nearest bowling alley where a pinsetter was needed.

"You're hired," the wide-chested owner declared with a weak smile. His features were rock-solid as the bowling pins I had often set and neatly stacked. "You can sleep on the cot in back, if you like," he added in passing.

At the bowling alley the next morning, I met an ex-boxer named Mark. Every time a bell rang, Mark balled his softball-size fists thinking he was in the ring again. Mark, however, had become a mellow fellow. His strange diet included one bursting gallon of green peas he munched daily. At closing time, Mark gulped a bottle of beer while sharing his peas with anyone he called a friend. Scraggly alley rats loved to scuttle up Mark's bulky legs, patiently waiting for the crazy fellow to feed them handful after handful of his delicious green peas.

"These fellas are my buddies," boasted Mark of the scrambling, hairy rodents. "They give me plenty of comfort and love." With bristly hands like a lion's paws, Mark could not be pinsetter. So he pushed his broom around the alley cleaning up, sleeping in the back room, just like me. In no time at all I became an excellent pinsetter, clutching three of those heavy pins by their necks in one hand, and three in the other. Bowling game after game when the alley was closed, I quickly learned the proper way to lacquer the bowling lanes. By age fifteen I finally had some money in my pocket—enough dough for better duds, tailor-made cigarettes, and even some high-grade cigars. Bowling a game of 200 had become as easy for me as a ten-year-old riding a bike. But it was time to move on because big Mark was gettin' on my nerves. Besides, I sure couldn't stay in one town for too long . . .

All around America folks were listening to the popular tune, "Over the Rainbow,"[1] from Judy Garland's new movie, *The Wizard of Oz*. I couldn't seem to get a few of the words out of my mind:

> *"Somewhere, over the rainbow, way up high,*
> *There's a land that I heard of, once in a lullaby."*

"Once in a lullaby." I sure wasn't in any lullaby land. And I certainly got homesick as the muscles of my neck leaped like the dickens when that bowling alley gig suddenly shut down. There I was in this uncertain year of 1939, the same year some historians called "the greatest year in Hollywood history." 1939 was the year of movies like: *Gone with the Wind* and Bogart's, *King of the Underworld*. But hey, the split second the summer rains slackened I made a path back to the rail yards, my feet carryin' me straight to the depot. My thoughts were sharp as a chef's knife because I was thinkin' toward the place where I knew my far-off mother *prayed*.

---

[1] *"Over the Rainbow,"* (1939) Written by Harold Arien; Lyrics: E.Y. Harburg

CHAPTER 4

Testing the West

September, 1939 — "GERMANY HAS INVADED POLAND: SEPTEMBER 1. BRITAIN AND FRANCE DECLARE WAR ON GERMANY: SEPTEMBER 3."

"All abbboarrrd! All abboaarrd for points west," the uniformed conductor fired his message to those of us who had read the terrible news. The time-honored advisory absorbed the entire station, blowing through the lively crowd as we tried to forget the war across the pond. The train was packed with folks from all over the nation, many who were just like me, dips runnin' on the lam. My bundled sack of belongings was gripped tightly beneath my arm, but this time I climbed up the spick and span train steps with ticket firmly in hand. When the train whistle sounded, pages of my childhood scrapbook whooshed like steam engine exhaust over my being. Ever since studying *My Weekly Reader* at Divine Rosary School, the scenic sites of the Rocky Mountains and the wondrous Golden Gate Bridge had seized giant pieces of my wandering heart. Getting comfortable inside the clean snug coach, finally there were no cold steel pipes, no smelly urine cans, and few stinking bodies. No, that train car's chief aroma was the wafting whiff of choice cuts of sizzling meat and the rich flavor of freshly brewed coffee, steaming hot from the bustling galley. No more menacing wood chunks tottered dangerously overhead, loose timbers often jolted by a rattling boxcar, preparing to gore another innocent victim.

"Tickets. Tickets please," the creamy-headed conductor announced, punching my paper ticket. Coal vapors drifted in and out of the wheezing passenger train while whiffs of crackling bacon and roasting ham smelled like heaven to my continually groaning stomach. "Here you go, sir," the conductor said, dropping the punched ticket into the palm of my hand.

Sir? It sure felt good to be called sir instead of "Hey kid." Peering around the train car, I could barely take in all the sights, outside as well as *inside* this rushing coach. Vast cattle ranches, desolate farms, jagged sagebrush, and boatloads of tiny towns whizzed past my gleaming window. As we settled in for the trip, blonde, flattened-haired women wore the same high heels, decorated skirts, and fashionable hats, each carrying sleek, smart handbags at their sides. Chitchatting away in meaningless small talk, they paralleled the men who accompanied them. As nice as pie these people were but they were too formal and lackluster. Lipstick. Brisk cologne. Wads of money. Custom watches, shiny shoes and ornate hats. Observing one couple then another: *These people were not in survival mode like the hobos. Like me.*

Our train clicked-clacked over scores of miles of track as my eyes grew as weighty as those rolling wheels. Life was a gamble, like pitching pennies or slamming the baseball. Wherever it landed was anyone's guess. As the afternoon light sliced the syrupy air of the train, I dreamed of the sites ahead: purple mountain ranges, restful streams, rocky paths, and golden sunsets. Montana, Idaho, Utah, Arizona, California, Mexico. Where would I stop? My only desire was to test the west, every last ounce of it.

The same could not be said of Albert. Writhing his thin torso in the stark white hospital bed and still housed in the county mental institution, Albert regularly blistered his terror at the dutiful floor attendant. The crafty patient shrieked so loudly the whole floor rumbled.

"A bear is chasing me, don't you see it?" Albert queried the attendant with deathlike eyes. "A big furry, black bear. Watch out, watch out for the bear!"

"Calm down, Albert," the hospital attendant sternly scolded, shoving the explosive man deep into the bed's lumpy mattress. "There is *no* bear, Albert. I'll get the doctor. Just sit tight and relax."

Relaying to the doctor the fact his patient was experiencing yet another attack, the physician added that violent outburst to the long list of many others. Oh how he prayed for wisdom in handling this most challenging case. Combing his fingers through frizzy graying hair, a sudden eruption of laughter yelped from Albert's crooked grin. "Hah, hey, haaaaa, pizzz," the patient sputtered like a car without gas.

"Medication please, and get a leg on," the doctor hollered on the room's crank wall phone. A thick-armed nurse hurriedly scurried into Albert's hospital room, a tray filled with drugs calmly resting in between her quivering hands.

"Okay, Albert. It's okay," the nurse exclaimed, aiming the shiny needle straight into the patient's vein. "Now let's take a nice long nap. See you in the morning."

"Wake up, wake up, sir," the train operator with chocolate skin jostled my arm, rousing me from a rock-solid sleep. Like a bad nightmare Father's illness had lingered; it seemed impossible to remove the details of his breakdown from my own troubled mind. Clutching Mother's telegram within my quivering hand, "End of the line," the train operator announced. My lips were awkwardly unlocked as I had dreamed Father was after me again. Grabbing my bundle, I stuffed the telegram into the bottom of my cloth sack.

Heading straight for the depot, I shook off the dream. Refreshed by the view of a brand new town, I collapsed onto one of the station's crowded wooden benches. *Should I search out a bowling alley? Maybe get a room for 75 cents? Or, maybe go back to hopping the rails just for the thrill?*

When I was flat broke I never had *that* kind of problem, trying to figure out my next move. Was our parish priest right? *Was* the love of money the pathway to all kinds of evil?

"Cigarrrs … cigarettes. Cigarrrs, cig-ar-ettes," the strawberry blonde dish offered all of us live wires, the skinny girl selling her wares in the big bustling depot. The blonde had soft fair skin, and her mouth looked as sweet as candy, framed with a heart-shaped smile.

"Hey, girl, come on over here," I beckoned the good-looking kid.

"Yes sir; what'll it be?"

At long last rested, "Give me your best cigar," I commanded, feeling pretty good giving the salesgirl my order. Instantly her silky hands and cherry red nails presented me with a twenty-five cent cigar. Twirling around the rolled tobacco I sniffed, scanning it with my meticulous sight. No, that cigar didn't look like the best one to me. "This ain't no cigar," I grumbled. "Give me your *best* cigar, if you please."

A few folks amassed near where I sat, craning their necks, wondering who in the world was making such a fuss. A knot rose inside the salesgirl's throat as she lightly said, "Oh sir, the best ones are way up in the front case." Feeling like the king of this busy joint, I flaunted my order to the highest degree.

"Well, then why are you just standing there looking at me? Go to the case and get me one. After all, what good is money if you can't spend it on one of the greatest pleasures in life?" Now, even *more* folks were watching the hay-wired fray. Clenching her puss like some tuna in the Pacific, the girl nervously belted out,

"But *those* cigars are a whole dollar, sir."

"Here's the money," I stiffly said, scrunching the bill inside her soft palms. "Please, just go ahead and get me one. Scram!"

Shaking my head, in a thirty seconds flat the blonde reappeared. Reaching for the dollar cigar I rolled it between my fingers, inspecting it for overall freshness. Smelling it thoroughly, I then bite off the tip. Lighting it, a fragrant bouquet drenched every last corner of the depot. That beauty was one of the first of a million more fine cigars I would smoke in my lifetime. As smoke slipped from my lips, my heart did flips of joy. But not merely because I had bought that expensive cigar. No, I knew I had somehow been born to command.

"When does the next train roll out of here?" I questioned the egg of a ticket master, his tiny section of the depot swimming in my meandering cigar vapors.

"In about an hour, sir," the ticket master squinted through the dim haze. Studying the schedule like the evening newspaper, I stuck the train ticket snugly inside my right shirt pocket. In one hour flat I would be back on track, my bankroll holding strong at $146.00. Downing three sandwiches and a five-cent beer at the cheesy diner next door, the train whistle reverberated like a pigpen filled with squealing sows. *I'm blowin' this quack pop stand, this jerkwater of a town. I need some razzmatazz; some hustle and bustle.* Descending the train steps to this next town with a little more life, I grabbed a cheap motel room because I had no idea how long I was stayin'.

"I want *this* one," I firmly instructed the used car salesman, gaping at the '34 beauty with a swank V-8 engine.

"Don't you want to drive it first?" the salesman questioned in surprise. Explaining that the car, along with the license, would cost a grand total of $49.99, I handed over the dough. Filling up her tank, I drove my very first car, paid for entirely on my own. Pressing the gas pedal until I gritted my teeth, I shook that deadbeat town, leaving behind clouds of dust and swirling tornadoes of rising gravel. *Okay honey; let's see what you can really do.* Mashing down the pedal all the way to the floorboard, my mind escaped its miserable prison with no way out. Flooring the '34 as far as she would go, I didn't realize the gravel was slick, covered with moist dew.

One, two, three, four, five, six, seven, eight! Ye-ah! Whoa! Toppling over and over and over again like rolling tumbleweed, my lanky form went for the ride of its life. The steering wheel was spinning like a top, and silver stars were dancing like glitter inside my shaken head. Dizzily crawling from beneath the twisted wreck, I tapped on a few of my numerous bruises, checking for any breaks. Examining several dirt-filled cuts, I mentally noted how serious any one of them might be. Gathering my strewn belongings from a nearby ditch, I tossed them into my new suitcase with only one latch in tact. She wasn't a bad little ride, no siree. Checking the speedometer, that gal was stuck at 92. Lighting a cigar, I exhaled into the damp country air. Poking out my thumb to cop a lift, I was on the lam once again. After a short stint on the road, a chicken farmer pulled up, his dusty car creeping slowly along my left side.

"Hiya, sir," I flashed my kindest grin, the farmer's body willowy and wooly. "I was visiting my uncle down the line and got a little mixed-up; I really need a lift."

"Where ya goin', son?" The farmer asked, stroking his chin. His mustache was stiff; eyes soft yet sore.

"Wherever *you're* goin,' sir," I answered, heaving forward with an even broader smile. "Beggars can't be choosers ya know."

Stopping only for water and gas, the farmer's old Model T used as much water as it did gas, particularly when the car got a might warm.

"Here's my farm," the middle-aged man lumbered the Model T along the rocky lane.

"Thanks for the lift, sir," I grinned, thrusting a couple of bucks for the farmer to grab.

"Can't take yer money, son."

"Why not?"

"Well, ya never know. One day the wife and I may be hitchin' a ride and *you'll* be the one with the vehicle. Maybe then *we* won't have the two dollars for *you*. Wouldn't be right in my book, son. Don't know 'bout you."

I swallowed and managed to utter, "Thanks sir. You take care now," I said with a fervent wave to the farmer, my skin tingling over his unexpected gift.

Hoisting my suitcase from the back of the Model T, I brushed away a whirl of chicken feathers stuck to its side. There wasn't a single breath of wind so I brushed the rest of the fluffy feathers off with my fingers. Totally alone, the countryside sat brutally still. No pretty signs. No racket. No more fragrant cigars. In the far distance a car rumbled against the stony ground. Sticking out my thumb, I plastered on my largest sunshiny grin. Passing me by like a swift breeze at midnight, about $70.00 waited in my bankroll, saved from my bowling alley jobs. I rolled a Bull Durham and strolled the gravel road, my gut coiled like a snake. As the sun dipped, first my nose and cheeks chilled, then my hands became frosty as Minnesota snow. I prayed my toes wouldn't end up like hobo Al's blackened stubs.

"Need a lift?" a fellow in a suit coat and tie questioned, stopping his brand new 1939 Chevy near my side of the road. After tossing and turning a few hours at the bottom of a dank bean field for the last two nights, I knew better days were comin'.

"You bet," I nodded, examining the '39 Chevy glistening in the midday sun. Climbing inside, we briskly shook hands. "Where ya goin'?" I eagerly asked.

"Up north for a meeting," the salesman said. Needing someone to talk to so he didn't fall asleep, we chatted over miles of dipping valleys, narrow roads, and soaring hills. Whenever we stopped for food, he bought all my meals.

"Are you a good driver, Ralph?" the salesman inquired with a prolonged yawn, peering at my capable hands and sturdy legs.

"Yes sir, I am."

Pulling the car over along an empty stretch of roadway, the salesman mounted the Chevy's back seat like a horse. Plunging gently into the seat cushions, he curled into a comfy fetal position for some well-needed rest. Stopping for gas then breakfast, "We're almost there," the salesman announced at the wheel again, refreshed from his peaceful snooze. "Beautiful Butte, Montana is just ahead. We're having a big convention in Butte. Ever been there Ralph?"

"No sir," I readily replied. "Say, could you just drop me off at the biggest bowling alley in town? I'm lookin' for a job."

"You betcha. I know exactly where the bowling alley is."

Approaching Butte's train station, I wondered if it might be a swell town after all. The largest city for miles, purple-hued mountains rested at the town's edge, their jagged corners gazing at its residents like ghostly guards. Known primarily as a copper-mining town, Butte's night sky was as black as India ink. But hey, it was the action I wanted—the four "W's," (work, women, whiskey, and wine). Entering the bowling alley, I left my battered suitcase outside.

"Ma'am, are you hiring?" I asked the woman at the front counter. Blessed with waist-long red hair, her ankle-length, daisy-dotted dress matched those of pioneers living in the century past. Nearby, a younger gal sang the popular tune, *Jeepers Creepers:*

"*Jeepers, Creepers. Where'd ya get those Peepers? Jeepers, Creepers*" ... [2]

"Let me get the boss," the lady in the daisy dress said.

Framed with keen eyes and a jaw as rigid as Montana's

---

[2] *"Jeepers Creepers"* (1938) Music by Henry Warren; Lyrics: Johnny Mercer

mountains, the boss stared me square in the jug. "Jane says you're looking for some work."

"Yes sir," I bobbed my head.

Leaning both elbows on the counter, "You know anything 'bout bowling alleys?" the boss asked, thinking a kid like me was too young to know much about anything. Describing all the bowling alleys I'd worked so far—how I lacquered the lanes, set the pins, tended bar, and even taught folks the basics of bowling, "Might have a job for you then, Ralph from Minnesota," the pointy jaw boss stated. Leading me into a large room, a sea of wooden bowling pins sat silently on the floor. Each pin stood at attention like curved wooden soldier boys. "Ralph, here's the job. See those buckets of red and white paint over there? I want you to first paint all these pins white. Then, position each one near that far wall. When they're dry, I need you to paint red lines on the necks of each one of them, okay?"

"Okay," I replied. "I'll take the job." Hired on the spot, lunch break was half an hour; quitting time was six o'clock sharp. When the boss stopped to check me at six, he seemed pleased. "Not too bad for the first day, Ralph. See you tomorrow at 6:00 a.m. Here's a card for your room. It's three blocks down, 25 cents a night." In two months time I was setting pins and tending bar, pretty much running the whole joint. Real life cowboys, young and old, fellows looking for a good time had become my friends. After riding and roping cattle, the brawny scent of rawhide zigzagged through the smoky air. Those genuine cowboys had fought genuine Indians, their stories making my skin rush. With plenty of saloons and "jeseybells" in town, the boss was something else. Marking all the whiskey bottles with a thin line, he made certain no one was cheating him. One day the boss came over to where I was working. Swerving his head, he cleared his throat. Looking around the room, the boss softly whispered:

"Ralph, when you mix the drinks tonight, with the first two

drinks give 'em the good stuff. After that, when they're feeling pretty loose, pour them this cheap stuff—it'll be right here under the bar. Ya know, son, I gotta cut corners any way I can."

Watching scores of dusty-armed cowhands swig wine and bloody their noses, as 1942 approached I had been gone from Minnesota for well over three years. But as soon as the weather broke, (though I didn't know what I would find, or who I might meet), for some reason, I was thinkin' of *going home*.

CHAPTER 5

Going Home

"Bogart is my favorite tough guy; he was swell in *The Maltese Falcon*," voiced a jittery runt of a guy, badgering me about Bogart one night at the bowling alley. Nodding, I agreed. Bogart sure was *the* best. But let me level with you—I sure was thinking about home. Although held tight as a glove in the county institution, would I ever truly be able to go "home?" Stopping at a phone booth, I dialed the number of my girl in St. Paul. Polite and pretty as a picture, I met Betsy the last time I was in the Twin Cities. "I'm heading to St. Paul to see you, Betsy. And then I'm going home to visit Mother in Mankato," I spouted my intentions with ease. A dove cooed in the background and a lit Camel cigarette dangled dangerously from the left edge of my lips. "Can't wait to see you, Betsy."

"I can't wait to see you either, Ralph," Betsy sniveled with joy, a sweetheart of a gal. She was a good friend of my old pal, Wes Vanguard.

"I won't be there yet, but I'm coming as soon as I can. You write me, and I'll write you back," I said, hanging up the telephone then heading to work. For some reason my feet slogged down the street heavy as a sledgehammer. Holding my breath as the alley's coal furnace grumbled, my mind grew numb as a doornail. I felt as if a fifty-pound weight was about to plunge atop my head.

"The lines on the whiskey bottles didn't match up last night, Ralph," the boss reported when I saw him at the alley. The two of us were discussing the new state of affairs inside his private office. Lifting my brow, I was totally stunned. Struggling to curb my temper because I was getting that bum rap, "It wasn't me, sir; I think it was the other guy," I said, glancing over in a dire attempt to persuade the boss. Nonetheless, I was fired without delay. Beyond the boss's office door, the stale scents of last night's alcohol, burnt tobacco, and the mixture of cleaning fluids I often used to scrub the countertops and floors surged into the pores of my being. I was pretty sore at that sap; I should have popped him a good one in the kisser.

With the ten dollars I had saved in my bankroll I bought some Bull Durham, a few sandwiches, and a couple of my favorite candy bars. I hit the road with suitcase in hand, all set to hitch a ride. In half an hour I was bouncing around in a farmer's old dented truck. Riding twenty-five miles down rutted country dirt and gravel lanes, the raggedy farmer with a mangled left hand suddenly muttered, "Here's my turn, boy. Sure hope ya git another ride real quick."

"Thanks," I responded. Hustling down from the back of the truck, I was dropped like a dead fly on the hard ground, smack in the middle of nowhere. Thrusting my thumb repeatedly into the air, not a single soul wanted to stop. My broad feet and oblong face ached in this blank darkness. Parked at the border of some patchy woods, I snapped off a few tree branches for quick covering. The frosty damp air settled into the earth where I laid as motionless as a grave. A few hours later, the stillness was breeched. My ears had sharply turned toward the *Crrrunch! Crrreakk! Snap!* Were those footsteps?

Taking further cover beneath an old picnic table, I was ready to kill if need be. Yeah, either with my knife or with my bare hands.

How I would do it, I really wasn't sure. But I knew I could kill, if necessary. My icy hands quivered and my bony knees shuddered in the drafty midnight fog. Dare I breathe? The approaching footsteps were bulky—*two men, maybe three, possibly even four.* Filing boldly out of the woods, a large hulking shadow began to take shape. Straining my greenish-gray eyes in the dim moonlight, I began to make them out. Bears! A tidy toddling line—I saw a complete family of bears! Cuddled beneath that beleaguered picnic table I yearned for the Montana ground to give way. Underground I would have been totally shielded from the bears' gigantic appetite. Would I die by way of the razor-sharp teeth and claws of this marauding, wooly mob?

My suitcase was opened for added shelter and I had draped more tree branches over my crouched, coiled body for protection. The woodland's faint breeze suddenly shifted, wafting the opposite way. My protruded nose lightly exhaled. *Never again would I ride out into the middle of nowhere with some sap. Next time I would make sure to ask if the joker was going through a town.* After poking around the bushes and scattered brush, in thirty heart-throbbing minutes the lumbering bears finally moved on. Like an angel appearing from heaven, I heard a vehicle approaching that gloomy, empty road. Springing from my shelter with the force of a leaping mountain lion, I planted myself in the center of the moonlit road. If I got run down, my suffering would be over, immediately. On the other hand, if the driver decided to stop, I could thaw my ice-cold body and live. With truck lights beaming upon my leaf-flecked chest, the vehicle ground to a halt a few yards ahead. Dashing toward the driver's seat, "Could you please get me out of this misery, sir?" I pleaded with the driver. I was wide-eyed as a wild beast, a forest animal running for its life.

"Sure," he agreed with twin nods.

"Okay, wait right here, " I said, catching sight of my things. "Just gotta get my stuff." Gathering my suitcase and cloth sack,

I careened into the fellow's truck like a hot poker was pressed against my backside. At last, off we went. No, *never again.*

"Where ya headed?" I questioned the driver.

"This load is headed for Rapid City, South Dakota. That okay with you?"

"Sure. The next meal is on me," I offered, attempting to take the edge off our initial meeting. How my heart was soaring like a kite.

"All right, son. I know a great truck stop." Scores of towns and roadways pass before we reached Rapid City, due east of the famous Black Hills. "Rapid City," informed the driver, "is known as, The Gateway to the Black Hills." But after our meal was paid for, I was flat broke. Locating the Rapid City depot in less than an hour, I dove into a boxcar heading to Pierre, South Dakota. In a jiffy I landed on the high prairie shores of the Missouri River, at the foot of the rutted Black Hills.

Shuffling into the hobo camp adjacent to the tracks, "I have tobacco and rolling papers," I expertly announced. Anxious to meet that new motley bunch of men, unlike the musty Platte River camp where I'd spent quite some time, those fellows worked during the day on the railroad. Those men wanted to live full and clear in the open instead of mulling around, trying to survive secretly in the dark.

"At the turn of the century the four of us fought the Injuns," one of the seated men confided as we gobbled down tin plates of a chunky chili bean stew and sopped bread.

Recounting tale after tale of bloody massacres and gory brawls, "Can I come out tomorrow and work?" I appealed to the men, squinting through the sooty haze.

A thickset man in his late twenties (a two-inch scar crimping nearly all of his right cheek) instantly turned my way. "Think you can knock down this here spike with a 40-pound hammer?" The man with the most massive forearms I had ever seen smugly asked.

Holding up a giant metal spike glinting in the firelight he then questioned, "And say, Ralph, can you lift?"

"Sure I can," I replied, my chest already heaving.

"Well, eat these here beans kid, and hit the hay. I'll see you bright and early at 4:30—we start at 5:00. Quittin' time is six o'clock sharp."

Up at the crack of dawn, I finished the job the very second my arms could no longer extend. Keeping my belly full, I stayed in that camp for a good three weeks. Hopping a boxcar, once again I was filthy as dirt. Heading east to Sioux Falls, I then hitchhiked to Albert Lea. My vision clouded when the driver pulled onto the familiar streets of St. Paul, its swanky sights and welcome sounds exciting me to the very core. Staying with a pal of mine, I quickly cleaned up. Not wasting a moment of time, I looked up Betsy.

"I'm not going to step one foot inside that house," I told Betsy when we finally met. Eating dinner at "Dave's," the two of us were dressed to the nines and holding hands. As the sun set an orange-red along St. Paul's horizon, Betsy, with her dark curly hair smelling like flowers, looked more beautiful than ever. Clothed in a swell red and yellow suit, her eyes sparkled as the cleanest Minnesota River. After some weeks, I took the bus to Mankato where I met Mother in front of Divine Rosary Church.

"Your father is still in da institution," Mother winced. Her sweet face was marked with lines, and her dark hair had thinned. Her back was bent and hunched. Oh how Mother was so utterly thrilled to see me. The two of us embraced for the first time since my hasty departure from home, from everything.

"This is Betsy," I introduced Betsy to Mother. Living off the produce of her garden, Mother's friends and sisters helped wherever they could. Yes, Mother was well and she had kept her faith. Taking a bus back to St. Paul, I stayed with old friends, working in a nice bowling alley. Though he was locked safely away, one night I thought I saw my spiffy-dressed father strolling a downtown street.

Had they let him out, out to get *me*? After I lived several months in St. Paul, a gnawing urge suddenly cracked my soul. *I'd never hit California's coast; never yet seen Yosemite.*

Though the city was steel grey—grey clouds, grey buildings, the town painted with silver-coated bridges and roads, I was still happy to be in St. Paul after visiting Mother in Mankato. Settled on the eastern bank of the Mississippi River, St. Paul was opposite its twin sister, Minneapolis. Home of the Como Park Zoo, there was something about the "Saintly City," making me chime like a ticking clock.

"I'm making more money than my father ever did, even at the prime of his life," I told friends at the bowling alley where I set pins, lacquered the alleys, and ran the bar. Replacing cracked and broken boards whenever the alley needed them, Betsy and I went to fancy movie houses and nightclubs in St. Paul while I taught her the tricks of bowling. "You're getting to be quite a good bowler," I told Betsy one night after closing time. During the summer of '42, Betsy, her family and I rode on their boat, enjoying our free moments together, after work and on the weekends. I had saved $30.00, and was staying in a room near the alley. It was a fine bowling alley, one of the best I'd ever seen. My room, however, was located in an area loaded with cheap hotels, cheap women, and scores of cheap bars.

Fed up with these beggars, on my way to work all I heard was: "Gotta cigarette for a friend?" When I answered, "yeah," then they asked me for a match. Okay, I guess that wasn't good enough then they wanted a dime. "Hey," I mumbled, "that's enough. Go find some other chump, will ya?" I stayed in my room for a few weeks, eventually moving to a better part of town so every Tom, Dick, and Harry who came along wouldn't pester me. Plunking down a whole dollar for rent, my new room had a radio, a bathroom down the hall, and a nickel telephone on every floor so in half a shake I could talk to Betsy whenever I wanted instead of tracking down a telephone booth. Still in high school, Betsy went along with the program, the two of us livin' it up with the time we had.

"Ew, ah," I moaned, flopping down on my apartment-size mattress. Spreading out on the lumpy twin bed, I mulled over my days in the circus, the brief time I traveled from town to town setting up rides, then tearing it all down. *Eassy, whezzy, kizzy carney!* Eh, the stories I could tell about the days I worked for those characters. Everybody had a hustle, the rich as well as the poor. In all my learning, I had noticed the rich seemed to hide their hustle while the poor openly displayed it for the entire world to see.

Sitting on the top of the world, I was working in one of the finest bowling alleys in St. Paul: classy, clean, and swell. Checking on some dented bowling pins one night, a friend popped in the alley spouting off how great the bowling alley was a few miles away. Like a fool sap, I believed that chump and quit my good job, going to work instead at the alley down the street. In a week or two I was sorry I had left that classy alley. Why in heaven's name did I cheat myself because of greed, thinkin' the grass was greener on the other side? Wiping my hands from the chalky residue, you can bet your bottom dollar there was nothing on earth like a fine bowling alley.

TWO MONTHS LATER: I was still in St. Paul—it was a good city with a good hometown feel. In addition, I had a girl who was head over heels in love with me. Yeah, I stayed there a good long while and went out with Betsy, havin' *plenty of fun.*

CHAPTER 6

A Thousand Miles of Rail

Was I shivering from the rotten cold *or* from the fact Father was still walkin' God's good green earth, living in Minnesota? Was that why my mind jiggled like a box of rocks while I stayed in St. Paul, a mere hour and a half away from my own hometown? But it was as if everyone was shivering with the brutality of world war on that early December night. On December 7, 1942, the United States had commemorated the first anniversary of the day our naval base at Pearl Harbor had been viciously bombed. Guys my age were signing up for the war by the bucket load, even the runts, answering the call to fight.

After Betsy and I celebrated our November 4th birthdays, (both of us were born on the very same day and year) something suddenly pulled me away from everything in St. Paul. Anxious to hit the road again, I had to go without Betsy, though I knew that beautiful girl sure was carryin' a big torch for me. *Betsy; sweet Betsy.*

"Whew!" Catching a freight train heading west, I was in the hot seat again with those cologne-soaked railroad dicks. Same grease-heads. Same hiding out like a stinkin' crook. The only difference was those trains were jammed with a constant stream of soldiers, particularly army and navy men. Spending many a night under creaking bridges, the reek of human sweat, dirt, and urine merged with the musk of every animal known to mankind. Often making a stopover in a few small town jails, I washed and thankfully grabbed some delicious hot grub. Some of the hard-core bums I came across sipped *Sterno* to relieve their pain, smutty bodies either sopping wet or freezing cold, bones protruding through slashed, matted skin.

"Pioche. We're in Pioche, Nevada, boys," the conductor announced to our chatty group of work hands. The entire gang of us leaped off that choking train one after the other like sheep leapin' off a cliff. I got wind of the gig from a pal of mine, so there I was with the best of them. About 180 miles northeast of Las Vegas, all the men in my outfit had come to Pioche to work the mines, "getting the lead out," for the war effort. Mining in Pioche was *my* patriotic contribution so I wasn't greasin' a living soul. At any rate, I couldn't wait to get a closer look at that Old West town.

Strolling down the main drag of that two-bit town, there was a good-sized hotel, an old-time saloon, and a friendly café. But the opera house caught my fancy, drawing me to its doorstep almost every time I passed by. Shanties and half-cocked shacks were built for us miners, the temperatures 'round there getting clear up into the hundreds during the day, sometimes plunging down near freezing at night. My chest burned like a campfire from days and nights of poundin' rocks, and my parched throat gagged from the granules of filmy dust constantly coating my insides with their stain. My light European eyes were nothing more than narrow slits as they lowered us into that deep cavern of drear. Down, downward several stories below the ground we plunged, skirting the fiery pits of hell. Repeatedly plastered with grubby soot, my breath became mere curly puffs of lead-laden grime.

"Bullets for our military *must* be made, men," the mine supervisor pounded his fists and yelled. His chin and nose were triangle-shaped, each of them pointed as the bullets we were beating that mine to ultimately create. Scratching around that musky hole for two whole years, my belly was happy and round. Finally ready to move on, I was pumped enough to drift with the clouds overhead. Hopping a slowed freight train going further west, I decided I wouldn't be stopping anymore. Too much visiting, too many towns. I had to reach the West Coast. If I could get a job making just a quarter, I could stay in a roach-filled flophouse *where,* at least I had a place to lay my head.

Its clanging cable cars were music to my ears, the nifty open-air streetcars moving hordes of passengers throughout busy San Francisco Bay. The crimson Golden Gate Bridge (bright against the royal blue of the Pacific Ocean) brought me immediate wonder—one of the sites I had longed to see. Positioned on the southern edge of two hilly peninsulas, the city grew like a forest fire during the famous Gold Rush of 1849. I had yearned to see that hodgepodge of people, and I couldn't wait to discover that fog-bathed town. Before I knew it I was working the bowling lanes again, inhaling the ocean's sea-breezy scent every time I stepped out the alley's front door.

"Hey there, fellow," two stripe-shirted guys in bell-bottomed pants called as I wandered Fisherman's Wharf. Smirking at the two guys like a dizzy dolphin, I sprinted like a racehorse to the opposite side of the Wharf.

I jogged like mad along the ocean, *Holy Mackerel!* Royal blue was the dominant color in that whole city—royal blue water and sapphire blue skies. No more grey! No more caves! Fresh and free, that was Frisco. There were jobs galore and money was flying as fast as the soaring sea gulls. I finally visited beautiful Yosemite—its luscious falls, the Giant Sequoias, and those purple-brown granite mountains. I thought I might stay forever but then ...

At the very northwestern tip of the nation I slogged through

Washington State's mushy soil, but it didn't hold a match for me for very long. No, the air in Seattle was too clammy; the pace was sluggish and moody. And neither did Oregon's craggy coast, *its* drear failed to engage my interest—too desolate and too dawdling. Slicing through the state of California as if she was a supple piece of Mother's cherry pie, I worked near the famous Hollywood Bowl. One night in walked my all-time favorite star, Humphrey Bogart, along with a carefree Bette Davis. Those two took over the alley for an entire night, laughing and roaring, their bowling balls careening right down my lanes. I loved Los Angeles and Hollywood—the picture shows, the stars, fancy restaurants, and all those dazzling lights. But the whole affair was shut down whenever there was a blackout on the coast.

At California's southern border I reached San Diego, movin' north after a short stint in Mexico. Gobs of Navy guys were crowing those bustlin' streets, slinkin' in the arms of their swell babes. Those California gals were decked out with rhinestone earrings and long, red-painted nails. Guzzling down beer after cold beer, salty sea gusts tousled my hair into tumbled waves, mimicking the wavy mounds of the Pacific. Rolling around town on foot, I could barely move an inch. Soldiers, sailors, airmen, and carloads of dames, (eight deep in some places) were howling, dancing, smokin', and drinking hard. I couldn't blame any of 'em cause some of them weren't ever coming back. That's when I got an idea. Setting up shop in that ocean side paradise, I peddled booze to all those soldier boys, selling entire cases at a discount price, cheaper than any tavern or nightclub in town. It was a clever gig until the cops got wind of it. And then I was back in Frisco when one night everything suddenly broke loose.

"All Japs out of here! On the double, people. Out, out, out! All Japs out!" The five state troopers hollered, whacking and slamming their batons against the tavern's brass bar with all their might. Hustling short, thin Japanese bodies into the street, it all went down just a few feet from where I stood glued to the floor. Their shocked mugs outlined their inner fear because anyone who faintly resembled someone from Japan was ordered to stand outside in a stretched-out winding line up. A few days later all Japanese-owned stores, restaurants, and shops were boarded up, done for. Whole families were rounded up like cattle, preparing to be reinstated inside the governmental camps. Their eerie stares haunted me for weeks.

"Keep a goin', Mack. Get crackin'," the Greek cook sprayed his orders into my aching ears. His head was nearly the size of our five-gallon stewing pots. Ever since I'd taken my new post as cook's first mate on that traveling troop train, all I heard was "Huge Greek's" noise. Making a hundred eggs over easy at one sitting sure wasn't any picnic. My sole squawk was by the time I broke open the last egg on that blistering grill it was already time to go back to the beginning, turning them all over without fudging a single yolk. If I did mess even a single yolk, Huge Greek would get me good. The old sap even got so mad at one of the other cooks he smashed the meat cleaver down hard on galley's cutting board, nearly chopping off my partner's lowly hand.

"Come on, come on, kid; letz go, letz go," Huge Greek blistered. "We ain't got all day." The smell of fresh coffee was the only thing keepin' my glazed eyes open at that blasted early hour. "Letz get these soldiers fed, Mack."

We cooks never got one free minute on that sardine-packed train. Traveling down those train lines from the West Coast to the East, I grew plenty acquainted with California on the west, New York on the east, and all points in-between. I may have been the only soul in the U.S.A. who had worked on every railroad line in the nation including: The New York Central, the famous B&O, the Great Northern Railway, the Northern Pacific, the Burlington (CB&O), the Missouri Pacific, the Pennsylvania Railroad, the

Sioux Line, the legendary Rock Island Line, the Union Pacific, and the mighty Chicago Northwestern. Yeah, I heard their bells clanging and their shrill whistles blowing inside my brains. Their smoke twirled in my mind like clouds swirling atop the Rockies, and their wheels clacked-clacked forever as I rode a thousand miles of rail.

Stopping for a time to see Mother, I received a letter from Betsy but I wasn't sure how to answer it. I'd been writin' her cause she was always writing me.

February 20, 1943

Dear Ralph,

Honey, if you could only see me. I've got a cold & have to stay home cause I can hardly talk. I also have my hair up & mom says I look like a kid!

I'm glad you are having a good time at home but you should have. How is your mother?

I'll be glad when I can go out again! I went to the show yesterday & it made my cold worse. I'm supposed to usher tomorrow if I can talk, that is.

What does your mother think of your mustache? Does she think it's swell?

Honey, you should be here. I sure wish I had some books here to read. Donna is going to bring them tonight.

There isn't much news to tell you except I'll be glad when you come back, I'm getting anxious to see you again.

Later I'm going to find all the letters you have written to me since we started going together. I have them all in different places.

Last night we played basketball & it was to decide for champion games but I couldn't go. I

*really wanted to as yet I don't know who won. Well
I hope to see you soon.*

>*With lots of Love,*
>*Betsy*

Betsy. After sending Betsy a short letter (and one to Mother), I decided to move to Ohio, eventually shovin' off to New York City. Gazing out the front window of a posh bowling alley, the snazzy joint overlooked Manhattan's glittery skyline. I felt lucky because Betsy and Mother loved me, and I was also lucky because everyone in that jazzing town tipped really well. Those bigwigs threw around dough as if every last one of them was a movie star or some well-off king, loaded with barrels of money. Staying in Manhattan where the real action was, at those high-class New York bowling alleys we had what were called "betting pots." The bigger the betting pot grew, the bigger were my sweet tips. Depending upon how much beer those fellows guzzled, whenever they hurled their bowling balls down my lane where I was setting up pins, I quickly snatched up my tips. Say, I was grabbing singles, fives, and tens right out of the holes of those heavy black balls. *Thank you New York!* Yeah, from the Bowery to Manhattan, that joint was jumpin.'

New York City was sure swell until one day I came across some creep who was robbing a Manhattan deli. Throwing down his gun to make a run for, like a fool I picked up his silver pistol. And wouldn't you know it? Here came the cops.

"I didn't do it," I kept tellin' the cops time and again. Dragging my scared tail over to jail, there I was, not even twenty years old, innocent until proven guilty. "Please God," I prayed hard, almost busting my sides. "Please God, get me out of here." Before the next day was out, the warden personally came and opened my cell, explaining how they finally got the right guy.

"You are free to go," the warden said, waving his hands as if shooing away flies.

Thanks be to God Almighty! By fall, my mind swayed like a tree in the wind. On the outside I was hard as the steel of the Golden Gate Bridge. Inside, I kept pushing down those miles of angry thoughts. Taking a train to Buffalo, I visited the Niagara Falls. But after a few weeks of scraping by in that Buffalo ice land, I watched the snow pile up to the rooftops. Giant snowflakes had whitened the ground, snowflakes the size of ping-pong balls. Forty inches of snow careened down on the Buffalo streets as easy as an Iowa spring rain. No sir. I had to blow that city of snowdrifts.

"Chicago, and all points Southwest: Cleveland, Toledo, South Bend," announced the conductor. I sure knew the drill, it was etched like flint inside my mind, ridin' the rails until I could barely stand it one more night. Seated on the people-packed train, an unseen force was pulling me down the line. But every time I stopped, scratchy notions were pushing in my mind, especially at night when all of life stood still. I had seen the West and the East, and just before comin' to Chicago I stayed in the Motor City. Hustled a lot I did, making plenty of dough. But one of my gals nabbed money out from under me. Mad as a hornet, I stayed in Ohio for a spell, but the magnet kept pullin' me toward Chicago.

In Chicago's Union Station, I stood inside the terminal's Great Hall. Hiking up the station's jammed stairwell, hundreds of soldier boys, their girlfriends, wives, and assorted family members gathered like mounds of giant ants.

It was a miracle when I knew it was the right time to blow a place; so would Chicago really be, *my final stop?*

CHAPTER 7

Meeting Mike Sibley

Holding another letter from cocoa-haired Betsy, she was such a swell kid from a good St. Paul family. I was staying at the Plymouth Hotel[3] where I decided to take life as it came. My hands were too busy to think about being strapped down, and that's what I loved about Chicago—no questions, no ties, plenty of hustle, and heaps of money. And yes, there was a gal on every corner. When one gal took off, there came another one. My room at the Plymouth Hotel was so small, when I stood smack in the middle of it I could reach out and touch both walls. Living there for some months, I wanted to cover all bases. As sudden as an empty streetcar, to St. Louie I traveled to visit my big sister Katrina.

"Ralph, I can't believe it's really you," Katrina gushed, hugging me tightly when I showed up on her doorstep. Katrina's reedy figure was sun-tanned from the boiling St. Louis sun, and her stance was a bit off-balanced, nervous as a cat. Father, you see, did an unthinkable thing to Katrina when he caught her with another guy. I sure hoped she had gotten over that bum rap. Katrina and her husband were in the furniture racket, running an upholstery shop on Broadway Street. Refurbishing old furniture was a new gig for

---

[3] The Plymouth was a popular men's transient hotel in the south Loop.

me, so I sat wide-eyed as a cat, watching Katrina's husband work because it was a real gas. The tobacco-chewing character guzzled beer like lemonade, constantly wettin' his whistle with the stuff, chugging it down by the quart. Why that cat drank so many quarts of beer he blew bubbles out of his puss when he slept. Shoveling handfuls of upholstery tacks inside his thread-thin lips, he spat those tacks faster than one of Big Al's Tommy guns. Fastening the short silver nails onto the furniture's fabric, his bony hands moved as fast as the eye could follow.

"This one's all done, Ralph," Katrina's husband puffed like some big wheel businessman. "Come on," he ordered, tugging his finished product. Waving me over to help him lug the massive chair, "Let's throw this thing in the window for the customers to see right quick," he cooed.

Peddling furniture with my brother-in-law and sister for a time, I tested the scene, trying to figure if St. Louie was really for me.

"Come over for dinner tonight, Ralph," Katrina invited me one evening after work. Following a delicious dinner, Katrina's husband showed me a stack of war bonds about a half-foot thick. That costly stack was sittin' as nice as pie on a nearby shelf. Of course, I just left it alone. But just like those silver nails tacked onto that big chair's fabric, Chicago was tacked to my soul. On my way back to the city, a certain memory was threaded in my mind like a spiky needle.

Thrilled if a guy threw me a gleaming nickel or dime when shining shoes as a kid, I could well remember the day I found myself in New Ulm, Minnesota. New Ulm was a southern Minnesota town west of Mankato, a place where a fellow could buy an acre of the blackest dirt for one measly dollar. If I had only been bright enough to invest in New Ulm land.

Taking a whizzing cab directly into the Chicago's main business and shopping district known as the Loop, all I heard was noise. The sweet racket of the screeching El trains that looped around downtown, the zooming whirr of the cars, streetcars, and trucks oddly soothed my soul. The gust of human feet stampeded to offices, restaurants, and nightclubs, playing endless choruses inside my head. In no time I was working in a bowling alley on the Chicago's bustling North Side. The moment I trekked down any city street I inhaled men's secret feelings, conscious of what they were up to, the schemes they were planning deep within. Did they think I was some country-bumkin' chump from the sticks?

"Hey! I'm not some sucker, no sittin' duck," I told a hotfooted chump. "Get lost, buster. Scram," I belted out in one second flat. "I ain't no small potatas." Stuffing a few dollars inside my billfold, my big bankroll was tucked safely inside my shoes. I guess you could say, "I walked on my money." Smoking three packs of *Luckys* a day, I topped off the night with a three-inch cigar. I was twenty years old, having experienced more than most people had experienced over their entire lives.

"Clark Street, Clark," the streetcar driver yelled. Bolting down the streetcar's smudged steps, I had lived in my new Clark Street apartment for a few months, having rented a smaller, Diversey Avenue apartment earlier in the year. Chicago always boasted a room to be had, an apartment to rent, or a cheap flat to lease. Pouring drinks in a bar on madcap Clark Street, I was workin' the graveyard shift from 2 a.m. to 8 a.m. Since there was no such thing as closing time, it was twenty-four hours straight, day and night. Man, those big city guys were like no one you'd ever met, especially a fellow named "Silver."

"Hiya, Silver," I would usually holler. Just like clockwork, Silver came into my joint flanked by six coal-haired bodyguards. Each of their eyes were peeled thick on my fingers as if I was gonna slip big Silver a "Mickey." Yeah, a Mickey Finn that is, especially since the whole idea originated in Chicago. Word had it bartender and manager, Mickey Finn, of "The Lone Star Saloon," (a tavern joint popular at the turn of the century) began to lace certain drug powders in customers' drinks so he could rob them blind, allowing them to pass out cold. But that wasn't my style.

"Buy the house a drink, Jerry," Silver's mouth widened, his chubby olive hands flashing a thick wad of cash (about one hundred clams) in front of my tired eyes. Struttin' around the place like a spring chicken, Silver (so named because of a grey streak right in the middle of his hair) and his gang bopped into the tavern a couple times a week. I was then known around the city as "Jerry," since that's the way I liked it—Jerry from Detroit. Anyway, one morning when I was cleaning the bar from the last night's grunge, I peeked over at the coat rack, wondering where in blazes was my overcoat. *Thought I saw one of Silver's bodyguards by my coat last night. Holy Smoke—they swiped it just like that.* In Chicago, you learned real quick to never let go of your belongings because if you did, they would be gone as fast as one of those taxis speeding down Grand Avenue.

"Ain't seen Silver in a while," I mentioned to the boss on a slow morning a few weeks later.

"Haven't ya heard, Jerry?" The boss asked. "They found old Silver shot in the noggin a day or two ago. Don't know who did it and don't know why. Just plain shot poor Silver smack in the noodle."

"I'll miss the old guy," I said with a sigh. Putting on a frozen front, my mug registered a cold blank, uncertain why they rubbed out the old clown, seeing how generous he was and all. Once I was back at the apartment, the sizzling metal of the El trains clinked and sparked outside my window so loudly I could almost grab hold of their shrieking wheels. *PIZZZ! CRRRUNCH!* The second I fell into a solid sleep, there came another rattling train, shaking my room like an earthquake every ten or twelve minutes. Staying in that tiny room for six months, I spent the summer there while working in various downtown bars, some of them pretty swank. I started shootin' the breeze with all kinds of swift-talking, power hungry ward bosses and a few high-hattin' aldermen. Chicago's slick politicians were smooth as a newly lacquered bowling lane, just as smooth.

"Did you see *that*?" I questioned my newest boss. Shrinking like a raisin in bowlful of milk, my index finger aimed straight toward the kitchen floor. "See that?" I alerted the white-aproned Master Chef, (also known as "Big Tuna") from one of downtown's most razzle-dazzle restaurants. Showing that character the rust-colored roaches scuttling around his restaurant's kitchen floor, they were milling around as happy as they pleased. Yeah, those bugs were scootin' all over the place like crusty nail heads with legs. Besides that, there were water leaks trickling all over, gushing like tiny Yosemite Falls.

Watching a gushing water stream flow straight into the joint's featured soup, "What they don't know won't hurt 'em," Big Tuna hooted like funny man Jack Benny, stirring the soup all the harder. "Say, Jerry boy," the chef motioned. "See the lady in the fancy red hat over at Table Three? That woman is complaining her steak is so tough she can't eat it. Bring her plate back out to me, will ya?" Moments later I returned, handing the lady's plate to the chef. Positioning her twenty-five-dollar steak in the center of our kitchen counter, the chef expertly hurled the chunky slab onto the roach-infested floor. Big Tuna started trampling the meat underneath all his weight as if it was a cartload of ripened grapes. Flinging the flattened steak back onto the grill, Big Tuna then ordered, "Send it on back to her now, Jerry boy."

About twenty minutes later when I was refilling her water glass, the hoity-toity woman, all dolled up in her shiny red Santa suit, gazed up at me with a giant toothy grin and said,

"Sonny, this is absolutely the best steak I have ever eaten. It's delicious. Please give my compliments to the chef."

Spreading the woman's message to Big Tuna, the whole kitchen broke out in roaring laughter; we were all nearly choking. I guess folks like her didn't know it, but behind that famous row of restaurants a whole hoard of dog-sized rats roughhoused nightly in the alley, mulling around like miniature furry street gangs. Bars 'round there stayed open all night, and those fancy-dancy restaurants hardly ever closed because the Loop was crammed with people from every corner of the world. Someone, somewhere was always throwing food away, plenty of good-eatin' for those furry packs of rats.

Unlocking the door to my room, I gawked at the splintered ceiling. Once while in New York City, I was so broke I ordered a hot water Catsup mix, buying a package of crackers for one penny to munch on with my watery soup. Slurping whiskeys with the winos one minute, I drank with powerful borough politicians in Manhattan taverns the next, never certain where my next meal might come from. And oh those aggravating brown outs and black outs along the Atlantic Coast. Spending money as soon as it fell into my hot hands, my only answer was to medicate myself with alcohol. Many folks boasted how they never drank at the gin mill, but most guys in the country hadn't walked in my shoes.

Staying on north Clark Street where there was a gal on every corner, cute chicks followed me wherever I went. I soon got a job at a bowling alley I once worked, since it was suddenly under new management. The name? Well, it was Lincoln Lanes located on busy north Lincoln Avenue, not far from Western, the longest street in Chicago, north to south, by far.

"Jesus, Mary, and Joseph," my old pal bellowed with a grin as I trotted through the bowling alley door looking for a job. "Yep, I bought this businez awhile ego," the rosy-faced Irishman explained with a welcoming smile. Like most of my positions, I was hired on the spot. An honest-talking, joke-loving fellow, Mike Sibley and I became fast friends because Mike was a "straight shooter" like me. Performing my usual chores around the alley with skill and ease, in time Mike put me in complete control of the bustling north side alley. Every time we locked up the bowling alley, Mike routinely inquired, "Jerry, did you lock up?"

"Yes, Mike, I sure did," I answered with a mellow smile.

Nonetheless, the two of us incessantly jangled the bowling alley door, always finding it shut and tightly locked. Afterward, we hit the town for drinks. Irish whiskey was Mike's favorite, straight up and with no ice. Patting me on the back as the sun started to peek over the lake's distant horizon, another new day dawned.

"What do ya think, Jerry? Think I could make it outside the bowling alley racket?" Mike questioned.

"Sure you can," I replied, clapping my arm around smiling Mike's shoulder. Working for Mike four whole years, Mike and I shared loads of gags along with a whole heap of hard work. That was my first really good relationship with someone who treated me decently; he was a mentor of sorts. And Mike's alley certainly made good money, and it was a swell place to take the family to learn that amazing sport. Since working there I'd become a better bowler, so good I was a finalist in the amateur bowling league, bowling a whopping 299 match, one pin short of a sanctioned "perfect game." They say it was easier to pitch a no-hitter in baseball than it was to bowl a perfect game in bowling. And hey, I certainly could believe it.

"There they goooo!" I shouted, watching the balls spin down the alleys like twirling black tops, hearing the pins crash against the wooden floor even in my sleep. I'd gotten so good at the sport I really enjoyed teaching people how to bowl. One thing I learned over the years was it was much easier to teach someone how to bowl that had *never* bowled before, than it was to *un*teach a fellow's bad bowling habits, trying to *re*teach someone the proper method of bowling. I had found my nitch in Chicago. It was far enough away from home, and miles away from Father. In the fall of 1945, I was nearing 21 years of age.

"It's over! War's over!" People were shouting and crying,

hugging, and leapin' high into the electric air. Warm smiles painted everyone's face, happily replacing the sullen scowls of the last several years. Camera lights were flashin' and the newspaper boys were yelling at everyone passing by.

"Extra! Extra! Get your *Chicago Tribune* here. War is over!" screamed the newsboys. I, too, was thrilled the war was over. By then, I was livin' by one basic rule: if you treated me good and didn't give me any guff, I'd do just about anything for you, *and I meant it.*

PART TWO

Finding My Way

VIRGINIA

My name means: "Pure, virginal"

CHAPTER 8

Nice Girl Like You

"I hope you're not sore at me," Jerry jibed and flirted while thoroughly draining his glass. That happened the second time I was seated next to him at a downtown club.

"If I was sore at you I sure would let you know," I reasoned aloud. Stretching my legs under the polished bar, "I just love the stage and picture shows down here," I cooed, remembering the last vaudeville show I had seen. Strands of my hair were naturally colored in the same shade as my favorite dark coffee, bits and pieces were curled wildly around my puffy, linen-soft face.

"Can't say I've seen too many of *those*," Jerry chuckled with adorable dipping lips. Chattering on about the countless hours he spent in various bowling alleys and the weeks he had sweat bullets in fancy restaurants, as well as the rough-and-tumble basement bars down in the Loop, he suavely hinted, "Maybe we could go sometime, Virginia, ... to one of those shows, I mean. Vaudeville ain't too bad. The comedians are a real gas," Jerry laughed while lighting my cigarette.

"I just love vaudeville acts."

His lengthy slim legs wheeled nervously around the bar stool, Jerry's peachy crooked smile, his straightforward style, and those witty words intrigued me like a Zane Grey novel. That blonde-haired man owned characteristics unlike my other loves—flibbergiberty men drawn to my friendly personality, kindheartedness, and striking looks. Born in the Chicago Heights' house built by my Swedish grandfather, the Heights was a growing suburb south of Chicago proper. I, like Jerry, had lived in so many places I could barely keep track of them. Finding home mainly in the small towns and rural villages of Illinois and Indiana, my two favorites were Hoopeston, Illinois, and Williamsport, Indiana. Located on Illinois Route 1, Hoopeston was famous for its corn, corn, and more corn. And Williamsport was an adorable little town set along the shores of the Wabash River, the same river my mother warned us to never swim, or even wade. But like the fools we girls were, Adelyn, Jane, and I swam in the river's spinning currents, the three of us thinking there was no harm in it whatsoever. No harm until the river's undercurrents started to change course, causing me to lose my balance and nearly drown. From then on, I was terrified of water.

"Williamsport is the most beautiful little town in the whole world," I told Jerry in regard to one of my most favorite places. Charming Williamsport possessed the most beautiful waterfall (the tallest in Indiana, about 90 feet tall) and wouldn't you know it? Yep, there we were again, walking behind those falls, another of Mother's warnings gone unheeded. "Oh dear Lord," I sniveled to Jerry with a dull smirk. "If we'd ever fallen in those falls, that would have been the end of us."

My two sisters and I spent much of our young lives with our paternal Grandmother Rena on her Ambia and Williamsport farms. Since our father, Gram's only child, Floyd O. (the "O" standing for Orange according to Dad) was injured at birth, the poor soul never found enough work to support his own family. So Gram became our secondary mother, raising us three girls on her farm. But even during that awful Depression (when a single penny could get a sad sack of a person a cup of coffee) you wouldn't have believed the fun we had living out in the country.

"Even though we didn't have one bit of electricity, modern heating, or indoor plumbing, we ate the best food in the nation. Yes, we had the sweetest corn, the fattest chickens, the freshest milk and the juiciest berries," I constantly boasted about country life to Jerry. "Whether climbing up the windmill, playing with our new-born ivory lamb, running the grassy hills with Gram's farm dog, Betty, attending church suppers and sweltering, saw-dust floor tent meetings, my childhood memories were pleasant as homemade ice cream—creamy rich and soothing."

"I don't know much about country life, Virginia," Jerry admitted after ordering another drink.

"Let me tell you something, Jerry, it's the best," I readily confirmed. "Grandma Rena and Grandpa James smoothed out the rough edges that might have otherwise made Adelyn, Jane, and I dead as run down opossums," I declared with a smile. Twirling the ice cubes in my drink, distant strains of a "swing tune" on the radio interrupted my thoughts, carrying them toward my days on the farm. A faithful Christian, wherever there was a church meetin' Grandma Rena always found it. Gram was one of twelve children, born in 1873 to the family of Elijah Evans. Doing anything to make us girls laugh, Gram played all kinds of silly pranks with us around the farm. Why she was even involved in a few miracles, marvels unable to be humanly explained. One miracle involved Gram and her husband, Grandpa James. While driving down an old country lane in their chugging Model T, for some reason their car whacked into something on the rutted country road. The metal toppled and twisted until the whole car turned completely upside down, the whole shebang falling on top of poor Grandpa James. After praying as hard as she could, Grams lifted the clunky car off her husband's body, freeing him from the massive mound of heavy metal. The two escaped with only minor bruises and a few scrapes. Don't that just beat all?

"I plum done and tried pickin' up that clunky Model T again some time later," Gram often remarked, wearing her best wide smile. "But I just couldn't do it, Ginny Mae. No, the Lord was with me that day, giving me supernatural strength to lift that car off your Gramps, saving his precious life."

Needless to say, we were all baffled when strange occurrences began happening in Gram's 1800's, white Victorian farmhouse, real strange events let me tell you. One time, for instance, Grams, Mom, and us girls were in the kitchen helping to get supper. Out of nowhere the gaslight fixture in the dining room started swinging back and forth on its own accord. The five of us stared at one other with eyes as big as saucers. Then, we heard all types of movement up in the attic where Dad was taking an afternoon nap.

"Ginny Mae," Gram called to me from her place at the stove. "Will you please go upstairs and tell your father it's almost time to eat? It sounds like he's awake and doing something with those boxes up there." Despising those creepy stairs leading up to the third floor where Dad was sleeping, the closer I got to the top of the staircase the more the tiny hairs on my arms and neck began standing straight up on end. Peering through the room's doorway, I instantly saw Dad sound asleep. Everything in the room was in perfect order, hushed as a pasture fence. Without a doubt, whoever lived in that house before us left some spirits who sure didn't like Grandma Rena—her own strong spirit agitating them like a milk churn, causing the whole bunch to make quite a hullabaloo in the attic! One day that old white Victorian house burnt flat down to the ground. No, them 'ole spirits didn't like any of us one bit.

"I hope to find some work in Chicago," I heard Dad tell Mother hopefully some months later. So in 1934 I moved to Chicago's Hyde Park district with my parents and two sisters, eager to start the seventh grade. By that time I had attended numerous schools including a two-room schoolhouse in rural Indiana. In those days, the schoolhouse was heated solely by one lone potbelly stove. Kids all the way from the first grade to the eighth were crowded into the two adjoining rooms. Each school day our teacher cooked potato soup for us kids—how delicious that potato soup smelled, cookin' on the potbelly stove on cold winter days.

Hyde Park's focal point was the site of the 1893 "World's Fair," where the famous Museum of Science and Industry (the original World's Fair's Fine Arts Building) was built. I graduated from Hyde Park High School on 62nd and South Stony—that was how I started in Chicago—such a fine town; it always carried plenty of everything.

"He's the greatest trick shot bowler who ever lived. He's the best in the whole world," Jerry gushed, grinning from ear to ear. His face glowed like a cigarette, and his mouth gaped wide as our eyes were peeled on the great Andy Varipapa. Andy was bowling in the most prestigious bowling alley in Chicago, a high hat, swell place on Damen Avenue. Jerry quickly explained how a man named Louis Petersen had opened a bowling alley on the second floor of that building back in 1919. Staging a tournament two years later, Mr. Petersen paid $1,000 to the bowler who rolled the highest total of eight games. In time, the tournament, "The Petersen Classic," had grown to be a bowling tradition.

"Known simply as, "The Greek," Andy Varipapa was considered the greatest one-man bowling show on Earth," Jerry stated, his face as excited as all get out. Gazing into my eyes from the alley's highest stool, Jerry described how he was called Jerry because he fixed whatever needed to be fixed, "jerry-rigging" things to save his boss money. "I've never met anyone like you before," Jerry said, staring into the center of my eyes on our next meeting downtown. "And by the way," he added with his charming crooked smile, "I hate to say this, Virginia, but what's a nice girl like you doing in a place like this?"

Throwing my head back, I let out an awkward giggle. "Jerry," I muttered. "That's just about the oldest line in the book. I came downtown with some of my girlfriends, stopping a few minutes for a drink. Suddenly, here you are again."

"Can I ask you one more question?" Jerry leaned in closer, speaking as mellow as a morning cup of coffee. "Do you have a telephone and can I have your phone number?"

"That's *two* questions, Jerry," I countered, scribbling my telephone number in pencil on a crumpled napkin. "Give me a call if you would like to have dinner sometime, *and that's it.* I sure ain't no pick-up girl; that's not my style." Tucking the napkin neatly inside his pocket, Jerry said now he had two reasons to move from Chicago's North Side to the city's South Side—Petersen's Classic, and me.

"You remind me so much of my mother," Jerry's eyes again fastened onto mine on our next date, tightly clutching my hand. "You're not after my money, and you're not looking for a quick fling. Virginia, I haven't been able to get you out of my mind," he confessed a few days later. Dining at a restaurant near my Cottage Grove apartment, Jerry had a new job working at a bowling alley off Western Avenue. Tall and lean as a light pole, my handsome go-getter Jerry was constantly being promoted, succeeding in every bowling alley he stepped inside.

"I won the PBA patch! I won the patch!" Jerry prattled on a clear night in 1953. Winning the patch for, "Best-Sanctioned Team Play," how Jerry beamed, buoyantly toasting the crowd with his win. He worked steadily in prestigious alleys citywide until quite unexpectedly a new-fangled contraption arrived in some of Chicago's high-class bowling alleys. The blasted thing was called an automatic pinsetter, putting guys like Jerry right out of work.

"This is the end of an era, isn't it?" I questioned, blowing cigarette smoke into the tense air.

"Yeah," Jerry acknowledged in a mild sulk. "The man behind the pins will soon be a thing of the past."

So I began to wonder: *Now what would he do?*

"I can't believe we're finally married," I driveled to my sister Adelyn, unable to withhold the good news. "Right at the Cook County courthouse," I bragged, twirling my gold wedding ring. Filing away the acid sting of my first abusive marriage, after we started our new lives in one of those flophouse rooms in the south Loop, before long Jerry and I settled in a small apartment in the city's Englewood neighborhood near 69th and Green. There we listened to the woodpeckers nibbling at the trees instead of El trains clanging every four or five minutes. And there I watched bushy grey squirrels chatter and leap instead of meetin' up with that lousy, skin-tailed rat I ran into downtown.

"Thanks Jerry for Luke," I conveyed to my new husband with a generous hug.

"Luke is just the guard dog you need when I'm away at work," Jerry replied. Selling ice cream in the housing projects on the city's Southwest Side during the day, at night, Jerry kept his new hot dog wagon (a converted, three-wheel Cushman scooter) parked across from a tavern on 47th Street, smack in the area called the Back of the Yards, west of the Chicago stockyards. He sold hot dogs for ten cents a piece and tamales for five cents, as well as cherry, grape, strawberry, and tangy banana Popsicles for two cents each. Breaking them in half for the little girls and boys in the city, Jerry charged those poor sweet kids just one penny, if that's all they had.

1955, the middle of the decade, was also the year of Grace Kelly, President Eisenhower, and heavyweight boxer Rocky Marciano. I was also alive since I was expecting our first child. During Chicago's snowy cold winters, Jerry still set pins in older bowling alleys like Gateway Bowling on North Avenue, The Vermont, The

Marigold Bowling Alley off Broadway Avenue, C.Y.O., and Archer Avenue's spectacular Miami Bowl, holding strong with over 80 lanes. Although the city boasted one hundred sanctioned bowling alleys (with scores of smaller, homier ones) it seemed Jerry's true calling was catering, selling ice cream and hot dogs to his growing public. He loved the people and the people truly loved him. Yeah, he was no simpleton, let me tell you.

"What's your name?" A barefoot little boy asked Jerry one afternoon while he was selling ice cream in the projects. A good name, you know, meant everything.

"Name?" Jerry played. "My name's Sam. Sam, The Ice Cream Man."

Jerry had quickly realized his major clientele (many of them second and third generation offspring of European immigrants) genuinely craved a specific product—juicy, fleshy hot dogs and spicy "old country" sausages. So when Jerry's business mind connected with his doting fans, my "gun-ho" husband knew more than anything a good name meant everything. So as he began selling hot dogs full time, primarily in the Back of the Yards but in various other city locations as well, from that day forward he would forever be known in Chicago as,

Sam.
Sam, the Hot Dog Man.

CHAPTER 9

Lemon-Haired Girl

Hyde Park, August 1956 — "I think I interrupted his golf game,"
I clattered my tale to Addie, gabbing to my big sister, Adelyn, all
about my Jewish doctor. "Yeah, the old goat was perturbed I'd
gone into labor at the University of Chicago's Lying-In Hospital
on such a gorgeous summer afternoon."

"You are such a card, Virginia," Addie laughed. Addie (so
pretty her husband called her a "Dresden Doll") had adopted
a blonde-haired little girl of her own, about a year older than
Lynn—*our* new baby girl. Addie's little girl's name was Sarah, and
the two of us were equally enthralled with our babies. Whenever
I looked down at baby Lynn, snug as a June bug in her crib, I
couldn't stop thanking God for the miracle. Having previously
lost two children, I had made a solemn oath to God: *God, if
you will give me two children to replace the two I have lost, I
will dedicate them totally to you.* So the moment my baby girl
was born I prayed, "Lord, I dedicate Lynn to you." I had Lynn
dedicated publicly at the Nazarene Church on 83rd Street, also
having her baptized. Though our beautiful baby was awake at all
hours of the night then sleeping like a darling during the day, she
was *His* precious blessing.

Before I knew it, Lynn was walking around the apartment like a champ. With the cutest smile on her pursy lips, my little gal repeated all sorts of words—big long words like, antidisestablishmentarianism. Yep, Lynn pronounced that very long word, and many others. She said each of those words as clear as a bell when we were at home. But whenever we shopped at the supermarket, I would ask Lynn to say one of those big words for the women shoppers. Instead of saying one measly syllable, she clammed up and looked at me with her clear blue eyes as if I flipped my lid. Dressing her in frilly pink, white, and yellow dresses, Lynn was my little doll. By that time, Jerry, Lynn, and I had moved into a second-floor apartment near 62nd and Bishop in Englewood, an ideal spot for Jerry since it was above a tavern. And didn't I know how Jerry loved his drink, sopping it down like soda pop!

"Hurry, Lynn. Hurry! Wake up Lynn, quick!" I hollered one morning a few years later to my three-year-old sleeping daughter. Dense smoke had whorled into my nostrils, snaking like the devil into our second-floor apartment. Rousing me up from a solid sleep on that newly dawned, early spring day, I jerked open our squeaky back screen door. Grayish-white clouds had nearly suffocated my lungs. Prodding Lynn from her bed, I scooped her lightweight form tightly into my shaky arms. Wrapping my red cloth coat around her shivery body, the two of us were clammy cold in our thin nightclothes. Racing down the chipped wooden stairs with Lynn in tow, I soon realized someone had already called the fire department. The black-coated, muscled firemen were furiously spraying their giant hoses on the smoky blaze. Everyone on the block smelled the drenched wood and the sopping flames that clogged our throats.

"You okay, ma'am?" One of the firemen shouted over the drenching ruckus.

"We're fine," I hoarsely gulped. Clutching little Lynn's body with all my might, our eyes were caked with shock. "Who *did* this?"

"Don't know, ma'am. Didn't even know anyone was up there in your apartment."

"I finally found out what happened with the fire," Jerry fumed a few days later, still spittin' like a mule. Red-faced and ashen-eyed at the same time, my jittery husband spurted out how our lemon-haired little girl and I had experienced such a close call. Seated at our chrome kitchen table, "Some lunk was mad at the tavern owner downstairs because he got thrown out of the joint. The stooge was fallin' down drunk," stated Jerry, sipping straight black coffee between his words. "The guy was so soused up he went and got a can of kerosene, wantin' to set the whole place on fire." Shaking his head in angry disbelief, I had never seen Jerry so steamed. "We've got to get outta here," he suddenly blurted out. "Virginia, we're lookin' for a new place."

One thing I really loved about Chicago was there were always plenty of apartments available to rent. There were expensive apartments in the higher-class neighborhoods, cheaper apartments converted from basements and attics, and medium-priced flats falling somewhere in between. But the apartment fire proved to be a haunting memory because Jerry kept repeating, "If it happened once, it can happen again."

Settling into our new apartment (a large tenement building near 59th and Halsted about a mile away from our previous flat) I began to think about a strange occurrence happening some weeks before the fire. The whole thing caused shivers to run clear up and down my spine. One quiet afternoon I suddenly heard:

"Mommy, Mommy," little Lynn called to me in an odd, shaky tone. Mere moments after awakening from her afternoon nap, I rushed like crazy into her cute, yellow-walled bedroom. "What is it, Lynn?" I asked. Nervously scanning her bedroom, I saw our lemon-haired girl standing puzzled in the middle of the room. "Lynn, what's the matter?"

"There were all sorts of butterflies in my room just now," Lynn's brow furrowed in childlike uncertainty.

"Butterflies? What did they look like, honey?"

Using her pale hands in an attempt to explain, Lynn formed flapping wings with the bony fingers of her two dimpled hands, wings something like that of a bird. Or yes, even a butterfly. "They were all around, flying all around me," she continued. Fluttering her hands in circles, my heart beat faster than a whizzing truck.

"Okay, honey," I finally muttered, trying like all get-out to catch my breath. "Let me know if you see any more." After a few minutes Lynn tottered back into her bedroom, playing as usual with her little kiddy "do-dads" and pretty baby dolls.

"I hope she's not delirious; there's not something wrong with her mind, is there?" Jerry questioned with panicky eyes. Later on that night, the two of us pondered Lynn's experience over coffee and cigarettes.

"No, I don't think so," I jiggled my head, tossing Jerry a loose smile. Swishing the sugar and cream inside my coffee cup, I gave Jerry in a heartfelt promise. "I'll keep an eye on her and we'll see."

The next day while Lynn was playing with some little trinkets on the kitchen floor I stooped down and asked, "Lynn, have you seen anymore 'butterflies'?"

Shaking her head, I exhaled a sigh of relief. "Okay, honey. You go on playing then."

Relaxing that afternoon in our kitchen with a fresh cup of coffee, scores of religious accounts streamed into my soul. Old family stories and varied reports of angelic encounters unable to be logically explained weaved through my mind. Actually, when I was awakened on the morning of the fire it seemed that someone, some invisible being shook me awake. *Could have been one of those angels that visited Lynn, those so-called "butterflies." Yeah, just could have been.*

Within a few weeks, Jerry had purchased a television set. Lynn loved, *The Lone Ranger,* our little gal prancing around the apartment pretending to be "Tonto," the Lone Ranger's Indian friend. One autumn day while watching, *Sea Hunt,* with good-looking Lloyd Bridges diving deep into the sea, the next thing I knew, blaring sirens had shattered our peace-filled afternoon.

"Lynn, Lynn, we're being invaded!" I yelled, searching the sky for alien ships ready to steal us up into outer space. The sirens shrieked so loudly if it wasn't alien ships it surely must have been Russian invaders, taking over our city and the rest of the United States.

"What's all the racket?" My neighbor, Annette, hollered, sprinting from her apartment located directly to our right. Her delicate, toast-colored face was racked with twists and furrows as she too gazed toward the sky.

"Are we being invaded, Ann? Listen to those sirens."

"I doubt it, Virgie," Annette paused with a blank smile. Staring up at the empty sky she smartly suggested, "Why don't you turn on the radio? They may know something."

Switching on the brown radio atop our kitchen icebox, "WHEW, WHEW, YAH! THE WHITE SOX HAVE WON THE PENNANT! I REPEAT, THE CHICAGO WHITE SOX," the frantic-voiced announcer prattled in a non-stop yelp. "CHICAGO'S GO-GO WHITE SOX HAVE WON THE PENNANT. Ladies and Gentlemen," he added, "Don't worry about those sirens. Our Mayor, the Honorable Richard J. Daley, is the greatest White Sox fan in the world—he's a bit excited right now so please excuse those sirens. Why I do believe the Mayor's first date with his wife, Eleanor "Sis" Daley, was right here to see the Chicago White Sox," the broadcaster beamed.

"Oh, that Mayor Daley," I grumbled to Jerry on that night in the fall of '59. "He nearly scared the living daylights out of me."

"Have you flipped your wig?" Jerry joshed. "You mean you didn't know the Sox were playing for the pennant, Virge?"

"How am I supposed to know about some silly game?" I questioned with a full shrug.

With that, Jerry laughed his head off, thinking that was about the funniest thing he had ever heard in all his born days.

I really loved our new apartment because it was so close to all the stores, particularly the wonderful shopping on 63rd and Halsted Street. Right on that corner was a huge Sears department store whose motto was: "Sears has everything." Addie's husband, Ray, worked in the television department of that Sears store so one day Lynn and I walked over to see him.

"The old neighborhood in South Shore has really gotten torn up," Ray's double-chinned face grimaced. In no time at all his soft eyes were threatening tears over the way the old neighborhood had changed. An Iowa native who was too young for World War I and too old for World War II, Raymond had become an ardent businessman. "Yeah, they tore up everything in my laundry and beat up poor Bruce."

"Sure is a shame," I sympathized with Ray, silently praying Bruce (Ray and Addie's oldest child) would be A-okay. Shortly after arriving back at the apartment, Lynn and I heard muffled yelling in the tenement yard. That was followed by a series of bloodcurdling screams. "What's goin' on out there, Lynn?' I asked, my heart poundin' like a mallet. Upon opening the screen door I quickly discovered Annette was in another fight with her husband. "Oh dear God," I cupped my face inside my hands, immobilized on the wooden deck we all shared.

"Help me! Help me, please!" Annette screamed at the top of her lungs, tightly gripping her right arm. Squirting like a water fountain, sticky red flecks from Annette's arm dotted the chipped wood of our massive tenement deck.

"She's hit a vein, Lynn. She's hit a vein." Later on I realized I probably should not have involved Lynn in Annette's terrible ordeal because Lynn was very timid. Once the poor child saw the ugly flow of blood, Lynn ran and hid in a corner of her bedroom. Crouching down, I found her in the same place she often hid when Jerry came home roaring drunk like a blubbering fool. Dialing the ambulance, in no time they took Annette to the hospital. After she was gone, Lynn and I inspected the big window facing our tenement deck, the same window Ann had put her entire arm through when fighting with her husband. Our stomachs swished when the two of us viewed a large shattered circle in the windowpane; both of us could still smell the soaked blood. After several hours Annette returned, her arm bandaged from shoulder to wrist. The entire floor of our tenement building was the same—silent and subdued.

My expanded dress billowed freely in the electric fan's breeze as I pulled aside the sheer Priscilla window curtains, checking the street outside for any sign of Jerry. Jerry had been in an auto accident while driving with some friends and he was wearing a white plastic brace around his neck. But that old neck brace was causin' little Lynn to be more terrified of her father than ever. I think the poor girl thought her father was some sort of thundering giant, especially when he traipsed through the doorway of our apartment, ordering me around like a kid. I felt bad about the whole state of affairs and I didn't blame Lynn one bit. Stumbling home after drinking more than he should have, Jerry nearly caused me to faint dead away when the nut filled our oil heater all the way to the brim.

"Stop loadin' up that heater until it's red as hellfire, Jerry. You're spilling oil all over the apartment floor," I yelled like a wild woman. "You're gonna kill us all!" I raised my voice at that man of mine. All the while, however, Jerry stood by that oil heater grinning like a schoolboy, scaring me to kingdom come. "You'll blow us all up to high heaven," I managed, the flame flickering in my pupils.

"Noo, I I wooonnnt," Jerry stuttered.

And that's when Lynn hid; she had really grown petrified of her father.

"Why don't you bring her home a toy?" I suggested to Jerry since he too was worried about Lynn being so afraid of him. So there came Jerry, bringing home a toy for Lynn. The three of us were seated at the kitchen table and I was so proud of my husband because he was really trying to be a good father. Bringing home a new toy for Lynn, Jerry removed it politely out of his crinkled paper sack.

"I got this for *you*," Jerry's cheeks beamed like the summer sun. Setting the metal windup toy in the middle of the table, Lynn didn't seem to know what to do with the new toy. So Jerry wound up the black and red Mickey Mouse figure tightly. Scooting around the table, the three of us watched Mickey's clumsy movements as he flit and fluttered until Jerry grabbed it, saving the toy from toppling to the floor. Both of us gazed intently at Lynn, watching for her reaction.

"It's nice," she said with a cheery smile.

Jerry was somewhat disappointed Lynn wasn't more enthused about the nice windup toy, so when the weather grew nice he took our little daughter on the bus for a ride. Together they went, hand-in-hand to beautiful Marquette Park on 67th Street, just the two of them. Afterwards, our lemon-haired girl seemed a bit more welcoming toward Jerry, making me happy because that spring I was going to have another baby to care for.

Washing clothes in my used wringer washing machine, I flopped onto the full bed, my eyes brightened as I thought: *Maybe this time it would be a boy.*

CHAPTER 10

Held Hostage

"My water bag just broke!" I squealed to Lynn, cool liquid rushing down my legs onto the apartment's hall floor. Barely able to move my bulky body, I instantly reached over to telephone my neighbor, Leticia, a good friend who Jerry and I normally called Lettie. To Lynn, she was simply known as Mrs. M., the initial of the last name of her dearly departed husband, Sid Misner. Although she had what was known as, "St. Vitas Dance," stuttering her words and shivering her hands, Lettie was a loyal friend, a widow who would do just about anything for us. On the same token, she was also a gal who almost everyone else threw away just because she was different. In a fast Chicago second, Lettie was at our apartment, walking from the "Y," the YWCA, where she lived. Helping me telephone Addie, (who was going to watch Lynn) Lettie called a cab because Jerry was at work. Swabbing up the huge puddle of liquid with an old towel, Lettie wrung it out as I kissed Lynn good-bye. "Wait here with Mrs. M. until your Aunt Adelyn comes," I instructed Lynn. "You go with Adelyn, honey, so I can have this baby."

"Your little brother or sister is on their way," Adelyn informed Lynn as the two drove to her home in suburban, tree-lined Green

Park. When the doctor announced I had given birth to a baby boy, everyone, especially Jerry, was ecstatic. But the excitement soon died down when I gave Jerry the disturbing news. "The hospital won't let our baby Lee and I out of here until you pay the bill in full," I bemoaned to Jerry. "Six hundred dollars even."

In seconds, my husband's shining expression slipped into an ashtray-sized scowl since we never had expected such a large bill. So although on that April 10, 1960, (four days following little Lee's birth) it was cold and snowing outside, Jerry set up his hot dog wagon for business, pressed to make enough money so Lee and I could be released from being held hostage at Sacred Cross Hospital.

"As soon as Jerry has the money, Addie," I tried to explain to my sister by telephone, "I'm bringing baby Lee home. He's a remarkable baby boy, he really and truly is. His skin is still a bit rosy, but aren't all babies red as a rose when they're born? And say, I'm sorry about you having to watch Lynn for so long."

"It's no trouble, Virginia, she's doing fine," Addie soothed, calming my anxious nerves. "Only thing is, I had to bribe her to eat, making sure there are plenty of chocolate "Suzie-Q's" on hand for dessert. See you soon."

With baby Lee growing by leaps and bounds, and Lynn turning four in August, Jerry and I had soon realized the tenement apartment was no place for a family. Besides, in the past few months Jerry had partnered up with a new fellow, a cigar smoking, loveable Greek named Nick Dukas.

"Come on in, Nick," Jerry quipped to his new friend on moving day. It was on that lovely day Lynn and I met Jerry's new partner for the very first time. Panting deeply with a chunky cigar lit between his stout fingers, smoke curled unevenly throughout Nick's wavy, brown-black hair, sweet-scented puffy mists filling those tiny rooms. Gathering my houseplants, I was more than ready for the move, spending our final minutes in Englewood.

"Ho heh, heh," hooted Nick with a half-moon grin, his curved stomach jiggling like cranberry sauce. As his fat cigar smoldered, the simmering tobacco created a distinct aroma everyone had no choice but to soak in. "This is my little girl, Gwen," Nick introduced his friendly daughter, the two peering at Lynn with eager, blackberry-colored eyes. Blonde-haired Lynn and brown-headed Gwen played telephone and chitchatted like old chums, as they were only one month apart in age. How thankful I was concerning their acquaintance since we were moving right across the street from the Dukas family that included: Nick and his wife, Diana, their oldest daughter, Rita, their middle daughter, Amelia, and then little Gwen. Off our young family headed to the neighborhood called West Elsdon, the sister community of West Lawn. We were renting an attic apartment above some of Nick's relatives near 54th Place and St. Louis, a block east of some of Chicago's largest railroad yards.

"Our neighborhood is filled with young families and bucket loads of kids," smiling Nick noted.

"I'm sure glad you got your baby boy Lee out of the hospital," Gwen looked up at me wide-eyed when I relayed the circumstances surrounding Lee's birth. "He's so cute. Can I hold him? Pleeease?" Gwen pleaded.

"Sure. But please be careful."

Like a miniature doting mother, Gwen lifted baby Lee from my bed. Cuddling him warmly within her small arms, Gwen was gentle as a hospital nurse. Man, that girl sure loved babies, wanting to push baby Lee in the stroller, telling the whole neighborhood that he was *her* little baby boy.

"Nick is the king of his castle," Jerry spouted one night after work. "Whatever *he* says goes, yeah," Jerry boasted. His willy-nilly speech was taken straight from Nick's mouth, Jerry blabbering all this foolishness in front of the kids to boot. Belting out this idiocy about being kings after selling all day on their blue-paneled truck

(Jerry and Nick sold ice cream, potato chips, and hot dogs to South Side factories galore) I squished my forehead within my chapped hands. Then, I posed the million-dollar question to Jerry without batting an eye:

"What do you mean, king of his castle?" I probed. Puckering my cherry-slicked lips, I nervously thumbed my wooly curls.

"I mean whatever *he* says goes," Jerry wallowed, his own belly increased to match Nick's rambling waistline. Although I didn't say a word to Jerry outright, the next day I made my case to Lynn, telling her there was no such thing as a king in *our* house. So to Jerry *and Nick,* I said one big, hoop-de-do to you!

Nick, for practical as well as business purposes, started calling Jerry, Gus. *Gus? Hey Gus. Hiya Gus.* It seemed in the Chicago business world everyone had a nickname. Gus, of course, was city lingo so I guessed Nick felt Jerry was part of the family. When those two got together they jabbered like there was no tomorrow. They were like twin brothers to be honest, almost as if the rest of the world had suddenly stopped.

"How's the business?" Jerry excitedly shot the breeze with Nick each morning shortly after sunrise, the pair convening like two hotshot lawyers.

"Hey, you can buy fifty pounds of onions at South Water Market today, Gus," Nick pointed north toward the famous fruit and vegetable market near the Loop. Squinting between scattered drags on his moist cigar, Nick paused, waiting for Gus's response.

"Yeah," Jerry agreed, puffing out his own cloudy gust. "Ya know that kid from the ice cream plant got the flu so we won't be able to get the deal on dry ice until next Thursday."

"You still goin' out today then, Gus?" Nick asked, scanning the nickel-colored sky because it looked like it might rain.

"Yeah, I'm goin', Nick. Gotta make the scratch. Rent is due and I ain't got no time to waste."

These two were real cards—but *kings*? Huh.

"Thatta girl," I encouraged Lynn, boosting her up onto the tall kitchen stool. Her delicate form was settled on the black kitchen stool since our little gal was helping me slap golden wafers atop each of the three-flavored chunks of ice cream. Slicing the huge block of vanilla, chocolate, and strawberry ice cream Jerry had given me, I was helping him make those sandwich novelties to sell. Wrapping each one, I stored them neatly in wax paper for he and Nick. "Here's one for you, Lynn," I offered, passing the ice cream sandwich to our daughter. A few hours later, I was wheeling the baby to the Hi-Low supermarket just across the tracks in order to buy food for the family. Exactly as I had taught her, Lynn tightly gripped the metal baby stroller with her left hand as we navigated the bumpy train yards of the Grand Trunk Railroad. I sternly warned her time and again. "Lynn, never go near those tracks because there's a big hobo camp there almost every night. Those men are dangerous." Yep, the railroad yards were filled with odd-looking ducks giving me the willies. And as for the five dollars Jerry handed me each day to feed our family, it was certainly hard to stretch that measly pittance, trying to feed a family of four. But I watched the newspapers and caught the weekly sales—a pound of bologna and a loaf of bread for 29 cents a piece, a sack of chicken for $1.00, delicious raisin spice cake for 79 cents, and thankfully, we got our milk delivered right on our doorstep.

West Elsdon was jam-packed with Catholics, like much of the busy Southwest Side. There were only a few rare exceptions like me. I soon realized the Dukas family was Orthodox Greek. I had begun sending Lynn to a local Sunday School with a lady friend of mine, trying to get her used to being with other kids. The poor girl, however, came home sobbing something fierce, and then suddenly she wanted to go back. Kids! I needed not have worried for one second about any of it since as soon as Lynn started kindergarten, she loved it. Chumming around with all her neighborhood friends like Gwen, Camy, Olivette, and Laura down the street had helped a heap.

Ever since she was around four, Lynn had an invisible friend who she talked to constantly. "Don't you know he's right there? Don't you see him?" Lynn asked me with a creased brow, peering to her right as if someone was standing there next to her.

"*Who's* there, Lynn?" I questioned in a puzzling tone.

"My friend—he's right here, talking to me."

Just as that childhood stage seemed to fade, and school finally let out in June, it seemed as the hottest summer on record had begun. "I'm sweatin' like a bull," I moaned to Lynn.

Lynn was often silent as a church mouse but her sharp mind watched every little thing anyone did, observing the world like a country hawk. My chalky white blouse was glued to my back as I scrambled through that broiling attic apartment. The twin window fans were squeaking in the front living room window; the big floor fan near the back door was off-balanced and swirling, intending to suck out the entire apartment's stifling, muggy air.

"It's got to be 100 degrees in here, even with those three fans running," I groaned, my body bogged down in sweat. Peering at the skeleton key hanging next to the back door, more often than not we didn't even lock up. I was thrilled when the Nick and Diana asked us over for a picnic and swimming in their pool because I knew the kids were roasting like I was. "Did you get him? Is Lee okay?" I yelled in panic about an hour after we arrived. My sandaled feet raced to Dukas' swimming pool on that blazing hot night; my blood ran as cold as one of Jerry's Popsicles. Quizzing Nick's daughter, Amelia, my heart thumped like a tack hammer against my chest. As the backyard chatter grew eerily silent, all eyes were plastered on little Lee.

"Lee's just fine," Amelia shouted with drippy lips. Bobbling in the water, Amelia held our little Lee, water twirling like a liquid tornado from the tangled mass of drifting kids.

"How'd he go down so fast?" I questioned Amelia and some of the others in the pool who were playing and watching him.

Shrugging their shoulders, not one of them knew for certain what had happened to Lee. But I was sure glad that angel Amelia was there to save him.

Besides the heat and humidity, another bad thing about that apartment were the squirrels. Yep, there was an entire family of squirrels climbing to the top of our apartment building. Every day those mutts found ideal shelter underneath the building's roof, directly above our flat. The moment everything in our house calmed down, (usually when Lee went to sleep) those noisy rodents went to chewin'. All we heard on most afternoons were the hair-raising sounds of *GNAW! CHEW! CHOMP!* The worst thing about the whole mess was when those squirrels got to gnawing, scattered pieces of paint fell flat into poor Lee's crib, frightening me like crazy because the falling paint chips contained lead.

"There are squirrels up there under the roof, Jerry, I'm not kidding," I griped to my husband when he came home from selling with Nick.

"There are *no* squirrels under the roof," chortled Jerry, as if I was nutty as a loon.

"Aren't there squirrels up there in the attic?" I probed Lynn, my sole alibi. A second later I paused and thought: *I should have known better; she won't utter a word, not that girl.* Lynn just shrugged like I figured she would. But then, she surprised me and piped up like a champ.

"We hear them in the afternoon when Lee is sleeping," Lynn shyly confirmed.

In light of Lynn's surprisingly clear admission, Jerry made a rapid complaint to our landlord, Sonny, who lived downstairs. The very next day, Sonny and his teenage son mounted a tall metal extension ladder to the top of our apartment building. While checking the whole thing out above our ceiling, the two ran smack into the family of squirrels. Loading the roof eves with poisonous *Decon*, in no time those squirrels were thankfully gone.

"Boy oh boy, Lynn. You'll need to wear just about every stitch of clothing you own today," I informed our daughter. Getting ready to go to first grade on that bitterly cold January morning, Lynn had to walk five blocks to the Sawyer School. The temperature outside registered minus 16 below zero. Since all schoolgirls had to wear dresses or skirts to public school, on a day like that Lynn heaved on heavy knee socks over her tights, tugging pants on over all that. Removing the pants when she got to school, Lynn stored them with her coat in the coatroom before the bell rang at nine o'clock sharp. Along with a knit hat, white sweater, a long scarf to protect her face, gloves, boots, and a thick winter coat, I still wasn't sure she'd be completely warm.

"You'll never guess what happened on my way to school this morning," Lynn's face beamed when she skipped into the apartment, rushing through the back door on that dim January afternoon.

"What happened, hon?"

Darting around the apartment like a wild monkey, Lee was getting into all sorts of things as usual. My busy toddler barreled around those rooms in his own bulky pants, dressed in thick wool pants and stockings.

"Well, Lynn began. "Just when I started to walk to school, Nick and Dad pulled up in their truck. Then Nick yelled out, "Hey, Lynn, it's too cold for you to walk to school. Wanna a ride?" So I walked up the stairs and held onto the truck's silver pole. The floor of the truck was real slippery and Dad was laughing. So Nick drove me in the big blue truck. No one ever had a ride to school like that before!"

I was surely taken aback by Lynn's bouncy words since our

little girl didn't really talk that much. "You're right, Lynn," I grinned and shook my head. "I am so glad you got a ride on such a cold day." Sometimes I worried myself to death about the kids, particularly as Lee had just gotten over a bout with Scarlet Fever. His entire little body had broken out in red, welt-like blotches, scattered all over his fine skin. Pleading for the doctor to make a house call, after my intense prayers, little Lee recovered just fine.

"No, Lee, no," I was hollering like a crazy woman one afternoon in spring. About the time God had finally sent the first spring breezes whisking through our back screen door, silly Lee went and whacked his head. That young whippersnapper of ours was doin' his best to run away from me. "Come back, Lee," I yelled. Clutching my hand mirror between his tiny dimpled hands, Lee just kept runnin' like a racehorse, crashing straight into the iron rung of the back room's low bed. "Come help me, Lynn," I screamed, my mouth and eyes awash in sheer panic. But Lynn hid like a scared rabbit in the front room because I kept yellin' like a fool, "Lee cracked his head open! Lee cracked open his head!" Thank God Trudi downstairs was at home is all I can say. Immediately giving me a lift to the doctor's office so our son's shattered forehead could be properly stitched up, out of all that mess an odd thing happened. Would you believe those stitches ended up looking exactly like a miniature cross? Yep, there was a small cross smack dab in the middle of Lee's forehead.

Dressed in starched blue uniforms, two Chicago policemen stood soberly in the middle of my kitchen, making me nervous as a cat. It was about ten minutes before Lynn was slated to come home from Sawyer School.

"Ma'am," one of them calmly said, his shoulders squared and stiff. "Your daughter was choked by a boy in her first grade class," the officer reported. "We just wanted to make sure you knew what happened in case there was any further trouble."

"Are you *okay*?" I quizzed Lynn the moment she walked through the screen door. Checking her over from head to toe, I threw my arms around our poor little girl, grabbing her tightly as I could. Nodding her head, Lynn explained how the boy who sat behind her had suddenly grabbed her throat, trying to strangle her neck with both hands. When the teacher called me on the telephone, I could hardly believe it. The teacher would change the boy's seat immediately so he wouldn't be sitting behind Lynn anymore.

"He's sitting in the last row, in the last seat," Lynn detailed the swift change after school on the following day.

Although I was thrilled to pieces Lynn would be safe from that little boy's awful violence, the police officers mentioned something I couldn't get out of my mind.

"Is there only one entrance in your apartment here, ma'am?" One of the officers firmly inquired, his astute eyes carefully inspecting the apartment for a second doorway.

"Why yes, just one entrance," I truthfully responded. "It's an attic apartment."

"Well ma'am, do you know that's illegal? If there ever were a fire here, you and your children would have only one way out. And it's an awful long distance down to the sidewalk from this high attic. If I were you, I'd look for another apartment," the officer advised.

"Those officers warned me that this apartment is not legally safe, especially in case there was a fire," I sheepishly reported to my husband, knowing how much Jerry loved bein' across the street from Nick. But since we'd been in that fire in Englewood, Jerry had no choice but to hunt out a new place. Though I also loved my neighbors, particularly the Dukas' family across the street, it was better safe than sorry.

"Don't worry, Virgie. We'll get another place in no time," Jerry stated with a smile.

Quickly I started to wonder: *When we moved, would we still bank at the Talman Federal Savings and Loan?* Talman Bank on 55th Street held gobs of memories for our whole family. Especially memorable was the time I took the kids to see Santa and all poor Lee did was scream and cry while Lynn sat on Santa's lap happy as a clam. How well I recalled trudging to that bank every Saturday, rain or shine, lugging money from Jerry's earnings, socking it away in our safety deposit box. Jerry stashed his money in the vault because he didn't trust regular bank accounts for some reason, even though it was Talman Bank. All sorts of coins and bills were stockpiled inside the gray metal box I lugged weekly to the bank, more money than I really cared to count. Anyway, Jerry's money was Jerry's and no one would dare to mess with a bloody cent of his private stash.

"I love the sparkles on the sidewalks in front of Talman Bank," Lynn happily remarked every time she joined me on our Saturday morning outings. "They sparkle like the stars." But let me tell you, that bank was always bustling. There were even armed guards behind the teller lanes because we normally saw their long guns poking through the round glass holes, built high on the second floor. Yes, it was such a friendly bank, providing free cups of coffee colored in the same hue of Garfield Avenue's fancy brown bungalows. And everyone in the neighborhood loved their sweet chewy donuts, along with free goodies like candy for the kids.

In all my born days I had never seen a kid like Lee. Little Lee was certainly remarkable, and to tell you the truth, they were both remarkable kids and I was so thankful to God for allowing me to be their mother. It might sound strange, but when we moved from that apartment there was one thing I was really gonna miss and that was *The Talman Bank*.

LYNN

CHAPTER 11

To the Slaughter

Bony, and sometimes hard to control like a bouncy spring, my long arms balanced my whole body as I skipped down 54th Place. Settling my turquoise eyes on all the mothers of our block, I observed much more than I spoke. Wearing fashionable *muumuus*, (knee-length, cotton flowery dresses similar to "housecoats") they were tailor-made for busy housewives who scrubbed, cooked, did laundry, and mopped, women normally adorned in waist-hugging dresses, skirts, short heels, and faux pearls.

"I see you had spaghetti for dinner," our neighbor next door, Monica, commented with her naturally puckered smile. Perched atop the landing of her cement staircase, Monica gazed at me with a wide grin. "How did I know?" She questioned my thoughts exactly, blowing a circle of smoke from her dwindling cigarette. "I can see the red stains on your nice white shirt," she replied, pointing to my short-sleeved, fuzzy white play shirt. Monica was the watchwoman of our block, somehow aware of every *one* and every *thing* that happened. In fact, she was the one who had recently approached Mother. "Virginia, have you seen anyone around that car out front, the one between our two houses?" Monica probed, her eyes big and twitching. Aiming her chin in the direction of the eerily still automobile, it sat evenly between her house and our high, two-story white frame.

"No, I haven't seen a soul around that car, Monica," Mother wobbled her head in uncertainty. "Actually, I was about ready to call the police," added Mother.

"No need, Virginia," Monica fluttered her hand. "I've already called."

When the police arrived, they expertly pried open the car's rear trunk. Within seconds, a dead body was discovered. "Must have been the outfit," I heard Dad whisper to Mother later that night. "Just happened to dump the car on our block. That's all."

It was pretty scary knowing there was a dead body in that car in front of our house, but I was sure glad it was taken care of. By then, I had realized my city could be a pretty dangerous place, especially if I didn't follow what Mother and Dad said. All the same, that summer I was fascinated with the new blonde-haired Barbie doll Mother had bought for me at the drugstore on 55th Street. And how I enjoyed watching Trudi's teenage son rev up his motorcycle, toting around a new kind of radio called a transistor. The little radio was so small it fit inside his hand. And since Lee was a bit older, I start teasing him. Getting a kick when Lee's face turned rosy red, I joked with my kid brother after playing outside with Gwen and my other friends. Noticing his eyes were glued to the program, *Girl Talk* on television, it was a show for women Lee often watched with Mother.

"Are you watching, "*Girrrl Talk*," Lee?" I grilled, poking fun at my little brother.

"No, I'm *not!*" Lee insisted, stomping angrily around the front room like a mad bull. Lee did a lot of stomping, by the way.

"Lynn, now don't tease your brother," Mother chided. *Girl Talk* is a great show for anyone to watch. I just love Virginia Graham."[4]

---

[4] Virginia Graham (1912-1998) "Girl Talk" (1962-1969)

"Virginia is your name too," I smartly informed Mother. Plopping wiggly Lee's body down on a small chair, I wanted desperately to teach him how to write his name. "L-e-e," I spelled the letters, trying to play different kids' games with him. But Mother said Lee was still too young to learn much. Instead, I went back outside with Gwen and her cousin, Camy, and Olivette, Trudi's daughter from downstairs. The July air was syrupy and sluggish, and a wispy breeze from Lake Michigan eased inland, cooling our clammy skin. Teeny scents from the lake tweezed our noses, piercing the air where Greek, Polish, and Slavic mothers were cooking meat, cabbage, and potatoes for their families. The hunch-backed, elderly knife sharpener strolled haggardly down 54th Place as his knives clanked and clinked.

"Knife Sharpener, Knife Sharpener here. Sharpen your knives here," he yelled, trudging his clanging cart down our sidewalk as the sun set over the railroad yards. The gallon glass containers of empty milk sat silently on our doorstep, waiting for the next day's delivery that would bring an egg-white liquid tasting creamy, cold, and farm fresh. Snacking on a bowl of candy-sweet green grapes, that summer I was allowed to stay outside until nine o'clock when the tall, green metal streetlights started to shimmer. Playing outdoor games like, "Hopscotch," "Red Light, Green Light," "Tag," and "Catch the Lightning Bugs," with Gwen and all my friends, we had so much fun it seemed like summer would never end. One day after lunch, there was an excited rapping at our back screen door.

"Bruce!" Mother exclaimed, smiling cheerily through our dusty screen door. My oldest cousin, Bruce, stood even as a ruler on the floor of our back porch. All our apartment fans were whirring on that blistering hot day; the window shades were pulled down tightly against the 96-degree sun. "Lynn, unhook the screen door so Bruce can come in," Mother directed.

"Hi there, Lynn," Aunt Adelyn's eldest child, Bruce, said with lips fat like licorice. His skin was healthy, muscular, and cool, but his mood was held back like my jump rope, stretched with feelings too great to understand.

"Hi Bruce," I expressed with my timid voice, swollen in his warmth like a comfy blanket.

"Do you have any ice water, Virginia?" Bruce panted. Mother's short-sleeved dress was flowing yet belted, and my shorts did little to keep me cool on that lollipop-sweet afternoon.

"Sure," Mother quickly offered. "There's a pitcher in the refrigerator." Opening the refrigerator door wide, Bruce sought out the pitcher. Pouring himself a glass of the ice water, he filled it to the brim. "Bruce is going into the service," Mother boasted with a grin. The three of us were seated at our kitchen table—three like-minded spirits—three assorted generations. Though I was not completely sure what Mother meant by the "service," nonetheless I was happy to see Bruce who had come to visit all the way from Green Park. Mother and Bruce chatted for a while, then he stood and said it was time to go. "You be careful now," Mother playfully wagged her finger at my oldest cousin. Rising from his chair, Bruce waved good-bye to me then he unexpectedly placed both of his saucer-wide hands around Mother's belted waist, hugging her as tightly as I did my baby dolls. "Bye Bruce," declared Mother with a sad half-smile, his footsteps fading as he galloped down the wooden staircase. "That sure was nice of him to visit," she mentioned in a mixture of happy and sad, causing me to wonder.

Using my left hand to color with waxy crayons in my Lennon Sisters' coloring book, my mind traveled to the beginning of the school year. My first grade teacher had repeatedly tried to get me to write my letters and numbers with my *right* hand, but I could not do it. Coming home in salty tears because the teacher was forcing me to use my other hand,

"It won't work," I whimpered to Mother. "I have to use my left hand, but the teacher keeps making me use my other one. My right one doesn't work that good," I moaned.

"I might have to march down to that school and get this straightened out," Mother sighed, sipping her lightly browned coffee, loaded with sugar and cream. In a few days, Mother was at school, trying to persuade my teacher. "Lynn is left-handed just like my father was," Mother strictly informed my teacher. "She needs to use her *left* hand to write, not her right one." After Mother's visit, I was finally able to use my left hand in peace. Writing my letters and numbers perfectly with my left hand, I brought home an excellent report card. But at the next PTA meeting, Mother got into it again with my teacher. This time things were different.

"Lynn is pressing down extremely hard with her pencil on her papers, Mrs. Polachek. Is she unusually nervous about something? Are you having trouble at home?" She grilled. Students, you see, were able to attend those meetings with their parents, proudly showing off our classrooms. Standing at my mother's waistline, I fearfully sensed Mother's boiling fury, brewing like her hot morning coffee.

"No siree," Mother briskly insisted. "Everything is fine. Just fine."

After that meeting, I made it a point to press lighter with my pencil in order to satisfy my teacher, and not embarrass Mother. After finishing first grade, I was looking forward to attending second grade at Sawyer School until Mother gave me the news we were moving to a new neighborhood. My mind suddenly floated dreamily to a night earlier that summer, the night Dad, Mother, and I strolled down the street in order to attend a Christening party for Nick's new baby girl, Suzy. It was a joint Christening party for Suzy, and Camy's new little sister, Mona. When we arrived at the dinner hall for the Christening, all the Greeks happily waved to Dad, Mother, and me. Nick and all his family fondly greeted us.

"Hi, Gus, hi Virginia. How ya doin', Lynn? Good to see ya," Nick chimed like the church bells of St. Gall's.

Dressed like a movie star in a sparkling golden dress, that night Mother was a queen. She was more beautiful than any woman in the entire world. I was dressed in my frilly party pink dress, matched with pink-tipped lacy stockings. My whole body was washed squeaky clean with *Ivory* soap and my hair smelled pretty from using golden *Breck* shampoo. Heading for a huddle of chattering Greek men, Dad jibed about business, Chicago politics, and the ups and downs of our weather. Mother and I talked to some of Nick's family as the music suddenly began to surge.

"Um-papa, Om-papapa, Um-papappa," the midnight-haired Greeks shouted and clapped over the music, their hand-held circle growing ever larger. Nick's brother, bushy-haired Tony, sauntered into the hall like a Grecian king. Though the air was pithy with cigar smoke and sweat, everyone was laughing. Without warning, the women in the big circle began to wield sheer white kerchiefs, swishing them about like angelic fabric swords. "Umpapa, pa," the music grew louder as the Greeks danced faster and faster. Faster to the right. Faster to the left. And then it was time to eat.

"Those babies look like little angels," Mother sweetly remarked, the two of us amazed at the babies' flowing white costumes. The wide hall door on Kedzie Avenue was left ajar because it was sweltering inside the noisy crowded hall. Just before the sun set, Mother, Dad, and I said good-bye to the Greeks. Walking home on that quiet Saturday night, all the stores were dark, and the traffic was next to nothing. With the streetlights illuminating our path toward the apartment, on that night I felt as if I was a princess. Holding the loving hand of my gold-adorned Queen Mother on one side, I cozily grasped the broad, powerful hand of my important father, businessman Gus, on the other. No, there was no greater place on earth other than what was right then, on that night of nights.

Passing the newly built, glassy St. Gall's Church on the corner of 55th Street, I reminisced about the Sunday morning I attended Mass with Dad. My vision still held the reverent, robe-draped priests and the well-dressed parishioners filling every seat. The pungent incense and heady scent of blazing candles stirred our senses, and the mysterious Latin words carved something deep inside our souls.

"How did you like it?" Dad quizzed on the way home from our morning at St. Gaul's.

"It was good," I answered simply. "Good."

"She's going to Sunday School at *my* church too," Mother sternly reminded after I had attended St. Gaul's with Dad, causing me to feel yanked in two opposite directions. One Sunday morning when Mother sent me to Sunday School, the teacher who possessed kind puppy-like eyes, hoisted up a large picture to show our young class.

"This is Jesus," the lady explained to our class of five and six year olds. "This is Jesus. He's holding little lambs like you." Staring deeply into Jesus' tender eyes, I could somehow see behind His drawn features, the true part of people that is usually hidden.

And how well I remembered my birthday party, the day Aunt Adelyn came over and suddenly blurted out, "I feel God in this room." Searching the room for the slightest hint of God, I finally figured out He could not be seen. So how could I face moving away from all my friends, and the neighborhood where Dad had become calm and nice, even though he still talked about being king? I could never forget our first Christmas on 54th Place; the night Dad lugged home our Christmas tree, leaving behind a winding trail of thin pine needles.

"Turn off all the lights in the apartment," Dad excitedly told Mother when the huge tree was fully decorated with big colorful bulbs. Lettie had joined us on that Christmas night, giving presents to Lee and me. But even so, Lettie (Mrs. M.) arrived promptly on moving day, helping Mother with little Lee and telling me about our new neighborhood. Gwen was my best friend and I wouldn't see her anymore. Her cousin Camy was my good friend too, and I wouldn't see her either. Inside, I was crying a thousand tears, tears only tender-eyed Jesus truly could possibly see.

"I don't like this busy street for you kids," snarled Mother with a bent face as we scurried up the long flight of stairs on 51st Street on that summer day in 1963. Several miles southeast of our attic apartment across from Nick and Gwen, everything in the new neighborhood was dull and grey. Grey cement was rolled onto the soul-rattling grey, commercial thoroughfare called 51st Street. Our three-flat apartment building was colored in a dark gloomy grey. And even the sidewalks were brushed in a cheerless, brownish grey. The jumbled air was permeated with exhaust, soot, and the fleshy scents from the city's "Back of the Yards," where the stockyards were located a few miles to the east. Formerly known as, The Union Stock Yard & Transit Company, the stockyards had been Chicago's busy meatpacking district since 1865, helping our city to become known as the, "hog butcher of the world."

"Those stockyards changed the whole country," Dad sputtered out the importance of our new home. "Gives meat to the whole nation," he smugly boasted. Whenever the clattering wooden trucks tottered down 51st Street, I usually spied more cows than hogs going to their slaughter. But it was the distinct, blood-dried stockyard scent that became as familiar as Dad's steaming hot dogs, the quaint odor as certain as his tart cigar.

"Just look at the park right across the street," Dad brightly highlighted the area's chief amenity, sporting an upbeat smile. "And the bus stop is just a few short steps away from our apartment— you can't beat it with a stick. And Virgie," he extolled, since Dad was the one who found the apartment, "you've got all the shopping you'll ever need, practically in your own back yard. There's a meat market on the corner, a barbershop for Lee and I, the bank on Damen, plenty of churches, a supermarket, and even a dime store, all within a few blocks. And the best part is this apartment only costs sixty bucks a month, with two entrances to boot, front *and* back."

After unpacking our boxes and clothes, one muggy afternoon Mother once again moaned: "Kids, it's hotter than blazes in this apartment; my clothes are stickin' to my armpits." So Lee, Mother, and I crisscrossed hectic 51st Street, heading straight for shady Cornell Square Park. Forever a country girl, Mother inhaled the leaf-filtered air, pointing out the scattered oak and maple trees. With a wide grin, she sniffed the swishy bushes and celery green grass. "Look Lynn," Mother propelled her fingers toward the cracked path further ahead. "There's a water spout. It'll be great to cool us down on hot days like this." Taking off our shoes, Lee and I rushed into the spitting spout of cool water, allowing its drenching fingers to spray and douse our skin. Eagerly eyeing the swings, we tested the seesaw and the shiny silver slide. Only later did we discover tiny bits of glass and sharp edges of tin had littered the spout's cement floor. After supper, Lee and I busily patched up the jagged cuts on our feet with assorted sizes of sticky *Band-aids*, a clear warning not to stroll the park without shoes.

And because we had moved into the area a short time after the public schools had let out for the summer, there were still a few workers at the Robert Fulton School where I would attend in September. So Mother set up a meeting for me to tour the school in order to familiarize myself with the building before second grade started in the fall.

"Well I'll be," stared Mother at the street directly in front of Fulton School. "These are genuine cobble stones, old-fashioned, red cobble stones. Reminds me of the horse and buggy days, Lynn,"

Mother beamed, the three of us shuffling our feet on the uneven stones. "When I first came to Chicago, milk was delivered by horse and buggy in many neighborhoods," she fondly recalled. "And many streets still had these same kind of stones." Mother's story made me smile, keeping me warm in the new coldness of the strange and different region. But indeed, on Hermitage Avenue and 53rd Street where my new school sat, the entire street had never been paved. The chunky cobblestones caused our feet to wobble and bob, mere moments before we crossed the threshold of Fulton's massive front doors.

"This school was built in the early 1900's," the school clerk explained to Mother, little Lee, and I. "Here's the new addition they put on the building a few years back," the woman remarked. "We have a large population of children so we needed the extra room." The inside of the school seemed friendly enough, built with gigantic wooden windows and creaky slated floors. The outside of the building, however, felt shadowy and mean. The bark-hued brick was coated with soot, threaded with scarlet streaks unable to be explained. Climbing the front staircase leading back into our apartment, my sight locked onto the long wooden trucks rumbling down 51st Street. The see-through wood slats were bursting with jittery cows going to the slaughter. *The slaughter of death . . .*

"They're taking them to the stock yards," Mother said, reading my mind, the two of us pondering their fate. "Now try to remember how you're going to walk to school and then get back home," Mother illustrated the route with her hands, her cotton dress puffing in the city's shifting wind. Trying hard to memorize the five-block path, I quickly forgot and would need added practice before the start of school on the day after Labor Day.

Most of the houses in the neighborhood were two and three-flat wooden frames, and most were built with steep staircases ending only a few feet away from the busy streets. All the houses were placed closely together so when standing between the buildings with outstretched arms, I could easily tap both of them. For some reason, I could not get the school worker's words out of my mind: "Built in the early 1900's." Ever since moving into the neighborhood, even though I could not set eyes on the men, women, and children who once lived in the frame homes, somehow I could feel their bitter jagged souls.

Since our new apartment had only two bedrooms, Lee and I shared the back bedroom off the big kitchen. With a small living room near the front door, one bath, and a front bedroom for Mother and Dad, there was a handy pantry since there were no cabinets in the kitchen. A roomy storage shed on our back porch was supplied with a padlocked wooden door.

"That door is raggedy," Dad remarked in disgust. Dad and Mother had been talking about getting a dog for Lee and me when one day Dad toted home a shaggy-haired mutt named Candy.

"That dog is getting into everything," Mother carped when Dad got home from work, having followed the jumpy dog all day and night. "Where on earth did you get her?"

"She's the best," Dad bragged, trying to pet the frisky dog's springy-haired, bobbling head. But all Candy did was spin around in circles and chew on our shoes, making Mother more nervous than ever. And whenever Lee and Candy got together, they raced like the wind through the whole apartment, knocking over Mother's knick-knacks and making mess after mess.

"Look, Jerry," Mother brought the plain evidence to Dad one night. "That dog chewed up one of your good house slippers. And besides that, Opal downstairs is complaining about all the racket." At that painful turn of events, in a hushed flurry Dad finally took away our mad dog. That dog was Dad's way of trying to make us feel better because Mother and I were still unsure of our new place, the home of the slaughter. I sure didn't realize how good we had it living across the street from Nick and Gwen, but oh well.

Happy to have our apartment back in tact, Mother speedily advised Dad of her plan. "Next time, you let *me* pick out the dog, Jerry." Fingering her curly mass of weighty blonde hair, Mother soberly then relayed, "Because if it's one thing I know, *that's dogs.*"

CHAPTER 12

Flickers of Whiskey and Fire

You are late *again*!" Mother's voice broiled like searing catfish, sizzling in her cast iron fry pan. Her curvy lips generously sucked a Bel-Air cigarette as her hazel eyes narrowed in the lazy drifting smoke. Dad (known primarily as "Sam") had bolted noisily through our massive front door, his scuffed shoes plodding steadily across the living room. "I've been waitin' for you all night," Mother huffed. Selling hot dogs across the street from the neighborhood tavern on 47th Street in the warmer months, Sam still worked intermittently in Chicago's bowling alleys, mainly during the winter when he couldn't sell. Since parting ways with his pal Nick, Dad had been lugging home all sorts of what Mother termed, "barflies," randomly found men who hung around with Sam. Snagged by his invisible, almost irresistible spell, Sam was driven around the city by his private chauffeurs, taking their king wherever he desired to go. Since we didn't own a car, Sam's pals catered to his needs at all hours of the day and night. "What's wrong with you comin' home at this time of night?" Mother yelled because Sam had stumbled home at 3:30 on that Wednesday morning, having guzzled down countless shots of whiskeys and scores of bottles of beer.

"Tain't nooothin', Vir-gin-i-a," countered Sam in a ghostly slur, waking me up with his familiar blasting voice.

"Is too something, Jerry," Mother rapped back, since *she* would never, ever, call him Sam.

"Somethin', somethin', somethin'," Sam repeated in silly mockery, his two buddies chuckling like cocky teenagers in the hazy background, glued to Sam's every word. "Just get us some coffee, will ya?"

"Don't mock me like that," Mother shrieked.

"Mock you? I'm not mmmmoocking you, Virrr-gin-ya." Listening to the nerve-shattering ruckus I grabbed my pillow and squished it completely over my head. Lodging it tightly against both ears, I tried with all my might to stifle the earsplitting squabbling in the kitchen. My whole body stiffened hard as the sidewalk cement so I could barely move, or think, or feel. Hoping beyond hope Lee was asleep, around and around the cruel jabs circled our smoky apartment. How I wished I could stuff Dad down, down, down, exactly the way I did with the clown in Lee's jack-in-the-box, slamming and locking the door. Instead of screaming out my feelings, I rammed them into a secret corner inside my stomach, weaving them back through my mind. In my opinion, I thought it was a bad idea Dad sold hot dogs across from a tavern; it sure couldn't be good for Mother, Lee, and me, especially when he came home like that, the whole apartment reeking of sour beer, stale cigars, onions, and mean sweat.

"We're going to the pet shop to look for a proper dog," announced Mother one Saturday morning, some weeks before I started second grade. The snowy-haired man who ran the pet shop asked Mother a few questions, speaking in a kind, restful tone. In minutes, the pet shop owner brought out a darling, six-week-old fox terrier puppy. Her coarse white fur was painted with black markings, cute as a button. "She's just the dog we need," uttered Mother to the man. "We live in an apartment so we need a small dog. Yep, we'll take her."

"What are we gonna name her?" I questioned Mother on the way home.

"Well, it's up to you kids," her voice floated through the air with sugary gentleness, Mother's twin sturdy arms hauling the cardboard box bearing the tiny pup. Thinking about it briefly, I peeked inside the box Mother held. Velvety soft and curled into a fist-sized cottony ball, I instantly sensed the dog's sensitive heart.

"Let's name her Gwen," my soul burst out, considering how much I missed Gwen Dukas.

"Yeah," Lee put in. "Gwen, like Nick's daughter—she was real nice to me."

"Okay," Mother agreed. "I once had a dog named Betty, so Gwen is a good name. She's gonna be a good watch dog for us too." The whole experience reminded me of the day I listened to my first song on my first record, the music spinning around on my red-topped record player. Singing and twirling about the room, I was lost in the song's beauty and sweet words. Everything else, everything ugly, just faded smoothly away.

All kinds of entrepreneurs relentlessly tried to make a living in the Back of the Yards. One in particular was the ragman who turned up every week in his own mismatched clothes. Pounding the cracked pavement with equally battered shoes, the wrinkled-face man cried out to the entire neighborhood,

"Rag man. Rag man, here." Upon hearing his decree, many of the area's housewives, haphazardly clad in washed-out print housecoats, scuttled from their apartments like sprinkled ants. Capped in pink curlers, bobby pins, and *babushkas,* the women clutched spotted, tattered rags for the ragman to shove inside his cart. Bundling the area's grimy rags to ultimately resell, our local knife sharpener also rambled down 51st Street. Those same women buzzed like bees from a hive toward the busy knife sharpener so their dull knives readily sliced their families' juicy stockyard meats. *That* knife sharpener had a bicycle with a treadle sewing machine bottom. Pedaling the large rolling stone wheel faster than I pedaled my bike, the guy sharpened his customers' steel kitchen knives to a razor's edge. Entrenched in that inner-city world, for summer fun we raced into the stinky back alley to watch the rubber burn off the electric lines. Snickering and hooting as the lines glowed and flickered, some of those sparks started the wooden garages aflame, lending us a real show.

"Look at that, Lee," I screeched, an orange glow painting the dim night. "Hey, here come the firemen; they're comin' down 51st!"

"I've got to go to the store," Mother called to Lee and me, retrieving her metal shopping cart from the back porch storage shed. Through rain, cold, and even heavy snow, Mother devotedly trekked her metal cart west to the Certified Grocery. In front of the store was an old shack where a man sold daily newspapers like, *The Chicago Daily News* and *The Chicago Sun Times,* along with a host of current magazines like *LIFE.*

"Get your papers here," blasted the man. "Read all about it," he screeched. Hawking the weekly neighborhood newspaper, residents lined up for ethnic newspapers in Polish, Lithuanian, and Czech. When the middle of winter brought a half-foot of snow, the newspaperman placed a metal garbage can near the shack's shabby doorway, burning armloads of wood in order to keep from becoming a sheet of ice in Chicago's cold. Selling Christmas trees in December had caused the guy's sales to further grow.

"What beautiful Christmas trees! They're just like the evergreens in the country," Mother noted with reddening checks, our eyes tearing from the icy wind. So vicious was the winter Mother carefully positioned plastic on our windows, stuffing old washcloths and rags on the windowsills in order to stave off the freezing drafts. And in the summertime it was so stifling hot in the neighborhood you could feel the heat bounce up like beach balls from the sizzling pavement. Throbbing like a blast furnace, the boiling air was trapped between the buildings; the tall apartment houses were piled high as the sky, one atop another. Of course, we still had our trusty, squeaky fans.

"Open the windows and get some of that good air-conditioning," snickered Dad as the stockyards' rotting scent mingled with precious wisps of Lake Michigan's cooling breaths. "Yep, it's all free." The people of Chicago, you see, believed our Mayor Richard J. Daley was the President of Chicago, that was the way he wanted things to work out. "Daley is the king of problem-solvers," Dad wryly acclaimed. "If there's a problem, 'ole Mayor Daley will take care of it. Take care of da bizness," our Dad, Sam, the hot dog man laughed. "He's king of Amerika, da Mayor, King Daley." Dad just loved imitating the Back of the Yards' numerous Poles and assorted Eastern Europeans, a unique mixture of broken English and Chicago slang. And oh how Mother hated it!

A shaky beam shimmered across my face since I'd grown accustomed to Fulton School. I deeply adored my second-grade teacher, Miss Harris. An elegant woman and very poised, her dresses and skirts were as neatly appointed as First Lady Jackie Kennedy's. Although my ink pen often leaked creating a nasty mess, I tried hard to please Miss Harris and she seemed to understand. Like most of the kids at Fulton School, I went home for lunch. Scarfing down a bologna sandwich on buttered white bread alongside a handful of salty Jay's potato chips, I coupled that with a fresh glass of milk. Twin ring-shaped Salerno's butter cookies were ready for me to munch from around my right index finger, Mother's daily treat. Hurrying back to school at 12:35, I left home immediately after watching, *Bozo's Grand Prize Game*. The game of six buckets was played everyday on WGN's *Bozo's*

Circus. About a month before Christmas on a dull November day, our lunchtime excitement of *Bozo's Grand Prize Game* was suddenly interrupted.

"Ladies and Gentlemen," stated the announcer in a cracked, panicky tone. "This is a SPECIAL REPORT: President Kennedy has been shot. I repeat: President John Kennedy, who was in Dallas, Texas with his wife, Jackie, has been shot. More details are to follow."

Staring at Mother with skipping heartbeats, a thick knot tightened my throat. I faced little Lee who was sitting quietly on the floor. Shuddering, Mother's eyes instantly watered. "Oh dear God, Lynn," Mother cried, her spongy heart nearly broken. "Who would *do* such a thing?" She questioned. Shrugging, my shoulders fell limp in stunned silence. Regardless, I had to return to school. A gloomy balloon had inflated over everyone in Fulton's normally boisterous schoolyard; a shocking tension had cruelly gripped the damp air.

In class, Miss Harris gently urged, "We must get back to our work since no one is sure what is going to happen either way." Strangely, our usually shut classroom door remained widely open. A teacher's helper began rolling a large television set on a squeaky metal cart down the hallway, passing our classroom, Room 202. No one could concentrate; everyone alive hungered for news even though we all sensed the worst. After the one o'clock bell rang, Miss Harris stepped into the hall. Her mouth was grim as she spoke with a few of the higher-grade teachers. Upon returning to our classroom, my teacher's drawn face marred her natural beauty. "The President has died," Miss Harris announced plainly. "We won't do much this afternoon, maybe just some reading. Or if you want, just put your heads down on your desks."

My narrow feet flogged through puddle after puddle following our 3:15 dismissal. A nasty rain ruthlessly battered the deadened ground as if heaven was weeping, mourning the young president's brutal death.

"After you left for school this afternoon Walter Cronkite came on television and told us the President had died, Lynn," Mother whimpered, wiping her eyes as I trudged into the living room at 3:30. "Who could *do* such a thing?" she repeated with a crooked frown. "I burst out in tears, then little Lee just started crying too. I feel sick, Lynn. Sick." All weekend a pitch-black sorrow engulfed our nation; the bitter anguish was as thick as Sam's smoky cigar. Nobody felt like doing anything but watch the nonstop television coverage. And when the man who killed the President was suddenly killed himself, no one felt secure as we once did. Mother and Dad suddenly began using the skeleton key to lock our doors. And although lanky President Johnson from Texas was our new president, it wasn't the same. No, nothing would ever be quite the same.

Shivering in her flimsy bathrobe and wearing fuzzy open-toed slippers from the Discount Department Store, Mother's torso was nearly frozen solid as we awoke from a winter's sleep, our apartment cold as the icicles hanging from the tall roof.

"Jerry, we're gonna need a new space heater," Mother notified Dad immediately. As soon as Dad installed our new gas space heater, Lee cozied up to it, waking up before the rest of us. Perched in front of the flaming furnace, our dog Gwen was snugly clutched between Lee's crossed legs. The two of them were thoroughly mesmerized by the flickering red coil. One day before school I had positioned my good winter boots near the new space heater, hoping to warm them before walking in the bitter snow and ice. I tried any way I could to keep my slim feet from freezing.

"My good boots got melted," I moaned, showing Mother the front edge of my boots where they had been scorched, the rubber curled and ugly.

"Well, you'll just have to wear them like that," replied Mother matter-of-factly. "Next time, be more careful." Wearing my ugly melted boots for the rest of the winter, I sure hoped no one noticed.

The New Year of 1964 brought the news I had to get my tonsils removed—I was missing too much school because of frequent sore throats. My ears were always sharply attuned so I cautiously listened as Mother spoke to her younger sister, my Aunt Jane.

"Oh Janie. I'm just frantic because our great uncle died having his tonsils removed, remember Jane? You know we're from a family of bleeders," Mother fitfully acknowledged. My heart nearly thrashed through my skin at those facts, especially when I was taken to the hospital. Stretched on a polished operating table in a nearby hospital, I counted backwards from 100, drifting into a deep sleep. When my eyelids finally unlocked, two robed figures appeared before my hazy eyes. No, they were not angels as I supposed. Instead, the two sisters, (Mother and Aunt Jane) were robed in blue hospital gowns.

"I thought we lost you, Lynn," Mother smiled down with moist eyes, gazing directly into my groggy face. "You fought the doctors and almost bled to death."

"Yeah," lean Aunt Jane gasped. "Your Mother was really praying." After Mother and Aunt Jane had gone home, I was ordered not to speak a word so my operated throat could properly heal. Lying mutely in my sterile hospital room near 60th and Green, there was no television, no radio, and no toys. My muzzy eyes shifted longingly out the window, searching for any hint of comfort. In the distance a few blocks west, the huge red Sears sign on Halsted Street blinked, bringing me familiar, satisfying calm. Though totally alone, all the good times Mother and I had experienced in that bustling store strengthened me like the best medicine in the whole world.

When Lee turned four and was adorable as a puppy, and I was eight (blessed with wavy hair and a petite, skinny frame) we often dreamed up all kinds of fun things to do. Whether playing elevator in our dimly lit pantry or trying out various board games, we always had fun.

"Come on, Lee. Ya wanna play Checkers?" I questioned Lee, though I knew he would most likely say yes. Dad had taught us how to play Checkers, and while he usually beat me, a few times I actually beat him. Playing Chinese Checkers, Parcheesi, Authors, and Old Maid, Lee and I swished around in the nearly grassless dirt making up our small backyard, pretending to be on some distant planet. Almost predictably, Dad arrived home at all hours of the night and early morning, starting angry shouting matches with Mother, leaving her red-eyed and in a jittery, weepy state. Since there was no more bowling alley work, Sam stayed home in bed much of the time during the winter months when he couldn't sell hot dogs, sodas, and tamales on his wagon.

"Don't ever touch that radio dial, Virginia," Sam bellowed from his creaking bed, even when we thought he was sound asleep. Sam loved listening to the radio day and night, the brand new "All News" station—*Neeeeuws* Radio 78, WBBM. The new twenty-four hour news station continually reported Chicago's killings, robberies, fires, sports, and weather, droning on endlessly from atop Sam's bedroom dresser. Getting out of bed only to eat, Sam shaved, attended Mass at St. Michael's Church on 48th, and then drank at any tavern he found to his liking. Smacking a few sugary sticks of Wrigley's gum between his teeth, "I'm lookin' for work today," he spryly announced to Mother on a brisk Monday morning, hoping to cheer her desperate mood because there was not enough money to go around. But after Sam was gone for several hours without a word, we soon realized he was at it again. Finding himself at any one of his favorite bars, Sam repeated the same cycle over and over again. Nearing age forty, Sam was his own man. Despising factory work, he particularly loathed some chump manager ordering him around like a harebrained kid. Disappearing, drinking, then coming home to eat and fight, Sam regularly passed out into a deathlike sleep as NEWS Radio 78 droned on in low mumbling tones.

Sleeping and drinking, then eating and sleeping more, Sam awakened frequently and declared with an odd-shaped smirk, "Virginia, you live like a queen."

"You fool drunk," Mother responded with fiery red cheeks. "Some queen, huh."

"Lynn, you need your own room," Mother stated unexpectedly on a cool Saturday morning. Lee and I had been sharing bunk beds in the front bedroom for some months, but because Mother said I was getting older, I figured I needed the privacy of my own room. "Let's put Lee's things in the pantry," she said with a level smile. "There's plenty of room in there."

"Do you like it in here?" I questioned Lee a few days later. His clothes were packed neatly in the three-drawer pantry storage unit, and his toys were placed handily on the wide white shelves. Little cars, plastic trucks, and gray army men were haphazardly scattered between cans of coffee, boxes of cereal, and packages of sugar, flour, and saltines.

"Yeah, I sure do," said Lee upbeat. "I get to eat whenever I want, grabbing crackers and peanut butter when no one is looking." Though all Lee's things were in the pantry, he slept on the pullout bed in our living room sofa, Mother faithfully stashing away the heavy iron bed every morning before school.

Blessed with a feisty, resilient spirit that got her through the Depression, Mother habitually repaired broken furniture she had found in the alley. She loved to decorate our apartment anyway possible since Dad rarely had any spare money for sprucing up the house, things he dubbed, "foolishness."

"I'm going to recover this piece and it'll look good as new," quipped Mother, dreamily imagining the shabby chair she brought in from the alley, redoing it in a clean modern fabric. When cutting some linoleum for the kitchen, however, Mother sliced her arm and had to rush to the nearby medical center. A long red strip of infection had run dangerously up her whole right arm, but thankfully she quickly recovered. Saving up twenty-five dollars for an old upright piano, Mother ingenuously trimmed it with a bank of square mirrors. "We *always* had a piano in the house when I was a girl," Mother remarked, stepping back to admire her handiwork. "And I want you to learn to play too," she beamed, peering straight into my blue eyes. Taking me to ballet and baton lessons at Cornell Park's green field house across the street, I practiced dancing to the *Nutcracker*. Twirling my baton, I almost bopped poor Lee flat across his forehead.

Scanning Mother's bookcase, filled to the brim with books from the 1920's, '30's, and '40's, I often searched for something interesting to read. Turning to the little hardcover book, *The Passing Throng*, by Edgar A. Guest, I focused my eyes on Guest's signature poem also called, "The Passing Throng." I read and reread the first stanza of Guest's famous writing:

"From newsboy to the millionaire,
The passing throng goes by each day;
The old man with his weight of care,
The maiden in her color gay; [5]

Wondering about the author who watched men and women much the way I liked to do, I thought hard about life and its weight of care. Buying those old books for ten cents each at the secondhand store on 47th Street, Mother's purchases gave me a welcome outlet to my scrunched feelings: *Did anyone else live like me, carrying such a big load of care?*

"I'd die for you kids if need be," Mother honestly confessed,

---

[5] "The Passing Throng" - Edgar A. Guest (1923) Reilly & Lee Co., Chicago

widening her bloodshot eyes. Painfully aware of the unstable home life Sam had created (especially since living in the Back of the Yards) in recent months Mother was jumpy as a cat. Continually worried about our circumstances, she gripped her forehead, sticking a cold cloth up against her clammy skin. "My head is beatin' off my neck," Lynn. I'm having a nervous breakdown," Mother groaned. "That man is makin' me lose my mind."

In the Back of the Yards, unless we were shopping on 47th Street in the busy stores, riding bikes in Cornell Square, walking to the Methodist Church on Sunday, or visiting my aunt, there was really no other place to go. The three of us never knew what Sam was going to do, the cringing words he was certain to spew out, when, or with whom, he was going to show up, or if there would be enough money to pay for what we needed. My stomach tightened whenever Dad was around; Sam's angry brawling words had caused my wobbly teeth to twist like screws until my lower jaw hurt, making me bite my fingernails so hard only the quick of the nail remained.

"Stop biting your fingernails, Lynn!" Dad hollered whenever he spied me gnawing my nails, even though he was the one who had caused it. When we couldn't run, we just made due, watching television, playing games, and romping with our dog. More often than not, Mother's pretty curly hair was wildly askew, and her cheery attitude had frequently turned into a blank hopelessness. Whenever Dad *was* home, we routinely heard him harangue: "You people have it too good. Yeah, you peasants live like kings. Yous guys are peons." His crazy declaration brought Mother's blood to a boil, hoping to agitate her into yet another new fight, always seeking a new verbal brawl. Carefully watching the three of us like a towering hawk, Sam's sharp eyes inspected every little thing we did, desperately wanting to persecute us for any minor infraction.

"Stop running around these rooms in your socks, Lee, you'll wear out the floor. And put on your house slippers. You're makin' holes in those socks. Where are your house slippers, Lee?" Sam barked. Turning to Mother he harshly interrogated: "Virge, why are you always sewing? Phewwee, there are stickpins all over the place. Are you tryin' to kill me? Why don't you keep these kids in line, huh?" And to me Sam inquired, "Lynn, don't you know how to clean a table properly? I should send you kids to Catholic school, better. Yeah—you kids go to Catholic school, those nuns fix up real good." On and on Sam's intimidation raged, burning like the endless flames of our space heater, making my stomach whirl and stiffen like a solid block of ice.

"If you say something's white, he says it's black. He's an old stick in the mud," Mother proclaimed in sheer exhaustion, a hopeless panic having wrapped her like the heaviest winter coat. So whenever she repeated those terrifying words about a nervous breakdown, I began bawling inside, trying to visualize life without Mother. It would have been unthinkable for me to spend months and years alone with Lee and our senseless, beer-loving father, Sam, our apartment regularly enveloped with flickers of whiskey and bitter fire. As the voiceless cows and pigs rode to their deaths in the huge wooden trucks traveling down 51st Street, Mother, Lee, and I oddly matched their plight.

Nevertheless, the most important thing to anyone in the Back of the Yards seemed to be your nationality—*What nationality were you?* People constantly asked that question, no matter where you traveled, no matter who you were. It was especially important on St. Patrick's Day, March 17th,, the Mayor's favorite day. All the Irish kids flaunted their emerald green dresses, skirts, or sweaters, making the rest of us feel like outcasts, particularly since I was not Irish. The Poles got their revenge two days later on St. Joseph's Day. On that day, all the Poles wore red. But I wasn't Polish either.

"*You* are a *Swede*," Mother declared proudly when I asked about our nationality. "My grandmother was born in Stockholm. And your father is some kind of European, though he won't say what kind." That information did not help me much since most of the kids in the neighborhood were either Polish or Irish. So, if you were neither Polish nor Irish on those special days in March, you really were not much good for anything, especially when you didn't belong to a specific Catholic parish. All the same, every day and night the three of us went to Sam's slaughterhouse where there was only one person who was right, only one way, and only one voice. Constantly threatening Lee and me with a strict Catholic school education, (something I would detest because I loved my school and especially my teacher, Mr. Wiles) I finally figured it could never happen since Dad was unable to fork out enough money to pay for such schooling.

My own personal slaughter caused my inquiring mind to slowly grow numb as my soul was beaten down to mere shreds. Our Dad, Sam, did not hug or easily smile. No, Sam kept pushing and pounding with his hammer, so down I went along with Mother and Lee. Often I could hardly utter a single syllable; I was too afraid, too fearful of the hammer of words ready to beat and squash me like a thick nail. Mother and Dad frequently remarked, "Boy, is Lynn ever timid—she is an introvert." But how could I be anything else? It just made sense to keep quiet. Then, without a hint of warning, the doctor told Mother she must have an operation. Horrifying questions began to strangle my brain. *Was she gonna die? Was she leaving me alone with Sam?*

CHAPTER 13

The Snack Shop, A Fair, and Mr. Wiles

"I got mixed up and thought I was at home, Janie. Huh, I nearly fell off the blasted hospital bed because of the medicine they gave me," Mother joked with Aunt Jane on the telephone while Lee giddily jumped up and down on the living room sofa. Thankfully, Mother's operation was a routine hysterectomy and she recuperated just fine. Success for Mother and Dad seemed to come in coughing spurts, much like one particular day I would never forget. Tightly grabbing the black dial telephone with his wide, leathery hands, Sam yelled like mad to all three of us,

"I got the shop! I got it!" Lee was leaping around the apartment like a mad frog, and Mother's smile was as broad as Ashland Avenue. I was almost ten years old and the year was 1966. Across the street from Lindblom High School near 61st and Wolcott, Sam, Chicago's hot dog man, had rented a small snack shop. For several years he sold hamburgers, French fries, chili, his famous hot dogs, Polish sausages, and tangy orange and grape soda to the hungry high school kids. Smothering the grease-stained floor with shiny, red lacquer paint, Sam expertly installed a steam box, new grill, and a genuine jukebox, as well as a baseball and pinball gun game machine for his customers to enjoy. On the day Mother, Lee, and I took a bus ride to visit what became known as, "Sam's Snack Shop," the walls were vibrating as passionately as the floor's garish paint.

"Baby, baby, baaaby. Baby, baby, baaaaby. Baby, baby, baaaaby," chanted Sam in brain-loosening repetition. When he finally came home from the snack shop, his head still swirled in sluggish rotation from the pulsating music. "They must've played that new pop song a hundred times," he griped. Releasing a long sigh, Sam's pores reeked of onions, relish, and slimy grease. Though the area where the snack shop was located rested at the far edge of the neighborhood, the whole area was quickly changing.

"They tried robbin' me again," revealed Sam some weeks later, swishing about his dilapidated paper sack. At that upsetting news, our hearts beat like thumping kettledrums. "No sweat," he continued, his bucket-sized head stretched in rosy, revenge-filled ire. "I loaded my .38 Huskavarna and put it squarely on the snack shop's counter. Then I asked those fools: 'Which one of you would like to go first? Cause if you're ready, then so am I!'"

Foot soldiers from a notorious South Side Chicago street gang, (their members wearing distinct berets) one by one the threatening thugs gradually slipped out from Sam's Shop. Tough Sammy then guzzled down a swig of whiskey, belting out to the few customers who remained, "Let's go, letz go, bud. Yeah, who's next? Here girl," Sam directed a regular customer. "Throw a quarter in the jukebox—I wanna hear G-8." Prancing around the garish red floor and singing at the top of his lungs like a television star, from that point on, Sam was treated with respect by everyone; the neighborhood quickly learned if you ever crossed Sammy, God have mercy on your soul.

Those uncertain days of racial change brought havoc all over the city. Jive-smacking kids angrily hurled their metal lockers out of

Lindblom's tall narrow windows as if they were mere lunchboxes. And restless gangs regularly shattered scores of windows around the super-charged South Side as hoards of young men shouted curses, flinging rocks at our bus and yelling obscenities when we traveled to a lakeside museum. The violence terrified our whole family, all of us, except Sam. One day while we traveled by bus, Sam stepped up and ruthlessly chewed out the CTA bus driver. "Why you puttin' up with this mess?"

"Eh," the CTA driver sheepishly muttered. "Nothin' I can do about it."

Back at Sam's Snack Shop, not one window had been broken. "Yeah, a couple of those kids were gettin' outta hand the other day," Sam snarled with tomato-colored lips. "No matter," he said, drizzling equally red-hot sauce over his perfectly fluffed scrambled eggs. "Ya know what I did?" Sam asked Mother, Lee, and me. "I cocked my trusty .38 and swirled the barrel. Then I shot that .38 at the back door. Boy did those kids' eyes chalk up like silver dollars; few of 'em scattered right outta there," Sam ended in a chuckle.

After a while, whenever we went to the snack shop, Lee and I began to notice several haphazard holes all over the shop's back door. Sam continuously filled the holes with putty. And on many Saturdays, Lee and I twirled around an old rusty flagpole, once again pretending. Placed in a desolate, dust-laden lot adjoining the snack shop, the two of us waited patiently for Dad to finish his work. It seemed as if the whole area was perched upon a jagged cliff, ready to topple at any moment.

"Ya wanna go a little faster?" The carnival worker's liquored breath roared over the screeching of the ride's rickety brakes. His scraggly hair was swathed in so much "greasy kid's stuff" it actually looked wet. Yelling his taunts in between sucking on a dangling cigarette, and sipping a hidden bottle of *Schlitz* beer, the blinking lights of the Himalaya's speeding cars flashed like circular white infernos, shocking the centers of our eyes.

"Yeah! We wanna go faster, faster," we countered, screaming in return. Helping the bumping ride along by pushing the rocking cars with all our might, we rode hard and fast through the smoky evening air.

"*I'm Hennery the Eighth I am, 'Enery the Eighth I am, I am ...* "[6] The pop melody quaked inside our ears, and quivered our organs until we couldn't help but giggle. Lee, Mother, and I rolled around the various carnival rides, dazed by each section of the Free Fair's mysterious allure. Meanwhile, Sam was perched against his hot dog wagon on 47th and Seeley, across the street from the Back of the Yards' annual summer fair. Laughing like harebrained clowns, the three of us staggered crazily to the next ride and the next since Sam had supplied Mother with plenty of cold hard cash to spend on that wondrous night of nights. The Free Fair was one of the major highlights of our summer, especially since moving into the Back of the Yards.

"You two kids be careful up there, no horsin' around," Mother cautioned as Lee and I mounted the swinging seat of the flickering Ferris wheel near the far end of the fair. As metal parts squealed against burnished steel, when nearing the top of the giant wheel my gaze turned northward. Snared by the mountainous downtown buildings, they glittered like a million stars against the silky black sky. Stopped at our vantage point high atop the giant circle, I peered down and spotted Dad. His bulky form was intently bustling around the hot dog wagon. His fragrant cigar smoldered, touching the shadows of the night. At home, Sam's colossal stature completely filled every doorframe he walked through. But on that night, Sam suddenly appeared strangely small. Oddly, he almost equaled Mother's feminine outline, as well as everyone else crowding around Sam's popular stand. Steam ascended like

---

[6] "I'm Henry the Eighth I Am" - Herman's Hermits, (1965)

miniature swirling tornadoes from his shiny metal boxes, the hot dog vapors purposefully merging with the reckless odors of tobacco, alcohol, exhaust, and human sweat. His trusty Coleman lantern was dimmed as another good-sized crowd gathered like flies around Sam. Assorted families of mismatched Poles, stout Slavs, proud Germans, mysterious Gypsies, a few Italians, a smattering of Mexicans, as well as the familiar Irish, all eagerly awaited their hot dog dinners or tamale snacks from Sam.

How tiny Dad looked! As the night wore on we sampled every ride, trying some twice. Watching curiously as teenagers snuggled, beer-bellied men dressed in rust-stained tee shirts and patched pants suddenly burst into fights in the scratchy air. Before leaving, I begged Mother to buy me a stick of mysterious cotton candy.

"No, Lynn," Mother cringed. "That stuff is just one sticky, airy mess. Why don't we just get some popcorn, okay?" Crunching the salty treat, "We had lots of fun," Mother applauded Sam with her words when we were finally ready to go home. Riding the near empty CTA bus a few miles back to the apartment, *why couldn't every night be just as good?*

Over the muggy summer, Mother escorted us up to the towering Prudential Building's observatory overlooking Lake Michigan and the rest of downtown. Bringing Lee and I on the scenic boat rides drifting along the Chicago River, we dipped and coasted through the locks leading into the blue-capped, choppy lake. Stopping in regularly at the air-conditioned Peoples' Theatre off Ashland Avenue, we habitually caught the latest *Elvis* or *James Bond* movie, usually after shopping at Goldblatt's and Meyer Brothers, the two largest department stores on 47th Street. The washrooms at Goldblatt's each cost a quarter, so Mother told Lee and me to, "scoot underneath the stall doors or else you'll have to wait until we get to Meyer Brothers where we can go for free." As the overhead fans of the Discount Department Store whirred and scraped in a futile attempt to refresh their customers with cool air, for a few restive hours we lost track of the agitation waiting for us whenever we returned home.

"Why do we have to go home, to *him*?" I questioned Mother. The harsh intimidation occurring every time there was an encounter with Sam was sure as tomorrow, throat-clenching bouts heavy as August smog. How often my heart wrenched in fearful pain: *God, why did you give me the wrong father? Why?*

Sam had easily befriended, Jeb, the man living in the basement flat downstairs. Jeb had mounds of unruly gray hair, and he carried a sagging beer-belly. Though Jeb was intrigued by Sam's late night antics, the hot dog man had fitfully angered Jeb's elderly mother, Opal. But Jeb was just another of Sam's blind-eyed followers, stuck beneath Sam's magnetic spell.

One overcast summer morning Sam unexpectedly made an announcement. "Lee and I are going for a bus ride, Virginia; we'll see you later."

"Where are they going?" I probed Mother, watching enviously as Dad took Lee somewhere interesting on the bus.

"Just for a ride, I guess," she sheepishly responded, fully aware Sam knew the city like the back of his hand—North, South, East, and West. Sam had traveled every inch of those assorted regions, knowing precisely what Catholic church was here, and exactly what tavern (and who owned it) was over there. Spending the quiet Saturday together, when curved shadows settled on our quieting block and the streetlights began to glow, Mother's troubled eyes peered toward the corner bus stop. "I wonder where they are," she frowned. Shrugging my thin shoulders, my tummy knotted. Mother's heavy worry lines extended deep inside of me like a yardstick, fear shrouding the rooms of our first-floor apartment like dark clouds of rain. Threading her metal bobbin case with colorful new thread, Mother stayed busy with her sewing. Meanwhile, I watched the Saturday night television shows until it was ten-thirty at night. That was when the bottom of the black-and-white screen warned of the city's curfew. The television eerily read:

"It is 10:30. Do you know where your children are?"

"Oh dear God," Mother gravely prayed, falling hard to her knees on the sparsely carpeted floor. "Where on earth is Lee? God, please don't let him take Lee."

I never thought Dad would "take" Lee, but that was exactly what had been ravaging Mother's uneasy mind ever since the city had grown dark.

"Look," I called to Mother, peering from my window perch over 51st Street, mere moments following her passion-filled prayer. "Isn't that *them*?"

Rushing to the bank of front windows, "Oh thank God," Mother's face eased then hardened like the stone fountains in Cornell Park. On the hushed street below, Sam was clutching Lee's six-year-old puckered hand. The two of them were strolling the dimly lit street as if it was high noon. "Where have you two been?" Mother cried out as they piled through the front door, my own heart thrilled to finally see little Lee.

"We went to Lincoln Park Zoo," Sam dryly stated. "Ain't nothin'."

"Lincoln Park Zoo?" Mother solemnly inquired. Yet, somehow I felt something else had happened, a secret bond of sorts. And indeed, Lee later told me his trip also included a visit to the chili house, a few taverns, and a host of other hangouts, *in addition to* going to the north side zoo. In fact, Sam had worn out Lee's feet almost to a raw pulp. Though our down had gone up, something in the air had changed, and it sure wasn't for the better.

"*You* think Fulton School is a dungeon?" I posed to Lee at the beginning of the new school year, tossing my little brother a quizzical stare.

"Yeah, it's wreal ugwily," he nearly spit out the words from his crew-cut head. For some reason, my kid brother was scared stiff of our lovely school. Then again, on the way home from school I had constantly raced away from the neighborhood's countless Catholic kids who tried pouncing on me because I didn't go to Confirmation classes or practice Lent.

"What are you giving up for Lent?" A girl in my class asked.

"Nothing," I answered. "I'm not Catholic."

Hurling me an angry stare, I skipped down one side of 52nd Street in order to zigzag away from the marauding kids. On the opposite side of the street, I regularly dodged packs of growling, motley-haired stray dogs.

"Don't even *look* at those dogs or those kids," Mother warned when I grumbled about the shaggy hoards and the mean, bullying kids. "And don't ever *run* from them, Lynn," Mother cautioned. "Stand as still as a mouse or just cross the street."

Unlike Lee, I truly adored Fulton School, and particularly my new teacher, Mr. Wiles. Mr. Frank Wiles made learning fun, doing things most teachers would never dream of doing in a public school. "I like trying new things," young Mr. Wiles voiced with enthusiasm. Drawing massive colorful charts and funny painted murals, nearly every inch of our classroom had something interesting to look at, awarding us one new subject to learn after another. Showing us movies, giving us projects, and taking us to the Field Museum of Natural History instead of the Science and Industry Museum like all the other teachers normally did, I really admired vibrant Mr. Wiles, a man so different from my harsh and opinionated father.

"Don't ever believe men, Lynn," Mother sobbed one night following another bitter quarrel with Sam.

"But not *all* men are bad," I attempted to reason, battling Mother's flawed view.

"Most men are bad, Lynn. Most are."

But when I thought of my two kind uncles, some of the nice men at church, and I considered Mr. Wiles' patient love for his students, though I paid attention to Mother's advice in many areas, on that point I could not agree. I knew Mr. Frank Wiles was good; yes, he was very good, and he was my teacher for three whole years. One late January afternoon in 1967, the sky had turned a dull whitish grey. Opening to snow continuing to plunge without the slightest hint of stopping, large plump flakes cascaded onto the city's hundreds of sidewalks, streets, and yards. Falling in pasty ashen blankets, the snow descended faster than I had ever seen it fall. After sliding down all of our thirteen, icy front stairs (nearly landing headfirst onto busy 51st Street) the massive blizzard did not want to quit.

"I've got to go out and shovel, Lynn," Mother accurately figured, bundled securely against the snowy onslaught. "Please keep an eye on Lee." By six o'clock that night, 51st Street was piled high with ivory drifts and whirling heaps of leaden snow. Not one single automobile, and not a single bus, nor even the big rattling trucks crossed the mountainous drifts. A few hours later, Mother was at it again, heaving the shovel in the dark, trying to keep up with the raging storm. Flanked by wafting hills of white, Mother's feet were damp and freezing as she finally trudged indoors. Suddenly, the telephone rang with the news Sam was stuck just south of the Loop.

"All the buses have stopped in their tracks," Sam described the scene firsthand. "They're trapped in the snow banks, abandoned by their drivers," he relayed to Mother straightforwardly.

"He's walkin' home," Mother conveyed with a shiver. But, *how many miles was it to our apartment on West 51st Street from where Dad was stuck, just outside downtown?* Lee and I laughed our heads off when Mother let our white fox terrier, Gwen, out in the backyard. Sinking into the bottomless snow bank, our little dog blended in with the curving, sugary hills glistening in the snow-flecked streetlights. Although my stomach constantly churned whenever Dad was around, I felt terrible he had to trudge through all that snow. On television they showed the hundreds of cars and trucks deserted in the city's numerous streets as the snow was nearly waist-high to the average adult. Mother had tried to buy bread at the corner store but the shelves were completely empty, except for a few day-old loaves, crusty and hard. Framing the doorway with a smile, it was very late when Sam finally appeared. "Jerry, you're home!" Mother turned toward the doorway with a pointed grin, stopping her work at the beautiful sight of Sam.

"T'ain't nothin', Virginia, all this snow," Sam huffed, shaking out his sopped overcoat. Removing his wet boots and pants in favor of his threadbare, red plaid robe, Sam slipped on his comfy bedroom slippers. There was no school the following day, and boy was Lee ever happy. So many hard things happened in the Back of the Yards, but there were also a lot of good things that happened too. On Easter, our landlord brought us a delicious white frosty lamb cake that Lee, Mother, and I couldn't wait to sink our teeth into. Dressed in white gloves and a white hat, we wore our very best clothes to the Methodist Church where we joyously sang, "Christ the Lord is Risen Today." Weeks later, Mother and I could barely stomach the news our nice Methodist Church had been brutally desecrated. Desecrated was a new word I had learned when all that happened. The modest sanctuary, and even the reverend's robes were horribly vandalized by the Catholics.

Whenever Mother and Dad's old friend, Smoody, came for a visit, he sat politely as a minister in our big tan-painted kitchen. Smiling kindheartedly, he drank sugared coffee and devoured frosted cake with Mother. Smoody had bone white, disorderly hair and was a handyman of sorts since Sam never did much hammering and fixing. Smoody's coat was stretched long and bulky because Mother said his coat was actually his home—everything he owned was inside his coat. At whatever time he couldn't find a spot to lay his head, Smoody slept in a chair in our apartment.

"Bye, Smoody," I waved to gentle-eyed Smoody as he left the

apartment. Nodding, Smoody lent Lee and I a warm smile, another man who was very good.

When two men from the new church we attended came to visit us at our apartment, they told Mother all about Heaven and Hell. "You must accept Jesus Christ as your Savior in order to go to Heaven," they declared, reading some corresponding verses from the Bible.

"I don't want to hear about that awful Hell," Mother raged hard against their words. "I heard all about it years ago," she chided the two men.

Standing behind my bedroom door, my heart was stirred. My insides cried out in their loudest cry. "Well," I attempted in my tiniest voice. "*I'd* like to accept Jesus."

Turning around, the visiting men hurled me a baffled gaze. "You are too young to accept Christ, young lady," one of the men woodenly confirmed. "Maybe when you are eleven or twelve."

Crushed to the core, I tried not to think much about Jesus until then.

"Mr. and Mrs. Pol-a-chek?" Questioned the starch-collared precinct captain, perched at our front door. On that overcast Election Day, it was just about time to eat dinner. "Folks, have you forgotten it is Election Day? Mayor Daley can sure use your votes," declared the dapper city worker who was dressed with a sporty tie and polished shoes.

"The polling place is just across the street at the field house, Lynn," Mother briskly mentioned. Pulling both arms into her brand new, faux fox-trimmed coat, "Your father and I will be back in a few minutes, so please keep an eye on Lee," she remarked in a serious tone.

Settling onto the chair in front of our high windows overlooking 51st Street, I watched as Mother and Sam walked together into the dusky evening, giving their votes to the city's beloved Mayor Richard J. Daley. He was the man everyone on the Southwest

Side deeply adored, particularly since the Mayor's neighborhood, Bridgeport, adjoined all of us in the Back of the Yards. Yep, there went my two parents, even though it was nearly six o'clock and almost time to eat. Before the night was over, Mayor Daley had overwhelmingly won, *the 1967 election for mayor.*

PART THREE

Sam, The Man

LEE

My name means: "Clearing, meadow"

CHAPTER 14

Never Fear, Sammy's Here

"Lee is *kicking* again!" Mother's voice bumped eerily through the air like breaking eggs. Fumbling to grab my flailing feet through the sheets and blankets of my bed, my slate blue eyes grudgingly spied Mother's shifting form. Her complaint about my forceful kicking was lodged to my sister Lynn; both of them disturbed at what had become strangely routine. Often, when awakening from a restless sleep, I jerked my squirming feet in opposition to the night. The darkness, for some reason, held very scary things. My dreams, frequently nightmares, were filled with twisting syrupy figures I was powerless to fight, other than to lash my toes and heels at them with all my being. In my earlier years I saw "little things," vivid, transparent wavy forms taunting at will. Why did those ghosts boldly invade the open space surrounding me, attempting to burn my soul with their hellish irons?

"Hiiiyya, Sammy," a crumbly-haired man stopped flat in the middle of the busy city street, waving with gusto toward Sam and me. Miles away from home, we were up on Chicago's North Side where that wrinkle-faced fellow, dressed in an ankle-length rumpled coat, somehow knew my father. It was the same wherever we went—North, South, East Side, and particularly on the West Side's Maxwell Street. Maxwell Street was the famous outdoor market where scores of Jews bartered their wares at the cheapest prices in town, the street where Daddy bought items for a quarter, selling them to some "chump" at his hot dog wagon for a fin (five dollars) thereby making a hefty profit. Even so, everywhere we traveled people seemed to know Dad—Sam, the Hot Dog Man.

Riding home to the apartment, the CTA driver stopped his relish green bus directly in front of our house. Unfastening the folded glass door to let Dad and I off, we landed at the foot of our stairs, even though the bus stop was several doors away. "See ya, Sam," the driver affectionately called. I had realized by then, Dad was somewhat famous because Sam was a legend to many Chicagoans. Truthfully, I believed Dad wasn't meant to be fully figured out; some people were just like that.

"Your father is such an odd duck," Mother grimaced, her chin puckered while pondering Sam's strange behaviors. His entire life, we had all noticed, was filled with peculiar traits sandwiched between his non-stop smoking and frenzied drinking. Daily, I spotted Sam either sporting a greenish-brown El Producto cigar (from the two to three boxes he smoked per day) snugly squashed between his sun-tanned lips, or perhaps smoking one of the two packs of cigarettes he usually inhaled as well. And his drinking? I regularly witnessed Sam gulp down a case or two of *Pabst's Blue Ribbon* beer in a single day, or every other day, for sure. That was the same beer said to have won a blue ribbon at the 1893 Chicago World's Fair. Partnering that with ten to twenty shots, along with the tart Bloody Mary's he faithfully concocted in order to finally sober up, how long he had been doing that was anyone's guess. Since drinking his first beer at the age of ten, Sam had been smoking since age eleven. Sometimes he would glug seventy beers plus a bottle of whiskey at one sitting, falling into bed at two o'clock in the morning, and then getting up the next day at six a.m. for work.

"You gobble your food like one of those thrashers we used to feed out in the country," Mother carped as she watched her husband eat. And sure enough, Sam ate a monstrous breakfast of spicy Polish sausage, fried ham, pan-fried potatoes, chopped garlic, green peppers and onions, eggs, buttered toast (burnt the way he liked it), strong coffee, tomato juice, and of course, a beer! Leaving our apartment early to get supplies for a full day and night of selling in the projects, and then at the Southwest Side's assorted factories, eventually he landed on his corner on 47th Street, wearing his cap backwards against the stiff Chicago wind. During his eighteen-hour day, Sam repeated the same practice of smoking, drinking, sleeping, and eating. That was how it went, day after grueling day.

On one early summer day, Sam forked over seventeen bucks to buy me a bicycle. It was a secondhand, 1950's, sixteen-inch bike, purchased from my Aunt Jane. Riding my new bike around and around the lanes inside tree-lined Cornell Park, "Weeeeee," I shouted. My body slid along the path in time to the fierce lake breeze carrying me like a soaring gull. For the first time in my young life, I felt as free as one of the chatty grey squirrels flittering from tree to tree. Freeeee at LAST! As the grassy park's scent filled my lungs, when my sister Lynn rode her big bicycle around the park, I rode right alongside her, trying to keep up. "Weeee," I yelled again. Last year I got a red, riding fire truck, but I could only ride it in our small backyard. One day I told Mother about the cute furry rabbits I saw on my ride.

"Those weren't rabbits, silly Lee," Mother chuckled like the clowns we saw at the three-ringed circus. "Those were rats!"

Rats? I really didn't care one bit what was in our backyard as long as Sam gave me a hot dog each morning, nursing the tasty red hot smothered with creamy yellow mustard and plenty of tomatoes, spicy relish, and catsup for minutes on end. Hanging on to Sam's masterpiece, I did not want him to leave.

"Daddy, can I please have a hot dog?" I raised the question every morning before Sam left for his route. Stretching up my head toward his, I thought about riding like the wind on my new bike. Removing a chilled hot dog and all the fixings from our giant brown refrigerator, Sam began its preparation, just as if he was at his stand.

"That'll be twenty-five cents, Lee," Sam quipped, sticking out his hand to collect the money. Peering earnestly at my snarled face, "No, sonny boy," Sam chuckled. "Here ya go." His eyes lit like a flashlight, he readily handed me the overflowing hot dog resting on a puffy golden bun. "Just remember where ya got it," Sam put in. Strutting from the kitchen into the front room to watch, *The Andy Griffith Show*, on the way out he turned toward Lynn and me, his mouth ajar, as big as a Lincoln Park lion as he roared, "Never fear, Saaammy's here! Heh, heh, heah. Yeah, Sammy is *here!*"

Sam was sure there, but so were all sorts of thoughts churning like thunderclouds inside my head whenever I thought of my life in the Back of the Yards. By September, I was in the second grade. One day that fall, my teacher at the Fulton School had plucked me up by the hair, yanking me straight out of my seat. Pulling the living daylights out of my skull, the teacher screamed at me hard because I had scratched a messy blotch on my paper instead of putting a line through a word the way she had instructed. At that turn of events, the girl next to me started bawling like a baby too. Her salty tears and mine were softly rinsing the wood-slated floor beneath us. I had not made that ugly blotch on my paper on purpose; it was just a mistake. Oh how I couldn't wait to go home to Mother, Lynn, and Dad.

Then came the terrible day when our dog Gwen got out of the backyard and darted into the middle of the 51st Street traffic.

In mere seconds, a long CTA bus ran smack over Gwen's little white body. Off went that speeding bus and I couldn't look. Lynn couldn't look, and Mother couldn't look either because we all knew our cuddly dog was dead. God, however (through some miracle) saw our poor dog didn't even get a single scratch. And God also wanted *me*, for some reason or other, to keep on living since I got a really bad sickness and nearly died. Whenever Mother prayed for me, I felt God's healing hand.

On a chilly fall night, two heavy black-suited firemen trudged up our back steps, each of them holding a gigantic axe. The bulging fellows started hollering like crazy through the back screen door,

"Where's the fire? Where's the fire, ma'am?"

My heart nearly stopped, and so did Lynn's.

"There's no fire here. Not even any smoke," hollered Mother to the firemen, everyone staring at one another in confusion. Tossing her eyes around the kitchen, Mom speedily scanned every nook and cranny of the room. We soon discovered a neighbor had called the fire department mistakenly thinking we had a fire. In reality, our clothes dryer was billowing exhaust from the kitchen window in curling vapors since the dryer was placed next to the washing machine on the east side of our kitchen.

While playing on our wooden back porch one afternoon I curiously thought: *What would it be like to slide all the way down the banister leading to the bottom floor?* Lynn and I had talked about doing that very thing hundreds of times. "Weeeooww," I yelled, gripping the chipped wooden banister with my hands. My body glided smoothly downhill, just like an indoor slide. But I hadn't realized, until getting ready for bed later that night, all the rickety banister's grey wooden splinters had gotten pushed deep into my backside.

"Hold still, Lee," ordered Mother in a stern tone, my patched blue jeans awkwardly pulled to my ankles. "Hold still so I can get the splinters out!" I sure had lots of fun whenever I could, but when Sam and Mother argued (as they did almost every day) it felt like a knife had cut through my belly. The thing I truly hated most was when Sam came home at three in the morning, purposely waking me up.

"Geeet uppp, Leeee," Sam stuttered his words because he had been drinking. Bursting like a wild bull into the living room, he headed straight for my bed. The gooey sweet/sour scent of alcohol controlled him the same way I controlled my bike. Rubbing my eyes, Sam set me into one of the chrome kitchen chairs so I could "shoot the breeze," with him and his drinking pals. For me, I only wanted peace. Circling Cornell Park's round pathway with my bike, I often thought about Sam. Only while riding my bicycle was I free from the twisting figures, the terrible fighting, and Sam's belly-twisting voice. It was that same voice oddly ordering me, "Get in your hole, Lee." Depressing into the couch's deepest springs, whenever Sam watched television he always went to sleep. It was that same voice calling me to scoot in behind him and get in "my hole," while stinky, icky sweat mingled between the two of us like animals in a pen. And it was that same voice ordering me to: "pinch the pimples on my back, son," and that is what I did—no questions asked.

"He's selling the place, Virginia," Dad stated to Mother head-on. Around the time when the trees again began to bud, I was seated on a stool inside the dull white pantry as I strained to overhear Mother and Dad discussing how our landlord was going to sell the apartment building; all the rents were then going to be raised. Suddenly, I remembered Sam tossing me to the top of the eleven-foot ceiling of our front room, throwing me high toward the sky then catching me like a sack of potatoes. But also while we'd lived at the apartment, Dad and Mother had fought like vicious dogs, continuously at each other's throat about everything, especially religion. "Catholic Church is the best," taunted Sam, prancing around the kitchen in his plaid robe proud as a peacock, trying to get Mother wound up.

"No, *it's not*," Mother volleyed back. "They're nothin' but goofs like you. You cavort over to your church on Sunday, then hang around the stinkin' tavern all day and night drinking like a fish. Now what good is a church like that? You can chuck it all, why don't ya?"

"I'm not chuckin' nothin', Virge," Sam snapped, thrilled to have gotten Mother's goat. "True church, Virge. Catholics are the true church. In fact, I should send the kids to Catholic Church. Better schools than public any day."

"*The* Catholic Church, Jerry. Stop talkin' like a D.P., will ya?"

"D.P.s are good peoples."

"People," Mother corrected, her springy hair framing her stirred up eyes. "And no they are **not**. Those Catholic kids have constantly been followin' Lynn home from school, pestering her like crazy just because she doesn't go to those Confession classes."

"Confirmation classes, Virge. Confirmation. And they're not following Lynn. She's not right about that."

"Lynn's not lying about a thing, Jerry," Mother tried to reason, squaring her shoulders taut. Puffing on her cigarette, she blew smoke straight into Sam's path. Leaving Sam speechless until he caught a second wind, Mother stomped into the front room to let off some steam, hoping to find a teeny tiny crumb of peace.

Shifting my gaze toward the front room windows, I mulled over the last year when I was six years old and got my first real job. Yep, I got a job at a tavern in the Italian section of a nearby neighborhood. While Sam drank from the early morning all the way to closing time at that local bar, his mechanic friend, Johnny Jim, knocked around on the pool table. His pretty girlfriend, Peggy, dozed away in her '56 Buick Century, waiting for Johnny Jim to finish his game. The German Jew who owned that particular tavern (a fellow dubbed, "Mack, the Dog Man") was thoroughly against any type of air-conditioning. That's how I got the job of killing flies. One day when Dog Man noticed Sam tromping through the tavern door with me in tow, he shoved a fly swatter into my unsuspecting hand. There were no flies buzzing 'round my head, nor anyone else's in that bar, better believe it.

Whenever Sam lugged me to the taverns, all kinds of things happened, things I couldn't tell anyone else. Not even Lynn; not even Mother. Sometimes the glassy-eyed women planted a cherry kiss on my plump check, leaving their smeary lipstick mess on my fair skin. Fighting over ball games, the best pizza joints, and various women, men argued wildly in curse-filled brawls, their fists balled and ready. By the time Dad and I finally reached home, my eyes were stinging with tavern smoke, causing my body to feel as if I had smoked an entire pack of cigarettes and a whole box of cigars. Watching folks tip, stumble, and topple from their whirling bar stools, and I witnessed violence galore. Eavesdropping on filthy language, my stomach growled from hunger while Sam sipped, slurped, and swigged as much alcohol as his huge body could hold. Nevertheless, Sam always made sure I had all the crunchy pistachio nuts I could ever eat, providing me with all the soda I could gulp down. Guys dressed in baggy, spotted pants munched shot glasses on a bet, while others vomited in the tavern's musty back corners, slobbering and using the street to relieve their full bladders. Copping a ride with some of Sam's drinking pals, all of us tavern hopped into the wee hours of the next morning.

"Come along, Lee," Sam summoned me like I was his own personal aid. Suddenly, we were riding in a car with a guy who was driving seventy miles an hour down quiet California Avenue, hitting the street down the wrong side! Only moments before we were in a bookie joint where a guy in a tavern's secret back room (a rickety-rack scrawny fellow) placed various bets on all the different horse races around town.

"Heeeello, there, Sammy," a wobbly woman in low heels greeted Sam and me inside a new tavern. "Whadya doin' *here*?" She questioned with an upraised eyebrow and a tinny smile.

"Yooo," Sam greeted the woman, using another one of his favorite expressions. "Say Lee, did ya get a load of that tavern?" Sam inquired after leaving. "That was a "lesbian bar," he coolly explained. "Yeah, a special tavern for women only."

And yet another time we were in what Sam deemed a sex bar. That particular bar was chock full of awful pictures hanging like dark stones on its dingy gray walls. Boy, I really wanted to run out of there fast. Yeah, that is what happened with Sam and me in the Back of the Yards, memories so different from the ones I had with Lynn and Mother. In those days I was really concerned about Dad because he was drinking so much. But I was equally concerned about Mother since she was always worrying. On yet another early morning, Sam had brought home more "friends," from one his favorite bars. That morning I played bartender in our smoky kitchen, since all the local taverns were closed.

"Wanna a bbbeeerrr?" Sam queried the dribbling trio, stirring Mother, then Lynn, from their peaceful night of sleep. Serving those fools as if they were still in the tavern, Sam even cooked them food until they all passed out. Shaking her head, Mother began to loudly holler.

"Jerry, you're makin' me as angry as a wet hen. What's wrong with you bringin' home those sloppin' drunks?"

"These are high class peoples, Virge. Watccha talkin' about? Ain't that right, Lee?" Sam quizzed.

Nodding, I had to agree with Dad, but I also saw eye to eye with Mother. When I finally got to bed, in a few hours my eyes were bleary as Mom shook me like her dishrag, waking me up for school. Even so, I had obeyed my father, Sam, the man who often boasted, "Never fear, Sammy's here." Yes, I loved my father with all my being even though he was (as Mother liked to say) a "boozer to the highest heaven."

Batting my eyes as the faded green city bus rattled and bumped down 51st Street, on a balmy Saturday morning, Mother, Lynn, and I were again riding the popular CTA. Traveling to look at an apartment Mom had found in the newspaper, the address was circled neatly in pen. The three of us bobbled up and down on the stiff vinyl seats as the bus jangled against a massive pothole, waiting patiently until we reached our stop. It seemed as if we were in one of those movies at the Peoples' Theater, each of us playing our parts in the only world we knew.

Blushing hot with confusion, I began to realize every human being must play his role perfectly so, *where we would live now? And what new school would we be attending?*

CHAPTER 15

Watching the Buildings Go Up

"I found an apartment," Mother disclosed to Dad when he arrived home from the hot dog stand, reporting faithfully as a secretary working in the Loop. We had almost rented an apartment in the Mayor's nearby Bridgeport neighborhood, an area known for its politics and rough-and-tumble Irish. Overlooking the massive, red-bricked McClellan Elementary School, the three of us stood naïvely as wandering pilgrims on the second floor of a very old, three-flat creaking frame. "How's the neighborhood around here?" Mother pressed the soft-spoken landlord who had somehow taken a liking to us.

"Not so good," the stoop-shouldered landlord truthfully answered. "Not good for the kids, I'd say. It's tough Irish, if ya know what I mean. They don't like outsiders."

Nodding her head in understanding, Mother crossed the Bridgeport apartment off her list. It was well known in our city when people accidently wandered into Bridgeport, they occasionally never came out alive. So Mom started making an appeal for an apartment in the more diverse neighborhood called Brighton Park.

Shuffling around in the refrigerator, "Where's the apartment at?" Sam inquired, wise as a cop concerning every inch of our sprawling city. Folding a slice of white bread inside the palms of his wide hands, Sam shoved a whole dill pickle into the bread, munching the whole thing with a few crunches.

"Brighton Park, Jerry," Mom began. "Near Archer and California. They take kids and a dog."

"How much do we fork over?" asked Sam, cranking out the magic question.

"$120.00 a month," shrugged Mother, holding her breath and fixed in her tracks. Looking pretty as ever, she was dressed in a new type of fashionable slacks called polyester. Her hair was washed and styled; her blouse was fresh and crisp. "But the heat is included," she added.

"Too much, Virge. Too many peanuts I'd say," Sam balked.

"At least take a look," she pleaded, having already fallen in love with the place. As soon as Sam saw the apartment was modern and clean, as well as located in a pretty good neighborhood, and right on the first floor, he seriously reconsidered.

"It's a nice joint," he agreed. "We'll take it."

"Mr. Atkins, the owner, says you've got to sign a lease," Mother abruptly inserted the sole requirement.

"Sure," beamed Sam. "You got a pen? Letz go, letz go, and get on the ball," he cursed under his breath. Shrouding the room with vapors from his chunky cigar, Sam puffed hard into the edgy air. "No monkey business," he blasted. Munching on another slippery pickle, he had slapped that one between twin slices of Polish rye, adding some stinky horseradish to the mix. "The good thing about a lease is it's made to be broken."

Our uncle's moving company hauled our boxes and belongings several miles northwest of our Back of the Yards' apartment, expertly unloading it in our new place a few blocks off Archer and California Avenue in Brighton Park. Separated into precise plots of real estate, Chicago's bustling streets, tidy parks, and varied parcels and lots were places every resident had to mentally compute.

From the Bridgeport and South Side Irish, to the Latino barrios, the scattered black areas, the Italian sections, and a whole host of Eastern European immigrant neighborhoods (led mainly by the Poles) those distinct areas were chopped into daring districts functioning with invisible borders everyone had to study. In June of 1967, our new neighborhood was an airy vicinity smattered with immaculate yellow bungalows and auburn brick apartment buildings, sprinkled with older and cheaper, two and three-flat frames. But a completely different atmosphere bathed the place. Gone were those scratchy spirits from the jumbled masses of the Back of the Yards' inner-city feel. In Brighton Park, something was being unraveled, something entirely new.

"I don't think they're Polish," Mother said, glancing at the immigrants we began seeing around Brighton Park. In no time at all, Mother, Lynn, and I discovered nearly half the residents in the area were Lithuanian. Many of them were broken-English immigrants, much like the immigrants in our last neighborhood, people who swarmed to America before, and immediately after, World War II. The other half of Brighton's population was Hispanic, primarily families from Mexico. Lynn and I were to attend the Nathan Davis Elementary School about five blocks away from our large, corner apartment building. The huge structure contained three private apartments on the first floor, and three on the second. We were on the first floor, to the left of the main entryway. All the apartments had only one exit, but since we were on the first floor it wasn't a major concern. As soon as I got a glimpse of our dark brick school, I was relieved since it didn't look like a prison the way Fulton School always did to my clear, simple eyes.

"Take it easy, breezy," Sam liked to say whenever Mother, Lynn, or I seem jumpy with tight hands and queasy stomachs.

"And don't let the bed bugs bite! Heh, heh," Sam tweeted like a robin. Trying to heed Sam's advice, another thing we noticed was everyone around Brighton Park walked everywhere since all the stores and shops were only a few blocks away. There were two large supermarkets and every manner of shops such as jewelers, shoemakers, restaurants, a library, a record store, a big department store, a couple of drug stores, and even a movie theater. Each one of those buildings sat on the ancient meandering Indian trail known as Archer Avenue. The well-known road was named after the Illinois and Michigan canal's first commissioner, William Archer. Boy, those folks sure had sweet smiles on their faces compared to the glum scowls of the poor souls in the Back of the Yards, where most of the families were poor, many unable to afford heat, hot water, or little more than a single light bulb.

"We can be downtown in a *half hour*?" Lynn shrieked. Jumping nearly as high the telephone wires, Lynn welcomed the fresh opportunities we were afforded by moving to Brighton Park.

"Yeah, the Archer Avenue Express bus can get us to the Loop in thirty minutes," Mother squealed, just as thrilled as Lynn. "Archer runs at an angle, so we'll be downtown in no time."

"I luv downtown," Lynn sputtered like a teakettle. The moment we got settled, Mother took quick advantage of the Archer Avenue bus. Like something in a dream, the three of us started shopping leisurely on State Street, that "Great Street," the famous thoroughfare filled with people, eateries, big theatres, and countless shops. And when the weather was nice we walked a few blocks to the beautiful shores of Lake Michigan. Often, we strolled down the "Miracle Mile," what was also called the, "Magnificent Mile" reaching the old stone Water Tower, one of the few surviving structures of the Great Fire of 1871. Deciding to explore the quaint historic buildings of Old Town, Mother also brought us to all the museums. While picnicking in Grant Park, Lee and I allowed the famous Buckingham Fountain's spray to douse our hot arms and faces, happily replacing the sputtering spout in glass-filled Cornell Park.

"This apartment building was once a working funeral home," we heard that fact stated from some of the other tenants. "It was a popular parlor during the 1920's," they interjected with a quivery tone. And believe it or not, whenever I opened my closet door to get my clothes and shoes, I saw a ghost. Yep, there was an actual see-through outline of a figure I really couldn't explain other than to say it was a ghost. And that dreadful thing began scaring the living daylights outta me. Bundling myself up every night compactly as possible beneath the covers of my bed, I hauled out my flashlight for safety. Shining the flashlight in the direction of my haunted closet door one night, I held my breath. An arctic chill crept up my spine; my closet door was opening up all by itself! At that, my seven-year-old heart was ready to explode.

"Mommmmy!" I shrieked at the top of my lungs. "I'm *not* staying in my room anymore. There's a ghost in here! It's in my closet!"

"Aw, come on Lee," Mother replied with puzzled eyes. "You're just having a bad dream." Nonetheless, I kept complaining about the strange goings on in my closet. Finally, Mother cleverly refashioned the dining room into a bedroom, *my new* bedroom, and Mother and Dad had taken my old room as their own. What's more, whenever Mother sent Lynn and I down into our apartment building's eerie basement (where all the tenants had locked storage sheds) the tiny hairs on our bodies stood straight toward the roof, giving us the chills. The grungy, funeral home embalming instruments sat as silent testimony, still preserved on warped wooden tables in mounds of dust in the far front section of the basement. Yep, it was a real creepy path down there because the mildewed-scented, dusty basement curled and coiled deep into the darkness for what seemed like a mile, whenever Lynn and I got up enough nerve to follow it. And every time I had to get my bike out of the basement storage shed, I galloped like a horse up the stairs with the bike, as fast as my feet would travel.

One more thing I had noticed since moving into Brighton Park was Dad and Mother were starting to argue again. Usually they launched their quarrels as soon as I was awake, fighting all day long until the streetlights turned on at night.

"I am the king of this castle," Sam postured repeatedly, as if truly believing his words.

"No, you are not," Mother corrected. "*You* are an old fart fossil. You are King Farouk, just taking up space and givin' me one royal headache!"

"Ehhh," Sam broiled, his eyes glued to *The Jackie Gleason Show* on one rainy Saturday night. Seated upright on the front room sofa, his stiff plastic coffee cup was clenched like glue inside his forever sun-tanned hand. With a loud sigh, Sam quickly churned, "Virginia, if you had a brain you'd be dangerous. Ewww, what's this?" He questioned in a sudden squirm. Plucking a shiny stickpin from the side of his wide behind, Sam yelled toward Mother. "You tryin' to stab me again?"

"Hahaha," Mother coughed. "Why Jerry, I was just tryin' to make this place look half-way decent. I was trying to cover that old couch I found in the alley, sewing on the material so the thing looked reasonable. Don't tell me about stabbing you, Jerry."

Thankfully, Sam still worked in Sam's Snack Shop in the winter, diligently working his hot dog wagon on the corner of 47th and Seeley in the spring, summer, and early fall. Dad's skin was so full of grease he frequently threaded his fingernails through the grunge of his massive arms, then he picked out his nails, loading scattered ashtrays and jar tops with the whole grubby mess. The tavern across from Sam's stand had been taken over by a friendly couple named Rick and Rosy, and gee, the whole area was hopping crazy, particularly during the Back of the Yards' annual fair. At that time I began accompanying Sam to his bustling stand, eagerly watching the new double Ferris wheel that caused all kinds of excitement. Featuring the wild bumper cars, the spinning red and yellow Tilt 'a Whirl, and the noisy, urine-doused Haunted House, the Free Fair was as popular as ever. Out of nowhere came a night I would never forget. All the Chicago Cubs' players came to the fair, and many of them got hot dogs at Sam's hot dog wagon! Quick, lean outfielder, Billy Williams, (my favorite Cub by far), strong, stout Ron Santo, homerun hitter, Ernie Banks, and many other Cubs' players were all there. Wooow, what a night!

"There's no place I'd rather be than here," I told Dad one night in all honesty. Yeah, helping my father on the wagon each night that summer, I packed the hot dogs and took the change. My gaze often spun far to the north, straight toward downtown where the giant, 102-story, jet-black John Hancock building was being built. Following its progress floor by floor until they hoisted the monster antenna onto the rectangular, mountain-like structure, it was situated perfectly atop the building like an upright crown. The whole thing was finally finished in 1969. Years later, I also watched the massive steps of the gleaming Sears Tower ascend high into the clouds with equal awe. That building soared upward like an iron peak, the pride and joy of Mayor Daley. Staring into the murky sky, my vision was swiftly interrupted.

"Sammy! Sammy!" People were hollering, yelling like crazy toward Sam's wagon, black men and women riding on the stuffy CTA buses. Many of them were traveling either *from* the projects near Cicero Avenue, or north *to* the projects at Cabrini Green. "Sammy, Sam-my, Sa-m-, Sa, S, ..." they chanted and cheered. As the green buses clattered past Sam's stand, with a faint wave and a smile, Sam aimed his cigar toward the passing buses, lifting it up as a toast as their voices, diminished in the smoggy city night. Boasting how he knew gobs of people in the projects, Sam had been friends with several of them for many years. At home, Dad was raw and "mean-streaked," as Mother frequently complained. But on the street he was jolly, charming, and steel-skinned. Yes, Sam was always joking, blessed with a captivating appeal, something you couldn't put your finger on. I'd seen him jiving with some Gold Coast hotshot one minute, then jabbering with a street hood the next.

Adding up the tallies of several orders at once, *how did he do it, figuring up everything as fast as a hurling Cubs' baseball in a few seconds flat?* "Dad," I called one night while helping him on the wagon, taking orders and wrapping them up. "This guy doesn't have enough money for a hot dog, whadda ya want me to do?"

A threadlike fishy breeze brushed our sticky foreheads on that oven of a night as Sam's needle-sharp eyes scanned like spotlights in every direction of the wagon. He had often wondered if one night, perhaps that night, he just might get robbed.

"Don't worry 'bout it, young Lee. When you give, you get. When you need it, keep it." Sam briskly stated, his motto on giving stuck in my mind even decades later. Many people in the Back of the Yards had absolutely no money to go out to eat. Even eating hot dogs at Sam's stand was totally out of the question. In those cases, Sam just let their bill go, giving them their food for free because he just seemed to understand.

But as the evening crowd subsided, someone foolishly tried tricking Sam out of some money. Almost instantly, Sam sniffed out the plan. "Have a nize day, pal," Sam advised the middle-aged huckster. Tossing him his famous adage, the fellow got nothing from Sam but the old "heave ho." For Sam, his slogan, "Nize Day," or, "Have a nice day," meant just about anything. Mainly it bluntly meant, "See ya later," or more likely, "Get lost, punk." Sam repeated that phrase more times than I could count, saying over and over again: "Nize Day, Joeski," "Nize Day, my man," or "Nize Day, pal." Standing around the wagon, Sam often gloated with a shimmery smirk, his armpits reeking with gritty slime.

"Ya know somethin'? I invented that saying, Lee Boy. Nize Day; Nize Day," he proclaimed between puffs on his cigar. "And it took off from there like a bird," Sam cackled, spitting out bits of tobacco into the weedy soil near the littered curb of 47th Street.

"It sure did," I agreed. After we had finally finished selling for the night, Sam normally plodded eagerly into the tavern. More than anything else in the world he was ready to buy the whole house a drink with some of the night's abundant earnings. Stuck to the tavern floor like one of Mother's stickpins on her velvety red pincushion fashioned like a tomato, Sam always stood while drinking. More than anything, he loved hanging out in the clammy, crowded tavern, milling about long into early morning hours. Sturdy as a construction worker, Sam was shaped with Goliath shoulders, holding fists as strong as a grizzly bear's paws. His influence was forever growing in the Back of the Yards, growing among the children of immigrants who played concertinas and watched as their relatives got married at Sacred Heart, St. Joe's, St. Cyril and Methodius, St. Michael's, or St. John of God, their cars cling-clanging with beer cans tied in the back, traveling to the nearest beer hall for the big party.

The weekly ritual occurred when Sam clinked shut the metal strong box where he stored all his weekly earnings, loading it up to take to Talman Bank's safety deposit box. How much did Sam really have in there? Truthfully, only the Lord above really knew. But by the time I was thirteen years old, I worked with Sam nearly eighteen hours a day, seven days a week, saving every penny so I could make my dad very proud. That's what was important to me, keeping Sam happy with my performance so I was accepted and approved.

"I'm putting this money in the bank," I solemnly notified Sam in regard to my earnings, waiting for his approving smile. Craving my father's love more than hot dogs, nuts, friends, or even money, in many ways street-tough Sam had tried to make me hard as a rock like he was, but he just couldn't seem to win. I was truly not like that—mean, vulgar, and steel hard.

In July, my Aunt Jane and her family came to our apartment for a visit. That afternoon a huge Sears' truck pulled up to our door with a long box filled with a 120-pound set of weights. Jane's husband, our Uncle Bert, a veteran of World War II, readily questioned, "Jerry, what's this? Who is that big weight set for?"

"That's for Lee," Sam exclaimed with a bent grin.

"Lee?" questioned Uncle Bert, his bushy brows lifting and arched.

"Yes, Lee. That boy of mine ain't gonna be no skinny kid anymore. Yeah," Sam's boxy jaw continually moved with his thoughts, his hide-like skin permanently burnt from relentless exposure to Chicago's harsh weather. "He's *gonna* lift those weights and I'm going to make a man outta him."

Hooting like a gathering of old country grandmas, little did they realize not many years later (weighing a mere 130 pounds at age thirteen and a half) I would lift an amazing 210 pounds right over my head. Besides making me physically strong, Sam also taught me how to be financially strong—the art of making and saving money. One of the first things I did to follow Sam's teachings was sell bubble gum at school. Depositing a shiny copper penny inside the gumball machine at the National Tea supermarket on Archer and California, out came a small pocketknife as a prize. That gave me the idea to turn around and sell the knife for a quarter, making a twenty-four-cent profit. Just like my Daddy, Sam, the hot dog man, I was ready to sell just about anything for a price. When I hit eight years old, I had saved up a whole three hundred dollars and was thrilled to open a brand new passbook savings account at the Archer Federal Savings and Loan. While other kids spent money on toys, candy, and trinkets, my chief concern was to save money and lift weights so I could make my father happy.

"I can't wait for school to start," Lynn spouted like a fool. As

Lynn and I attended the Nathan P. Davis School on Pershing Road, the first few weeks went pretty well. My sister seemed to like it, but she always liked school no matter where we lived. Both of us had made new friends, and many of Lynn's friends were Mexican. Most of my friends were Mexican too. But after three weeks at Davis, for some reason the non-Hispanic kids (the Eastern Europeans) were madder than junkyard dogs at me because I was friendly with the Mexicans.

BANG! SLAP! KABOOM! "Hi there Lee," the sour-faced kids yelled and poked fun at me. The flabby, honey-haired Lithuanian kids were at it again, smacking me down flat like a pancake. Those kids adored punching my lights into the cold concrete sidewalk, over and over again. One of the young toughs was in my grade, and he was just about my size. I wrestled that dude down so he couldn't beat on me, but the other boys, especially one mammoth kid, were way too much for me to handle. Those mean bullies continually clobbered me in the schoolyard's sandbox, smearing sand time and again in my eyes. Shoving those stinging granules down my throat, they kicked me with their run-down Buster Brown shoes. Sometimes they used their fists to cuff me in the neck, smotherin' my skin with jagged bits of gravel so I could barely suck in air. I guess that was called "bullying," but, nonetheless, I didn't tell a single soul. I didn't say a word until one day I finally bore my heart to Dad.

"Hey!" shouted Sam at the front doorway of one of the Lithuanian kids' houses, located on the corner near our apartment. "You tell your son to lay off my son Lee," Sam screamed to the boy's father.

Red-faced at Sam's charge, "Dat kidz problem," the cement-eyed immigrant bolted back. "Let kidz take kar of et."

"Well," reasoned Sam as the two of us walked home. "The next time he goes after you, just beat him up. You take care of him, Lee Boy."

Since I had always been instructed to obey my father and mother, and since I was a gentle person to begin with, getting an order like that completely overrode every one of my private convictions. The next day, like modern-day gladiators, the same boys flung me to the ground like a sack of potatoes. With spring-coiled grins on each of their plump faces, their shoes stomped on the tender parts of my stomach, depressing my delicate skin. Happy as larks, they pranced around my insides with their frenzied feet. Yet, I had my ORDERS. Thumping on the huge kid who was stretched over me like a black widow spider, I bashed him flat in the gut.

"Awwh, ooohh," the kid moaned, instantly doubled over. Like scared puppies, off scrambled the kid's brothers, along with the rest of his cowardly gang.

"Hey," I yelled, seated upright on the sidewalk. "You get back here." There was a whole pack of Mexican kids nearby; with hair and eyes colored as the darkest rye bread, and with immense curiosity, the group watched me fight. The Mexicans inched right along with the brawl because I kept whipping on the big kid, clobbering him all the way down the street. Whacking each other's bellies, we jerked our arms and wrestled, kicking up dirt, muck, and gravel. Our pants and shirts were ripped here, and awkwardly torn there. I could not stop the pounding because all those weeks of pent-up anger scorched inside me like blistering, black street tar. I had no mercy on that kid so he resorted to biting my leg. My fists, however, kept flying like Muhammad Ali's. I wondered how it was possible I knew how to fight like that. Could it be because I had witnessed countless brawls at the different taverns, whenever I went along with Sam? But I hated that fighting and I was sure not proud of it. When I finally got home, Mother nearly fainted. She was especially upset at seeing rosy teeth marks on her young son's leg.

"What on God's good earth happened to you, Lee?" Mother rushed toward me as I spilled my story.

"Good deal, kid," Sam said overjoyed, swishing my wavy, mustard-hued hair. Returning to class the following day, I stood right next to the boy I beat to a crisp. Suddenly, the kid whispered over toward me.

"*I* sure wouldn't have had the kind of nerve to do to you what you did to me yesterday," he noted with a couple shakes of his head. I didn't say a single word, but I was never bothered by a soul at Davis School again.

"Way to go, Pickle," the Mexican kids clamored, elated when they saw me at recess and lunch. They had dubbed me, "Pickle," because everyday I took a pickle to school at lunchtime, keeping it in my mouth like Sam's cigar. Playing bull rush with the kids from 12:30 until the school bell rang at a few minutes to one, what was bull rush? Well, that was a game we played on the gravel field in the schoolyard. In that game, everyone tried to run from one side of the schoolyard to the opposite end, tackling the first person you could take down. Everyone was trying with all our might to get to the other side, free and clear. Broken shards of bottle glass, chunky uneven stones, along with spiky gravel was haphazardly spread all over this schoolyard. So I rushed stiff like the wind through the jittery air, sometimes even winning, *making it safely to the other side.*

"Pic-kle, Pic-kle," the Mexican kids called. Truthfully, it really didn't matter what happened because when the game was over, I always kept a bit of a sour dill pickle wedged inside my mouth to chew on, knowing I would not get beat up, or possibly even killed. Since the day I was four years old and accidently swallowed a penny, I had never been so terrified as those awful days when kids like Big Pete kept beating me nearly to a pulp.

When January came I stood up high as a lamppost at the top of Davis school's green toboggan. Skimming down the icy slide full force on my feet, I made all my classmates hoot and holler. Everyone in the snow-edged schoolyard was watching *me*.

"Way to go, Pickle! Way to go!" they cheered, my own heart pounding with pride and joy. I finally had a new start. And yes, things were fine—*for a while.*

CHAPTER 16

Eat Hearty

"I can't wait to eat those mashed potatoes," I gushed my feelings to Lynn and Mother on a cold Sunday morning on our way home from church. Once in a blue moon, as Mother liked to say, our whole family sat down to eat Sunday dinner. Crusty, golden-fried chicken, buttery mashed potatoes with pepper and salt, supple homemade biscuits, sweet corn, and cake or silky pie for dessert demonstrated some of Mother's delicious offerings. As regular attendees of the Brighton Park Presbyterian Church on West Pershing Road, Reverend Weaver was our kind and wise pastor. Our souls were peaceful, and our spirits flowed as easily as the Chicago River as we returned home from the service. Anticipation of the good meal Mother had lovingly prepared was foremost on our minds. Greeting Sam as the three of us entered the front doorway of our apartment, he was dressed in his new bathrobe but donning the same matted down slippers. Mother, Lynn, and I speedily changed from our good Sunday clothes, eager to devour the meal.

Bowing to say the blessing we had said over our food ever since I could remember, one of us humbly prayed:

"God is great. God is good;
Let us thank Him for our food.
Amen."

Mother had taught us to always pray before going to bed too: "As I lay me down to sleep, I pray the Lord my soul to keep ..." But just before I was ready to scoop a large spoonful of Mom's creamy mashed potatoes inside my mouth, swathed in her deliciously warm chicken gravy, Sam blurted out with grating eyes and a strange gut-wrenching tone,

"Eat hearty, Lee Boy. This may be your last. Huh, heh, heh," chortled Sam in labored breaths. "Yeh, that goes for all of you— this may be your last." Extending his plate toward Mother, Sam was already asking for a second helping. "Yeh," he threatened again. "This may be your last!"

Once those haunting words were uttered in our joyous midst, a deathly chill sliced the air like Mom's butcher knife. Sam's five words caused the three of us to roll together into one tight ball— we prayed those words might never hold true. Yet, while living in the Back of the Yards there were several times when food was in short supply, particularly during the harsh winter when Sam had little or no work.

"How 'bout pancakes for supper?" Mother cheerily asked, probing Lynn and me with a meek smile. Doing the her very best to make ends meet, Mother regularly purchased armloads of boxes of macaroni and cheese, the yellow boxes marked down to 29 cents, sometimes priced at a mere 10 cents each, buying ten boxes at a crack. Eagerly chasing down the weekly sales on bologna, white bread, green beans, hamburger, fish sticks, packaged American cheese, and tomato or chicken soup, Mother scraped together whatever food possible so we had something adequate to eat. Something besides the cellophane-wrapped hot dogs and tamales forever lining our refrigerator freezer.

"You're *not* goin' hungry," contended Sam like a price fighter whenever Mother whined about the slim selection of food. "There are plenty of hot dogs in the freezer."

"We sure can't eat hot dogs all the time—not all winter long, Jerry," Mother nagged Dad with pouting lips, trying to figure any small way to make Sam understand. Dragging out her cast iron frying pan to cook round slices of bologna or make buttery-grilled cheese sandwiches, canned chicken noodle soup with salty soda crackers warmed our stomachs. That did well in providing enough good digestion (since Mother had made her best loving effort) making it miles better than tons and tons of rich food.

On a steel ice, wintry day I was in my new bedroom (the dining room made into a bedroom courtesy of Mother) listening to an earsplitting pounding outside. Following the commotion to the narrow alley off the side of our corner brick apartment building, a man was bashing an axe against a six-foot high, burled walnut secretary. That beautiful piece of furniture would have been worth somewhere in the neighborhood of $1,500.00 in the decades ahead. "What are you doing, sir?" I questioned the harried fellow.

"I'm choppin' up this old cabinet and putting it in the furnace. Ain't no good no more. Naw, it's just an old-fashioned piece of furniture from yesteryear," moaned the man.

But that didn't make an ounce of sense to me. But it was just as bad as when Mother took me to the Salvation Army store and told me to pick out a toy. Peering into one of the store's huge cardboard boxes, the whole thing was filled with old-time, iron arcade toys, each one selling for just ten cents apiece.

"I don't want any of those heavy old toys," I griped to Mother. "I want thin the metal ones, the modern toys." Little did I realize, however, that very box held about one hundred thousand dollars worth of antique toys. But that was 1968. What I had learned along the way was how you treat others is what really counted. If you punched a man or woman, whether in word or in deed, you killed *yourself*.

We had two television sets in our apartment—a 1960 Sylvania and a 1966 RCA portable. Both sets were black and white. Always looking for a deal, one morning Sam announced with the frankness of Walter Cronkite,

"I got a man comin' over to give me twenty-five bucks for this old Sylvania Console TV. We've got the portable, Virge," he reassured. "So don't worry," Sam quickly interjected. "I'll get a new color television set for us, you'll see. Anyway, that news is all propaganda no matter how you look at. Propaganda. Propaganda," he repeated.

"Yeah," Mother cut in. "I should live so long." And how right she was. We lived in that apartment until the end of May of 1970, and it wasn't until seven years later when *Mother* bought the new color television, not Sam.

"This ain't a bad little set we got here," Sam conveyed concerning the RCA portable. "Kid, move the antenna to the right," he ordered when we watched television together in the front room. "Better days are comin'."

"Yes sir, Dad," I pounced on the antenna like a guard dog. Scooting around the wiry antenna, my neck started to leak tiny beads of sweat. In a panicked frenzy I tried to flatten any curvy lines in the squirmy television picture, moving the antenna back and forth, up and down, backwards and forward.

"That's more like it. What time do we eat, Virge?" yelled Sam toward the avocado-tiled kitchen.

"We eat when the food is ready, Jerry," Mother hollered in return. "No one will appreciate me 'til I'm dead and gone. Yeah," Mother shook her head. "Dead and gone."

"Get me a beer, son," Sam then commanded like a five-star general. "And make it snappy. I don't want no pifflin' around. Move, move, move. Let's go, I ain't got all day."

We were all accustomed to Sam's barbed edicts, so I never thought a thing about it.

1968 was a radical, "rad" year for everyone in Chicago. Lynn had her ears glued to the city's two popular rock stations, WCFL and WLS. She tuned in to the top disk jockeys, learning as many of the pop songs as she could. Instead of listening to Mother's dog-eared scratchy recordings, LP's by Flatt & Scrubbs, The Ink Spots, and the musical score from the movie, *Goldfinger*, on Saturdays we walked to the record store on Archer and California in search of the newest hits. Lynn bought a new '45 record every few weeks, usually one of the WLS Top Ten. Her records included hits from The Beatles, The Monkees, and the Queen of Soul, Aretha Franklin, Lynn's favorite. Tuning into *Dick Clark's American Bandstand* every week, we caught the latest '60's fashions as well as the trendiest dances and most rockin' songs. In April, Dr. Martin Luther King was suddenly assassinated. His murder in Memphis started days of fiery riots on Chicago's South Side (southeast of Brighton Park) and the West Side (due north). Throbbing fear railed throughout the city, but not for Sam. Sam had to get stock for his wagon that week, but his usual supply company was completely sold out.

"I had to go all the way to the West Side for stock," Sam gritted his teeth as he spoke. "Made it right through those riots; didn't stop for anything, not even a red light. Had my hand on the Huskavarna all the way."

In June, Senator Robert Kennedy was also murdered, and no one could believe he too was gone. During the Democratic Convention there were riots downtown. Mayor Daley had strictly ordered a severe seven o'clock curfew.

"Lynn is almost home," I advised Mother, scanning the street outside. "She's coming from Little Mexico just in time to make the early clampdown."

"Oh this war is just terrible," Mother constantly squawked. Wiping a tear from the brim of her left eye, she grumbled with a bitter edge. "Every night on television we keep hearing about the death count in this Viet Nam War. I just wish it was all over."

In California, there were "hippies," and "yippies," and the women were burning their bras. College kids were rebelling with sit-ins; LSD was popular, but mainly in the suburbs where they had plenty of extra money. And '68 was the year Sam gave up his lease at the Snack Shop. The neighborhood had turned overwhelmingly violent, particularly after all the riots on the South and West Sides. The summer in Brighton Park was humid and sticky. "Sticky, sticky," Dad repeated. His body always reeked since he rarely bathed more than once or twice a week. And that summer we did something completely different. For the very first time we took a family trip, a trip north to Stillwater, Minnesota. Traveling with Dad's good friend, "Hank," (otherwise known as Henry Banes) we rode down the highway in his 1964 Chevy pick-up and travel camper, the vehicle smelling like the far woods. Rushing with a giant smile on his pale round face, Hank loved to fish so he visited Minnesota often. Exploring the small town of Stillwater was like turning back the clock seventy-five years. When some of the local residents discovered we were from Chicago, they shrank back and teased.

"Tattttaaat," they played, pretending to aim a machine gun at us. "Say, did you guys know Al Capone?"

"Of course not," Mother took instant offense, her cheeks shaded in a tarnished red. "Chicago is a beautiful town. Just beautiful."

Staying in a lakeside cabin, it was so pitch black outside we could not see the hand in front of us. There was no electric, and no running water. Not far from the cabin were outhouses and a squeaky, iron water pump.

"This is just like the one on Gram's farm," Mother grinned.

Grabbing the pump's handle with expertise, the metal pipe squeaked. When Lynn went outside to get water, she saw a slithering snake.

"Snake, snake!" she screamed, running like the dickens the opposite way. Staying in the cabin for three days, Lynn and Mother were soon ready to go home and take a bath, wash their hair, and return to civilization. Happy to return to Chicago, little did we realize Hank would introduce Sam to a man named Ernie Kipp. Mr. Kipp eventually sold his house on 67th Street in the Marquette Park neighborhood, the first and only house our family ever lived in all together.

As usual, there had not been many Christmas gifts under the tree that year as the stark winter months were limited on everything. So when New Year's Eve rolled around we did exactly what we did every New Year's Eve. Mother bought potato chips, French onion dip, and a few sodas at the National Tea supermarket, our extra-special treats to celebrate the holiday. Sam was nowhere to be found, so we tuned in to *Guy Lombardo's New Year's Eve* on television. When the bandleader played, "Auld Lang Syne," warm tears washed our faces like miniature rain, the ups and downs of the past year rumbling like trucks through our beaten-down souls. Minutes later, our tears turned to giggles as we watched Laurel and Hardy's comic movies. A few folks down the block were clanging and banging pots and pans in celebration of the New Year of 1969. Several hours later, Sam finally showed up.

"So you get off the State Street bus and get on the North Side's elevated?" Mother questioned the CTA consultant on the telephone. Her face as serious as a LaSalle Street lawyer, Mother clutched a pen and a jumbled mess of papers. Finally, she hung up the phone. "We're going to a Cubs' game," she eagerly revealed. Finding our way to Clark and Addison, that summer Mother took us to several Cubs' games at Wrigley Field. Lynn and I got to know all the players by heart, as that was the year the Cubs nearly won the pennant. Many of the games were jam-packed with people from everywhere around the Midwest.

WGN sports announcer, Jack Brickhouse, interviewed Ernie Banks, "Mr. Cub," early on asking the first baseman with an eager grin, "Ernie, what's your saying for this year?"

In reply, Ernie smiled and smoothly declared, "The Cubs will shine in '69."

In August, we breathlessly watched young left-hander, Ken Holtzman, pitch a no-hitter. Everyone was standing on their seats, clapping and hooting, cheering on the Cubs. Traveling back home on the crowded subways and buses, our hearts were still thrilled over witnessing that most amazing game. Most of the time when we visited Wrigley Field, we didn't want to go back home. Hanging around the field of sweet-scented ivy, we absorbed the stirring organ music for as long as possible, watching the folks of the neighborhood near the lake where the sea gulls pecked the scattered grains of popcorn and peanuts. Taking in a deep gulp of air, we inhaled one last fragrance of the searing meat, causing us to think: *What would happen when we arrived home and saw Sam?*

I sure didn't want to leave Wrigley Field because I adored my favorite player, Billy Williams. Born in 1938 in Whistler, Alabama, in 1961 Billy won the coveted National League's "Rookie of the Year." Hall of Famer great, Mr. Roger Hornsby, was an early mentor to Williams, predicting great success for the young player. How I loved to watch the level swing of Big Billy Williams' hot bat, the left-fielder hitting twenty home runs on average. Sucking in our breath when Billy made his crucial catch in Kenny Holtzman's amazing '69 no-hitter, sometimes I glimpsed over and saw how Lynn noticed my eyes tearing up whenever Billy Williams came up to bat. There was something sweet about Billy, something missing in our own hard-nosed, hardheaded Dad. Watching Sweet Billy play his finest season in 1972 when he rightfully earned the National League batting championship, he was named Player of the Year by

"The Sporting News." That year Williams batted a .333 average, collecting 37 (HRS) home runs and 122 (RBIS) runs batted in, finishing only behind Johnny Bench in the MVP. Yes, Lynn and I would rather soak in the atmosphere at Wrigley instead of going home, where we didn't know what was going to happen from one minute to the next.

Faithful as a preacher, Mother still took us to church every Sunday and on one of those Sundays, Lynn, at age thirteen, received Jesus in her heart, changing her life forever. That happened early in the year and she was never the same. So, not only did the Cubs and Lynn shine in '69, but also every Sunday *I* had to shine Sam's black shoes until he said,

"Okay, Lee Boy. That's good enough." Scrutinizing my job with meticulous military-style inspection, Sam got pretty peeved with me because I kept wearing out my twenty-nine cents' tennis shoes. Tearing them apart seam by seam (nearly one pair every other month), I suppose I *was* forcing Mother to buy me new shoes. The Archer Avenue Big Store was only a few blocks from our house so we were getting to know the folks there pretty well. Built in 1922, the Archer Avenue Big Store claimed wooden floors with wide wooden bins, each filled with assorted clothing, socks, and underwear. Wrapping our purchases in butcher paper and heavy string, there were mountains of toys in the basement where I secretly hoped Mother might take me after buying my new shoes.

"Can't you just walk places, Lee?" grunted Sam with a frown. Shutting the refrigerator door, a jar of pigs' feet was tightly clutched inside his right hand. Primed and ready to poke his silver fork deep into the pickled meat, "Do you have to keep runnin' around everywhere like a fool, wearing out your shoes?"

"Now Jerry," Mother stepped up to bat for me. "He's just a young boy; that's what young boys do. Don't nitpick all the time."

"Nitpick, nitpick," Sam immediately mocked. Wriggling his

hefty torso around and around in circles, Sam imitated a silly dance he saw chunky funny man, Jackie Gleason, do on his show.

On the way to shopping on Archer Avenue, we regularly took note of the other houses, wondering about the people who owned them. The street next to our building near Richmond Avenue held an avenue of houses I would never forget. Neat as a pin, not one shaggy bush or one scattered branch was out of place. Each two-flat, brick boasted polished stainless steel screen doors, coupled with firm, weed-free grass trimmed meticulously from the street curbs. Not one brick in the whole bunch needed tuck-pointing, and every single home's window frames were perfectly painted. And God help you if you even got your bike tire remotely near their precious grass.

"Git away from da grass," the homeowners barked at my sister and me. "Ve vill tell on you kidz. Ya, tell you parenz and da poliz." Walking on lawns around there was absolutely the crime of the century. Sure, the immigrant mamas and grammas swept the streets in the Back of the Yards. But man did the people in Brighton Park get hot about their property. I had seen millions of blocks of homes in my lifetime, but nothing came close to that street between Archer Avenue and Richmond.

"Lynn, check the newspaper to see what movie's playin' at the Brighton," Mom urged each week. For a special break, Mother, Lynn, and I often stopped by the Brighton Park Theatre to catch the latest movie. Ornately painted with faded gold trim, the Brighton was built in 1919. When the giant, red velvet curtains swung open, the newest *007 James Bond* film began, one of scores of movies we saw since the theatre was a mere hop, skip, and a jump from our apartment. Unlike the Peoples', that theatre showed everything from John Wayne to Elvis to Clint Eastwood, and sometimes triple X movies late at night, shown only to adults, of course.

"It's good to still be among the living," Mother commented as we took our seats, knowing all too well the uncertainty of our home life. From time to time, our cousins joined us at the Saturday matinee special—three movies for the bargain basement price of seventy-five cents. The floors of the Brighton were gluey and gummy, just like they were at the Colony on 59th Street, and the Peoples' near 47th. My cousin and I even scouted out the dimly lit ornate balcony to see who was up there, tryin' to see if they were kissing or not!

I was still working hard at the tavern as a fly killer, making a whole dollar a day. By then, Sam had paraded me through a vast horde of Southwest Side taverns, and I was pretty proud to know the names of all the different cops, many of the "big-wheelers," and all the taverns' multi-faceted patrons. In some bars, Sam drank *Michelob*. But in most of them he gulped his favorite, *Old Style*, along with a vast variety of shots. I had personally played thousands of games on the electric bowling machines, but Sam rarely lost a single one. Strutting into one bar after another, the guys quickly got out the dice cup. Sam normally won that game too, even though I couldn't understand how the whole thing was played. Whether a game of pool, craps, cards, checkers, or bowling, Sam exceeded at them all.

"YEAH, here's the winner, the winner's right here," Sam pointed to his own bushy-haired chest as a block-long grin soundly framed the bottom half of his giant oblong face. "Drinks on me."

More often than not, there was always someone fighting around Sam's hot dog wagon, knocking out some poor fool's teeth. Spilling their fights out of the tavern, they tumbled and tripped over the cracked sidewalks. "Hey you people," Sam hollered. "Stay away from my wagon; I don't want anything messin' up my mustard."

If Sam had run for office in Chicago, he would have won hands down. Black folks from the Southwest Side projects traveled by bus east to the famous Robert Taylor Homes, the massive concrete housing project near State Street. Boy did they love their Sammy! His hot dog stand was extremely popular—folks from all walks of life were coming from all over the city, since they too recognized good digestion was miles better than rich fancy food.

Unlike Sam who craved "shootin' the breeze" with anyone in sight, *I* clammed up much of the time since Sam was the one with the brains. Unfortunately, Sam had no interest in being a politician—he didn't have to since he was already the "King of 47th Street." Anyway, Sam had already won the game he was playing, and having a *terrific time doin' it!*

CHAPTER 17

The Day I Will Never Forget

While the months unraveled like the downy yarn Mother used to crochet into cozy, long winter scarves for Lynn and me, my mind jarred to a remarkable Saturday at the start of the year.

"Up and addam,' kiddo, socko, pal," Sam kidded with a whoozy smile. Boosting my sleepy body up from bed with his lively words, in no time flat I was dressed and ready. Before I knew it, the two of us were inside Maria's, an Italian-owned café a few doors down the block from the corner of 47th and Western Avenue, which some called Western Boulevard because it was wide with a grassy section in between. It was ten thirty in the morning and pretty, night-haired, satin-eyed Maria was chitchatting with Sam. "Come on, kid," Sam urged me from the diner's counter, sweetened coffee scenting his breath. "Let's get on the bus; we're going over to Rick's Tavern. Rick's kid is getting married and they're gonna have a big party."

The shuddering CTA bus headed eastward beneath a muted midday sun, our heads bobbling through Chicago's tidy Gage Park neighborhood. Most of the seats were filled with bundled up Polish women, Saturday shoppers wearing patterned silk *babushkas*, scarves so different from the ones Mother was creating to keep our necks warm as we walked to Davis School. Bounding like a spry alley cat off the crowded bus, Sam hurried to open the door to Rick's. Man, I had never seen the place so jammed with people. Awareness rolled in like a Lake Michigan fog when one, two, three, and then four people twisted their heads and viewed Sam and me ambling through the tavern doorway. Like an unexpected clap of thunder, something snapped in the air. I could only describe it as, astonishing.

"THERE HE IS! HEY, IT'S SAMMY!" Shouted tens of Rick's wedding guests, stopping their conversations and yelling our way. Their warm eyes were positioned like steel nails pointed toward Dad and me. Then, from the middle of that huge crowd I heard,

"HEY! IT'S SAMMY! BIG DADDY. HEY, IT'S BIG DADDY. IT'S BIG GREEN!" Everyone yelled, standing up in recognition of my very own father, my *own* Daddy. It was almost as if he was some famous rock star or a beloved king. "HERE'S THE MAYOR OF 47th STREET, THE KING. It's Big Sammy," they endlessly throbbed. My heart was pounding and swelling with the wave of enthusiasm, a thrilling current that had no longing to rest or recede. Tears flushed my turquoise eyes as someone else shouted from the crowd,

"Let's start the party; Big Sammy is here. NEVER FEAR," they chanted. "SAMMY IS HERE! Never fear; Sammy is here!" Brushing off two stools for Dad and I, the bartender poured all kinds of beer and shots on the long, glossy wooden bar. At that point in time Sam usually drank *Heineken* beer, the bottles with the green label. Flashing a grin as wide as that whole huge building, Sam relished the honor and proudly took a seat. That was the same Sam, my father the hot dog man, who usually stood in every tavern we had ever set foot in, ready to take on anything, and anyone. Turning up the volume on Rick's jukebox, the whole house started dancing in raw delight. Sam's good friends were here—the three brothers—Charlie Range, who lived a few steps down Seeley Avenue, along with his brothers Kenny and Lefty, sons of a Polish man Dad knew long ago. Kenny was peaceful; Lefty was softhearted and of course left-handed, as well as husky, a tailor living in a basement apartment set with an actual dirt floor.

Glancing over the crowd I saw Sam's other pal, Timmy, along with his wife and kids. Then, I waved to Dave and greeted "Lucky," and "Full Hand," and all their wives and families. All the local roofers were there, as well as Stan (Stosh) and his wife. Recognizing many of the neighborhood's painters, I greeted Sam's newest pal, friendly money-cruncher, Eddie Olinsk. Eddie had been driving Sam all over the city, and he even invited our whole family to his place for dinner. There were so many others I had never seen, all of them raving hour after hour about how great their Sammy was. That day Sam got more recognition than the bride and groom, more recognition than I'd ever seen any one man ever receive, *bar none*. That included any president, any actor at Hollywood's Academy Awards, any scientist including Albert Einstein, and any Nobel Prize winner throughout the world. It was Sammy all the way. *The raw love was unmatched.*

"Hiya, Sammy," another couple yelled and waved. Amidst the clinking of ice-laden glasses of beers and mixed drinks, puffy clouds of smoke roved into our skin and pores. The banging jukebox melodies thundered down through our bones, quaking the very soles of our feet. An inexplicable love streamed and bathed the entire room of wall-to-wall people from the Back of the Yards. Sure, those folks were drinkers and smokers, and there were even a few ex-cons waffled into the joyous mix. But what I caught sight of was true, genuine love. If he really wanted to, Sam could have solicited all kinds of money from any one of those local residents and they would have gladly handed over every last red cent they possessed. Why? Well, if the truth were told, when Sam appeared in Rick's doorway, those hard-working folks starkly realized he was someone different from the pack. Sam, you see, was painfully honest. There was absolutely no jive talk from Sam. So that day *he* was receiving more respect than I'd ever seen anyone receive. It was, if you can imagine, as if the Pope himself had shown up on that vibrating ground, a truly unbelievable thing for a nine-year-old to behold.

"Yeah, he just got here," I overheard scattered sections of people rant on madly about Sam's arrival, small groups chattering in the phone booths in back. At that, more and more people streamed in. The place was so stirred up people were standing outside in the cold, celebrating and drinking, jabbering and giggling, all enthused over Sammy. In fact, that day had become something of a legend in the Back of the Yards. On that special day of celebration there were more people in Rick's Tavern than there *ever* had been in history. I guess it was a record of sorts. Even when the Chicago Cubs came to the bar there weren't that many people at Rick's. Oh sure they were celebrating Rick's son's wonderful wedding. But they were also showing the love they had for Sam as well. Isn't there one particular day fastened to your mind like a button sewn tightly onto your favorite shirt? Well, that's exactly how I felt about that amazing Saturday at Rick's. I will never forget that day. *Never.*

But all that hadn't changed the love I had for my father one bit. No, I had always loved my dad no matter how harshly he treated me or how tough he wanted me to become. That day *did,* however, clearly demonstrate I was not the only one who adored my dad, Big Sammy, King of 47th Street. I was certainly not jealous of all the attention Sam received, but I certainly was proud. I could have never had a better present given to me by God, even if I tried. That day I also realized you never truly knew someone, even when you lived together in the same house. On that day I viewed my father in a totally different light—*My Father was a KING!* Though Mother sure didn't think so for one minute, the rest of the world knew the truth: Yes, he was a king.

"It's finally come to an end," Mom said in a meandering sigh. *Yes,* that mad decade of chaos, change, and crime was finally over. Our New Year's Eve celebration ended the madcap decade of 1960's, a decade changing the whole world. Of course, Mother, Lynn, and I were munching on potato chips and French onion dip as usual. But that year we slurped down cherry Kool-Aid as one of our special holiday indulgences. Guy Lombardo crooned and swayed with his satin shirt and silk-tie orchestra while everyone recapped the past ten years. Newscasters recalled the gruesome deaths of governmental leaders, the various riots, Woodstock and the sexual revolution, the popularity of all kinds of drugs, and the *un*popular war in Viet Nam. All that culminated in July of 1969, when we stayed up late with our cousins, (Adelyn's family who moved downstate), watching the United States' astronauts land on the moon. Sam did not have his Snack Shop anymore, and nearly all the bowling alleys had automatic Brunswick pin setters, replacing the brave, agile men who rushed for decades to set up those heavy white pins as their customers knocked them down, flattened hard against the gleaming wooden alleys. Having saved up some money from all those prosperous days of hard work, Sam set up his hot dog wagon early that year. Haphazardly running into his old friend, Hank, they met at one of the local South Side taverns.

"Mr. Kipp is 'bout ready to peddle that house on Marquette Road, Sam," thick-waisted Hank, with featherlike, tomato-colored hair mentioned to Sam.

"Okay, keep in touch, Hank," Sam said. "And hey bartender, give Hank here a beer and a double shot." Taking a prolonged drag on his seven-inch El Producto cigar, Sam then hollered to the bartender, "Come on, dude, I got business to take care of. Quit piffling around, will ya?"

"I'm comin', I'm comin'," belted the bartender in return, reaching toward the clean glasses beneath the bar.

"So is Christmas," replied Sam with a misshapen sneer. But still there were no drinks. Ten seconds passed and Sammy chided, "If ya move any slower, pal, you'll stop all together. What's with all the dilly-dallyin'?"

Finally appearing with the drinks, "I'm sorry Sam, for the delay. I was just thinking about somethin'," the bartender dreamily leaned against the bar. Setting up the drinks, the bartender swabbed the bar on either side.

"Study long, study wrong," Sam quipped in typical rhyme, one of the scores of sayings he daily repeated. "Time waits for no man." Swallowing another beer, "Let's go kid," Sam beckoned to me as the two of us rushed out into the mystery of another Chicago night.

"How many kids you got?" I questioned one of Sam's regulars, a lady who ordered seventeen, yes seventeen hot dogs every night of the week. Each and every night, Dad and I started up her order, getting the dogs ready as soon as we saw the lady coming.

"Got about half a dozen or so, give or take," she replied. A few of her kids were kicking in the scrubby dust of 47th Street, their faces dabbed with scattered blotches of mud. Some weeks later, Sam met up with another friend, one of his oldest friends in Chicago.

"Come on, Sam," Nick Dukas invited his old pal. Known to him in the old days as Gus, Dad was forever celebrated as Sam, even in the eyes of the Greeks. "Let's go the South Water Market, Sam. Let's go to South Water."

A few miles southeast of the Loop, bordered by Racine Avenue on the west, and extending to 14th Street on the north, bustling South Water Market imported produce from 48 states, Canada, and more than 20 foreign countries. The bustling market gave Chicago consumers one of the greatest selections of fresh fruit and vegetables on earth, a must stop for any food vendor around

Chicagoland. It was at South Water Market in fact, where Sam bought Spanish onions as big as watermelons. No kidding! Driving up in his panel van, Nick was in the driver's seat and Sam was in the passenger's seat, and I was seated atop the engine compartment. A wooden partition separated the front seats, and there was hardly an inch to spare.

Glancing around the familiar city streets and sidewalks, about five hundred pounds of man filled those groaning seats, between Nick and Sam. Yeah, it was Nick and Sam, all the way. And wouldn't you know it? Both of those guys were sucking on the fattest, longest cigars I had ever seen in my lifetime. It was damp and nasty in Chicago so all the way up to South Water the heat was turned up full blast and the windows on that vehicle were shut tight as a jar. There was so much smoke in there my eyes were sizzling; my soft pupils were smoldering with fire. I wondered, *how could Nick even see to drive?* Pulling in at South Water, upon opening the vehicle's doors dense cigar smoke spooled out from Nick's old van, much like fog reeling off Lake Michigan's shoreline. Stepping into the gigantic warehouse, there were enormous bags of tomatoes, gigantic onions, firm plump cucumbers, and every color and shape of peppers a soul could imagine. I felt so high from the cigar smoke I was wobbly and green. Noticing my unsteady stance, Sam looked at me and blurted,

"Hey kid, what's wrong with *you*? Why don't you straighten up and fly right?"

Nearly bowled over, I thought: *Yes sir, I sure was flying but I probably wasn't flying right.* I generally didn't talk all that much around Dad since his philosophy was kids should be seen and not heard. If anytime I even dared to say something to Dad, (especially if he hadn't asked me a question), he usually quoted one of his favorite mottos such as: "An empty wagon makes a lot of noise."

After loading the stock into Nick's vehicle and then horse trading for a few extra minutes with the savvy Jewish proprietor

Sam and Nick had known for years, the ride home mimicked the ride up to South Water. Man, that ride home nearly caused me to fly right out of Nick's van, even more shaky and queasy than on the way up. Thank God my stomach was running slow. After watching me stagger around like a half-drunk plumber, Sam spit, then jibed, *"Kid, I'm gonna make a man outta you yet!"*

RALPH

CHAPTER 18

What Don't Kill You

"Hey, Virge! Virge!" I hollered, unable to hold the news one second longer. Bursting through the door of our Brighton Park apartment with the force of a wild bunch of gangbusters I shouted, "Virge, I bought a house!"

"What? What did you say?" Virginia asked in a fuss. Racing into the kitchen with her frizzy tangled hair, Virginia's round face was dusty from another application of her favorite drug store product, Coty Face Powder.

"I bought a house in Marquette Park!"

Looking at me like my head was screwed on backwards, "With what?" Virginia grilled me like a cop, maybe thinkin' I had somehow nabbed an entire house.

"What do you think, 'with what'? I bought it with money, of course, Virge. Don't be so dense."

Hobbling over to where I was parked, Coty powder particles flecked through the air like miniature snowflakes, plunging down to the kitchen floor, mingling with the coarse white hairs of that dim-witted dog, Gwen.

"I know how to operate," I hinted with a solid grin. "I'm an operator; I made a deal with Ernie Kipp, see. I gave him $2,000.00

in escrow through my lawyer, Sal Irving." By that time, Virge was staring at me as if I'd landed from another planet.

"You got a lawyer?" She questioned in a more cheery tone.

"Yeah, the same lawyer I had for Sam's Snack Shop—Irving."

"Oh, *that* lawyer," Virginia suddenly recalled our prior deal.

"Sal Irving is a beautiful guy, sure knows da businez," I said, opening the refrigerator to see if there was anything even remotely good enough for me to scarf down. "Virge, why don't you wake up and smell the coffee, will you?"

"Well, how many bedrooms are there? I sure hope it's not a dump. It's heated, isn't it? Now, Jerry, where'd ya say you got that $2,000.00? And *how much* was the total?" She quizzed like a kid.

Heaving a stretched-out sigh, "The house is eight grand total, and I've got four years to pay the sucker off. You'll see the house soon enough. Just take it easy, Virge, before you blow your silly top. And of course it's heated—it's Marquette Park," I finished.

Plopping down into one of our kitchen chairs, Virginia allowed the news to sink in. "Jerry, this will be the first house we've ever owned." Before I uttered a rousing, 'Holy Moses,' Virginia was taking the CTA to West Marquette Road, touring our new house with Lee and Lynn. When she returned, Virge was in seventh heaven. Yeah, she was raving about this, and planning over that, tellin' me how beautiful it would be, living across from the park and how there was plenty of room for her to plant those prickly rose bushes she liked so much. Marquette Park was high class, see, the home of a park filling 323 acres of land. That joint was jammed with swank tennis courts, playgrounds, lagoons, a field house, flower gardens, walking paths, and even a golf course. Though our thirteen-year-old daughter, Lynn, was more concerned about Davis School and her friends, Lee went along with the program, just the way I taught him.

"Congratulations," said the lawyer as I signed all the papers for the house. With my customary glow gleaming on my oblong face, on May 29, 1970, I became a homeowner at last. Though Virginia, Lee, and I were happy as larks, Lynn, on the other hand, really dug Brighton Park's Davis School and all her Mexicano friends. So she started taking buses back and forth to the old neighborhood so she could graduate from eighth grade. *Yeah, nize day.* Meanwhile, that old, white two-story frame I'd bought (one of the area's original homes) had seen better days. In our new neighborhood called Chicago Lawn, besides the famous park, it also held claim to the largest bakery in the entire world—the National Biscuit Company, otherwise known as Nabisco. You could get a good whiff of those babies bakin' just about any hour of the night or day. Since my new property needed a bit of work, I got a few of my Back of the Yards' pals to work on the house. Building a sidewalk, they fixed the roof and cleaned the dumpy, gravel-floored garage. In payment, I shot them a case of beer or two—plenty for those characters. I couldn't do much work around the house because I was too busy with the hot dog wagon, making loads of bucks. But thank goodness I had a son. That's what I thought when I approached Lee one day and made an announcement.

"Lee, you've been playin' long enough, kid. I got a good surprise for you. We're going on over to Sears on 63rd and Western and I'm gonna buy you a present." Lee somehow thought maybe it was a bike I was buying him because that was the same store where I bought his bicycle years ago. Heading into the Sears store's huge home care section located in the basement, the familiar scent of popcorn struck our nostrils the moment we walked through the fingerprinted glass doors. "Here ya go, kid," I proudly showed Lee, the two of us staring down at a brand new, reel type push mower, a big leaf-catching bag attached conveniently in back. "Deliver this mower to our house on West Marquette Road," I told the chump salesman at Sears. "Boy, kid," I messed with Lee, "you sure are gonna have fun with that." Quick as daylight, and the minute the new mower was delivered, our son went right to it, cutting all the grass—front and back.

Once Lee got the grass down pat, I then had a second surprise for the kid. "Tomorrow's gonna be even better for ya, Lee Boy," I threw the words out with a straight mug. Right on schedule, thirty-two triple-track storm windows arrived at the house, along with a giant bag of small screws weighing a good ten pounds. Lee helped me install every one of these windows, caulking each one as we went. With *that* job completed, early one morning I got a joker I knew to come over and dig a ditch from one side of the house all the way to the back. Next, I bought forty, circular rust-red pipes, along with some adhesive, showing Lee exactly how to do the first one. Settling into the ditch I had that clown dig all around the house while Lee started hooking all the pipes up to the gutters, he installed those drains like a pro. "Heh, heh." The kid thought we were gonna rest but I noticed the lawn needed cuttin' again and the bushes needed trimming. "Yeah," I nudged Lee, the boy's shirt drenched in sweat on one sticky, 90-degree Chicago afternoon. "What don't kill you," I blurted out with a well-deserved burp. "What don't kill you, Lee Boy, will only make ya stronger."

Though I was tough as nails on Lee, he still had loads of good times. Making friends with a group of kids in our new neighborhood, Lee played all the sports—baseball, football, even fishing (just like his old man) in Marquette Park's lagoon, bringing home buckets of clawing crayfish and turtles.

"Yuck, Lee. Why are bringing those ugly things in the house?" Lynn questioned, shootin' her brother a twisted frown.

Lee and I laughed our heads off knowing full well Lynn was the studious one, staying in the house most of the time, reading and studying. In the fall of 1970, Lynn was a brand new freshman at Hubbard High School on 62nd Street. At Eberhart Elementary, Lee got his fifth-grade teacher named Miss Scott.

"She's the strictest teacher I've ever had," Lee whined like a squeaky wheel on the hot dog wagon.

"Good deal, then," I stated, remembering my teachers at Divine Rosary. "No more strict than the Catholic nuns," I added with a proud chuckle. Busting his breeches to get good grades in class, Lee just didn't get the picture with all that schooling. His grades weren't all that good, but he got an "E" for effort. So when the kid finally finished the fifth grade, Lee jumped for joy because he made it. Funny thing happened, though. When Lee got to sixth grade, there was 'ole Miss Scott again; she had moved right up with Lee, following him like a mother hen. Anyway, one day Miss Scott took Lee aside when the other kids were off to catechism classes.

"Lee," she expressed the same way some of the nuns did back when I was at Divine Rosary. "I would like to talk to you. I've had many students in my career as a teacher," she told the kid directly. "And I also understand your grades are not as good as many of the other pupils. But I would much rather have a student like you who tries as hard as he can and gets low grades, than a student who understands all the work but is too lazy to excel when they are truly able to succeed."

Lee never forgot what Miss Scott said and I shouted a hearty, "Amen" to that. That was exactly what I was tryin' to teach the kid myself, whenever I got the chance.

One day I clenched my fist solid as a hammer's head, poking my five-fingered ball of wax about six inches away from Lee's curled face:

"Do you see my fist?" I tested Lee.

"Yes sir," the kid gave the right answer, just the way I'd taught him.

"I wanna tell you something. In your whole life, how many true friends do you think the average person has?" I questioned, tryin' to jab the harebrained kid into reality. A crate full of anger was seething inside my soul like tamales simmering in water.

"Five?"

"No way!" I snorted at the kid's quack answer. "HOW MANY?" I rephrased the question.

"Three?"

"No."

"*Two?*"

Cupping my fist as hard as I could until it was nearly blood red, I got as close as I could to Lee and heaved up one finger. "If you have just *one* good friend in your entire lifetime you will have more than most people in all the world," I targeted my point, right on the money.

"Yes sir," Lee correctly stated.

Guess he was learning somethin' after all.

Working the hot dog wagon in the spring and summer, and as much as possible in the fall, during the cold months I tried my hand at "Add a Man," but not much was happening there since I wasn't takin' any razz from some idiot foreman who thought he was God Almighty. In the middle of December, we discovered the thermostat in the house was all jazzed up—either really cold, say about fifty degrees, or boiling hot, somewhere around one hundred. I sure didn't have money to fix the goofy thing so we had to make due. Buying cases of Peter Pan peanut butter (only the best), we chomped on that, scarfing down canned tomato soup when things got tight. Sometimes there was feast, sometimes there was famine, just like when *I* was comin' up in the forties. Life usually changed faster than you figured it out, but I had to rest sometime, and winter sure was a fine time for resting.

"Are you just gonna lay around all day?" Virginia nagged me like a sour-pussed cat.

"I'm not layin' 'round. I'm restin'. What about it?"

"Restin'? Who's gonna pay the bills around here, Jerry?" Virge yelled into my sun-bleached ears.

"Bills? We got plenty a money. Bills, bills, bills. I gotta rest.

Why don't you get you some coffee, Virge? You drink more sugar and cream than coffee, heh, heh," I razzed her good.

"What's it to you if I like a lot of sugar? Why don't you let me up, you old King Farouk? Let me up and lay off."

"Off. Off," I repeated, just so she heard me.

Every Sunday I headed to St. Michael's in the Back of the Yards, or over to beautiful St. Rita's on 63rd Street because I never missed Mass. St. Rita Holy Catholic Church was beautiful, even though some fools claimed it had been haunted since 1961. They'd probably been to the tavern *before* Mass instead of goin' afterwards, if you asked me. Virginia still hauled the kids to those Protestant joints—Baptists and Methodists—but the Catholic Church was the best.

"There's a high stakes poker game goin' on the second floor of that Greek restaurant joint," I told Lee while passing the place on the way home one night after selling. "They go in with $5,000 a piece. High rollers, they are," I emphasized.

Looking at me like I had a hole in my head, when we got home, Lee was our bartender as usual, always obeying his father just the way *my* father taught me, even though I wasn't sure if the old man, or mother for that fact, was still walkin' the earth. But once a boy learned to obey his father, it was a heap easier to obey God, *that's what the kid told me later on.*

VIRGINIA

CHAPTER 19

The Telephone Call

"There's no one here by that last name," I firmly verified to the woman on the opposite end of the telephone line, on an otherwise quiet afternoon. My hands shifted nervously as my white work shoes scraped against the filmy floor of our kitchen on Marquette Road. I was doing all kinds of jobs in the neighborhood—working at the dry cleaners on Kedzie Avenue, cleaning house for a few local elderly couples down the block, and I also sold Avon products. And yes, I certainly did say: "Hello. Avon calling."

"Are you Mrs. Polachek?" Pressed the strange woman on the telephone, forcing me not to hang up.

"Yes, I *am* Mrs. Polachek," I hesitated to concede.

"Is your husband's name Ralph? I'm his sister—Katrina. Katrina Polaieck."

Barely hanging onto the telephone receiver as if it was a cold block of ice, my throat constricted into a stiff knot. *Ralph?* "My husband's family is dead. His name is Jerry ... Who are you? *Katrina?* Born in Minnesota? Jerry?" I questioned, motioning to my portly spouse, his dog-like jowls munching on the slimy pigs' feet he so loved, eating this, that, and Lord knew what else. Plunked at the kitchen table a few feet away from where I uneasily stood, my eyes were fixed toward Jerry's brain. "This lady on the telephone," I took a quick breath then rallied a long swallow. "This woman says she's your sister, and, ... she says your mother is still alive, living in Minnesota." *Jerry told me he was born in Detroit! What a strange bird!*

Grabbing the telephone, Jerry's features numbed. His eyes were enlarged as big as dinner plates, and his twelve-inch feet shuffled beneath his chair. Never in all my born days had I seen a man like Jerry—never. Shaking his head, Jerry hung up the receiver. The stillness in the entire house registered something between total shock and storybook wonder.

"What's this all about?" I pressured my stone-faced husband. Seated like a baffled kid as he awoke from a strange dream, we were both in the center of it. "I don't understand any of this, Jerry. *Jerry?*"

"Katrina, that's my sister, Katrina. Remember I told you about her? Haven't seen Katrina since 1942. Haven't seen Mother since '42 either," Jerry muttered.

Katrina? His Mother? Drawing in my shoulders, to be perfectly honest, ever since I met that man I was never really sure what was going on from one blasted day to the next. Did I really marry a Ralph instead of a Jerry? A man from Minnesota and not Detroit? It seemed to be the story of my life—

Jerry: the guy who jerry-rigged things to save his bosses money.

Gus: the successful businessman, heartthrob of Chicago's Greeks.

Sam: Sam, Sam, the famous Hot Dog Man.

Ralph. Ralph? Those names weren't really anything other than nicknames numerous people had only labeled him. Why I'd even heard Lee say once someone called to Jerry yelling, "Hey Jack." Do you know how Jerry answered the guy? Shooting his words with the force of a gangster's bullet, Jerry aimed straight at the guy's gut, lashing back with a question,

"Where did you punk, where'd get that 'Hey Jack' stuff at? I'll jack *you* up, punk," Jerry snorted, adding a comment of his own, muttering some fool rhyme like:

'You got the story, morning glory,
No slip on the slide, eazzy way on the ride,
Ya know what I'm talkin' about.'

Lee constantly remarked how people from all over the city were dumbfounded when they heard Jerry's rhetoric since afterwards he usually spouted his famous ditty, "Nize Day." Yeah, Jerry loved talking like those fool rascals from the Back of the Yards. Why, just last week some folks innocently told Jerry at the stand, "Have a nice day."

"Hey, don't you be stealin' from me like that," Jerry scolded those kind folks, his warning accompanied by a toasty glare.

"We're not stealing nothing from you," those poor people replied.

"You are too—that's my saying, 'Nize Day.' I even said it before those yellow smile-faced pens came on the market, ya know what I'm talkin' about?"

I suppose after Jerry's fool discussion those poor people hurried out of there quick. No, there was no tellin' what would happen next with that nutty goat—Jerry, Gus, Sam, Ralph, whoever he was. Oh, how he drove me nearly to the edge, pouncing on Lee, Lynn, and me like cheese in the paws of a dirty rat. The whole mess started the day we moved into the Back of the Yards and away from Nick and his good family. Jerry started talking and actin' like the immigrant Poles, allowing them to think he was Polish, which I seriously doubted. To top it off, I nearly had a nervous breakdown when I was livin' with that bird on 51st Street. How my head pounded with biting migraines, my simple, carefree soul suddenly seething. Brighton Park was certainly a nice break, since our weekly escape to the Loop and the nearby shopping district on Archer Avenue really helped out. But since we've moved to Marquette Road, Jerry had grown crazier than ever. One day, for example, that husband of mine was sitting as nice as pie inside our house. Out of the blue Jerry moseyed to the front window and asked,

"Who is that lady sitting on our sidewalk in the snow?" Glimpsing outside to double check, I lobbed him a crinkled brow and replied,

"Jerry, that's not a lady; that's a man."

"Same difference," Jerry's bucket-huge head nodded with a yawn. Then he added, "Don't worry 'bout it, maybe she's hot."

"That's a man," I repeated, "a *he*, not a she."

But Jerry loved to argue, telling me, "Same difference—man, woman, or child. The dude is probably drunk or has to cool off. Maybe she got hot pipes or somethin'."

"Jerry, you are crazy as a loon. I feel like I am living in an insane asylum."

"That's where *you* belong, Virginia," Jerry pointed his silly fat finger toward my chest, his flabby stomach jiggling. Then I notified him in short *he* was the crazy one. Snortin' like a horse he then declared, "At least I ain't sittin' in the snow like that old lady."

"That is a *man*!" I defended the truth for a final time. "Can't you see his mustache and beard?"

"You've never worked in the carnival, Virge, have you? I used to help this fat lady with a mustache and beard in the circus," he abruptly revealed another one of his countless bizarre experiences.

"*How* did you help her?" I asked with a suspicious frown.

"I helped her finish off a half pint of whiskey," he shrieked with a loud hoot. "Yeah, maybe that's what the lady in the snow out there needs."

"That is a MAN!" I screamed at the top of my lungs.

"Same difference! God takes care of fools and drunks."

Oh that God-forsaken man. Discovering Jerry had a sister in St. Louis, and a mother living in Minnesota had really shaken our whole family. The kids actually had a grandmother, and I had a mother-in-law. That was someone I was sure lookin' forward to meeting. *What kind of a woman gave birth to that strange old bird? Yeah, that was what Lynn and I wanted to know.* Though that day, like most, he was testing my patience to no end, I tried not to get all riled up so I finally offered, "Well, maybe that's why you are so well taken care of because you are both!"

Showing his teeth like growling lion, Jerry grunted. At that point I waited to see which one of us would get the coveted "final word" in those harebrained proceedings.

"You're treated like a queen bee, Virginia," Jerry bolted back.

"Huhg! Some queen bee! You're the queen bee around here. You gave me five dollars for food in 1950, and you still give me five dollars for groceries today. Some queen—huh," I managed. "You're drivin' me to the funny farm with all your antics."

"Antics? Same difference," Jerry ended. At last our crazy quarrel finally fizzled out as he danced around the kitchen yelling in song: "Nize day! Nize day!" Whew, that man got me so agitated; he was always trying to get my goat, day after blasted day. He irritated me more than ten sore toes, bringing one hootenanny after another. I certainly knew my lot in life, and that hot dog man was my devil for sure. But you could mark my words: it would all come back on him. Yes, it surely would.

One grey morning Lee and I noticed our neighbors (the Italian family who lived three houses away) were heaving all their furniture into a moving truck. Those folks had gone to several Cubs' games with the kids and I, and the wife in the family had been a good friend. Lee, Lynn, and I had gone to the Italian carnival on 69th Street with them. Our other neighbor's boy, Jamey, was a year older than Lee. Jamey had a weight set holding around 120 pounds, more or less. Lee and Jamey regularly built models together, listening to the *Grand Funk Railroad* on the radio. On Saturdays they watched *The Wide, Wide World of Sports* on television. But every time those two kids trampled down into Jamey's basement, Jamey made terrible fun of poor Lee. Jamey, you see, always dared Lee with the same old taunt.

"You can't lift those weights over your head, Lee," scrawny Jamey jeered, pointing toward the big set of weights. "You can't do it, Lee, you're not strong enough." Though Lee had worked with weights since our Brighton Park days, when he tried to lift Jamey's weights he could barely hoist the giant things off the ground. It was the same thing every time they went into that basement: "You can't lift those weights over your head, Lee," Jamey ribbed again and again, ridiculing poor Lee to no end.

One amazing day Lee got so exasperated that he heaved those weights into his wide hands. With surprising might, our son boosted that colossal bar right over his head. From then on, Lee kept adding more weights, clinking and tightening them on the bar, lifting and grunting like a bear. Lee and Jamey even went to the Marquette Park's field house to lift since they had all sorts of weights there. By the time he hit age thirteen, Lee actually broke the field house record, lifting 210 pounds over his head, all the while the poor kid only weighed 130 pounds, soaking wet!

"What a family," I remarked, spying the new folks who had now moved into the Italians' old place. The new bunch had a big brood of kids, one of them a boy exactly the same age as Lee. I was so glad about that recent turn of events since Lee and the new kid, Larry, were doing everything together—going to the Ford City Mall on Cicero Avenue, riding bikes around Marquette Park, shooting BB guns in our basement, and just hanging out. Soon they became best friends, talking to each other all the time. Their relationship was even renewed several decades later. Larry was really helping Lee. But Lee was helping Larry as well.

Though my neck often struggled to support my aching head, before long I discovered Lee liked a particular girl at school. And it was my guess she was equally infatuated with him. But I was also aware Lee's hormones were startin' to rage wildly, so one day I sat Lee down for a talk. In no time, my sweet son conveyed with dancing, starry eyes how he knew all about having sex with a girl.

"Listen, I am going to tell you something right now," I gaped my migraine-prone head toward Lee. Holding his eyes with a fierce stare, my hazel eyes grew ironclad as Lee's heavy weights. Glaring like a lioness into his blue-green eyes, I handed out the sternest warning I knew how to give. "It is wrong to have sex with a girl, Lee. And it would sure hurt me terribly if you ever did, without waiting until you are married, that is." I knew Lee loved me greatly. But I also recognized several girls were interested in him because he *was* a very handsome boy, blessed with a sweet personality. Nonetheless, Lee didn't want to do anything to hurt me because he loved me with all his heart. Naturally, I knew he would love to have a girlfriend. But I also knew if he did, I seriously doubted he would be able to control himself. Though it was very hard for Lee, and because I always loved him unconditionally, bravely, our son waited.

"Please be careful, Lee," I lovingly warned our boy seconds before he left the house. That was the same year Lee started taking the bus all by himself from our house on Marquette Road, traveling several miles northeast to Sam's stand on 47th Street. Every afternoon there went Lee, our only son who was so sweet. In Chicago, like most big cities, you never knew who, or what, was waiting around the corner. It could have been a mugger, a killer, or something even worse. Those neighborhoods were like mine fields; everyone was trying to dodge a disaster in the making. The twitching in my head grew stronger each day as I felt like my whole body would crack into a thousand tiny pieces. Jerry had trampled me down so fiercely with his words there was not a blessed thing more I could do. So I prayed for Lee every night, pleading with God to bring my boy home safely. Faithfully bagging hot dogs and tamales for that father of his, the hot dog man continually infuriated me, especially on the night he made a staggering announcement.

"Say Virginia, I am gonna to break the kid in the business," Jerry said, clearing his hoarse throat.

"Oh, no. Lee's too young for that," I moaned with a twirling gut. Of course, my words went in one ear and out the other. Though Jerry was initially easy on Lee, over time he steadily watched our son grow faster and sharper at the stand. Then out of the blue, that blasted man started getting tough on our precious boy, testing him to see how much he could handle. Lee arrived at the hot dog stand at about five in the afternoon. Then believe it or not, the two of them didn't come home until two a.m., causing me to square off with Ralph. Yes, I was finally calling him Ralph, instead of Jerry, wrestlin' with that bugger the same way someone might do with a nasty field snake.

"What's wrong with you keeping that boy out so late at night, comin' home at two o'clock in the morning?"

"This is bizziiiness," Ralph stuttered. Before long, Ralph saw young Lee was growing up, getting to be a bit of a smart aleck. I, for one, didn't blame the boy one bit since it was just his anger coming out. Anyway, Ralph had no part of it. Blinking away my newest round of tears, Ralph and I argued about everything, but most especially about Lee, money, and a whole host of other things. The two of us brawled with words nearly every moment we were alive. Sobbing my heart out with my sore head sagged, I pleaded to God down on my knees: *Please God, have mercy on me; I need peace.* Then one night when sheer panic almost beat me to a pulp, I divulged my feelings to Lee.

"The only reason I stay with your father, Lee, is because of you and Lynn. If it weren't for you two, I'd march right out of this house in two seconds flat. I sure as anything would get a divorce from that brut—he's mean, Lee, especially when he's gulping down that whiskey," I said, weeping like a kid.

Lee had always been our negotiator. Agreeing with me one minute, he saw eye to eye with his father the next. Desperately trying to keep the two of us together, Lee patched up all our spats. All that heartache made me think of the day when Lee was little and he started acting up in a store. "Lee," I yelled, wagging my finger in his face. "If you don't behave I'll pull down your pants and spank you right here in front of the whole store."

With sparkling teardrops in his little eyes, Lee looked up at me and pleaded. "You wouldn't really do that, would you, Mommy?"

"Oh yes I will," I replied with a rigid frown, hoping he'd stop his foolishness, once and for all. And sure enough, Lee promised me he'd be good. Lee often remembered me spitting on my handkerchief, wiping the tears from his damp rosy cheeks. Lee says he even remembered what my saliva tasted like! But my words barely registered one wit because a few short days later, Ralph said some things to Lee that tore him apart.

"Why don't you go into the bathroom and cry like a little girl?" He mercilessly teased Lee. Not until decades later did Lee realize his father was harsh on him because he truly loved him. When Lee lumbered out of the bathroom, Ralph piped up. "Okay kid, eat your food, and then we're gonna go to work."

"He's so mean," I honestly admitted, nearly eatin' my hat when I heard how Ralph had turned up the furnace on Lee. He even made fun of our son in front of people at the hot dog stand, after Lee worked like a plow horse eighteen hours a day. But God often dropped surprises like eggs, hoping the broken ones might be used.

One day Ralph was under the wagon working and Lee plopped down on the wagon's seat without thinking. Feeling the metal hit sharply against his nearly baldhead, the hot dog man shrieked to the high heavens.

"Hey, hey! I'm under here! "You could have killed me," Ralph yelled.

"I'm sorry, Dad," Lee apologized, his eyes welling up in salty tears.

Then, as fate would have it, in Lee's junior year Ralph unexpectedly issued a horrible decree. "Why don't you people stop flapping your gums over nothin'?" the hot dog man declared, curling his lips in a funny hiss. "And say Virginia, I want you to call up that Hubbard High School and tell them, *Lee is done!*"

CHAPTER 20

Charmin' Lee

"Man, oh man!" Feeling like throwing up my hands and screamin' like a hoot owl, my curly-Q, fuzzy hair looked like Miss Ipswich. How I had been teased about my hair. When I was a young girl, they used to call me, "Ginny Frizz." "Hey, Ginny Frizz," the kids shouted and mocked. Ginny was short for Virginia, and frizz because my hair was always frizzy, even more so in the humidity. Fumbling my aching fingers through my sewing box, the long, wild nights slipped quickly by. After graduating high school, our Lynn worked for a downtown law firm, and she was dating a great fellow named Steve, making life a heap happier for all of us. Expecting another quarrel to spark the moment Ralph traipsed through the front door, my mind scattered toward the times I sang to charmin' Lee. When he was just a wee little tike, I jangled him fondly on my knee, helping him tie his shoelaces and comb his shiny hair. I was trying with all my might to guide him into the right things of this life.

After Lee was pushed to quit high school (following his wretched father's ridiculous advice) all the poor kid knew was hot dogs, Polish sausage, tamales, pickles, mustard, relish, onions, tomatoes, hot sauce, and propane gas. All the same, Ralph's silver coin changer clanged quarters and dimes all day and night, making money to fill their lock box to take over to the bank. With his .38 Huskavarna placed next to the propane tank running the gas to cook the meat and steam those buns, Lee was at it again with Ralph—Chicago's, Sam, the hot dog man—the two lollygagging around stinking taverns and beer joints until all hours of the dark night.

"I sure feel sorry for Lee," Lynn confided to me one day, her young face dour and lined, pondering the future of her little brother.

"At least he's got money now," I reacted with a weary smile. Almost regularly, my dear Lee moaned how he was watchin' people soar like jaybirds out the door of Rick's tavern. Drunken fists pounced on one goof after another, and vomit spewed like water in those nasty streets. Even when the streets were slick, Lee was out until the early hours of the morning when the poor kid should have been in bed. Falling asleep in reeking gas stations, in ripped up flophouses, on dusty garage floors, and in makeshift beds haphazardly thrown together in the back of pick-up trucks; it was no way for a young boy to grow up. Why didn't that husband of mine just "cease and desist?"

Watching some old tavern fool stop traffic on 47th Street very late one night, Lee revealed how some crazed lush was making everyone pay a toll in order to pass through the street. "That'll be a dollar," the soused drunk spouted, pocketing the tolls. Amazingly, the charade continued until the cops showed. Lee said on yet another night he witnessed a fellow sleeping in his car. The guy was all gassed-up and his wife stomped out of the tavern like a bull, stumbling into their car. The beer-trashed woman floored their '65 Chevy, slamming down those brakes to kingdom come. With the jukebox blastin' inside Rick's tavern, the old coot of a husband flew out of the Chevy onto busy 47th. Man! Lee sure had plenty of money, but since he quit school he was gettin' a street education instead. And I didn't like it, not one bit.

"How's it going, Lee?" I peevishly inquired, taking pity on my son. Looking straight as a needle into his bloodshot eyes, air snagged like a pulled thread inside my bone-dry throat. Suddenly, Lee started recounting the latest happenings at Sam's stand.

"Something nuts happened at the stand the other night," mumbled Lee nearly in a daze. Smoke from my Bel-Air twirled around his chest, swirling in roving clouds.

"What happened, Lee?" I probed. My pulse was skidding and my organs were heaving as I grimly held in my breath.

"Well, the whole alley behind the stand was full of cop cars. One guy, (this regular customer) came up and asked me a question."

"Samson, (they nicknamed me Samson—*Sam's son*). "Samson, hey where's Sammy? Has something happened to Sammy?" The guy asked, searching everywhere for Dad.

"I knew, of course, exactly what was going on," Lee continued with a sigh. "So I told the customer Sammy was just takin' care of business. What was really happening was all those cops were having a big beer and whiskey party; they set up their gambling contests right in Dad's garage, the same garage he had rented since '55. Dice, craps, cards—the whole bunch of those cops were havin' the time of their lives. Anyway, Sam knew all the Chicago cops, see. Ma, we never charged any cop for a single thing. When someone in uniform wanted a hot dog or Polish, they fished out their dollar bills but I shook my head, putting my hand up telling every one of them: Man, your money is no good here."

"Humph," I laughed, knowing too well how Sam operated.

"Ma, the cops always chuckled and told me I was just like my old man. But there seemed to be a cop car flying down 47th Street almost every ten minutes—day or night, no difference. Yeah, those guys sure had plenty of work around there. Once, a cop car was speeding about 50 miles an hour, bolting the wrong way up Seeley. It nearly crashed head on into the hot dog wagon. Helicopters regularly hovered overhead, and almost every week guns were shooting, even machine gun fire was sounding off, just like in the movies. On another night, a cop came to the stand, breathing hard after chasing a suspect. Just as plain as day the cop spilled the beans to Dad and me."

"We killed that rotten sucker, a clear dead shot straight through the head," the cop told us straight out. "Say, give me a dog, kid," the cop then ordered in the next breath. "This kinda work makes me hungry, and thirsty too."

"Oh dear God, Lee," I gulped, my insides wound like the stiff curls of my hair. "That area's getting really bad."

"Another night, this guy, Full Hand ..."

"*Full Hand?*"

"Yeah, he was a friend of Dad's. Anyway, they called him Full Hand because he had sticky fingers," Lee eagerly demonstrated, pressing the fingers on his right hand tightly together. "Full Hand was the nicest guy in the world, Ma. He slept in an empty building near Hermitage, nabbin' any bike not locked up. Then he went around the neighborhood selling the bikes like hotcakes in exchange for booze. One crazy night, Full Hand plunked himself down in the dirt asking Sharky's friend, (Sharky lives with his brother and always limps) to give him a beer. They nabbed a glass of beer from the bar and Full Hand grabbed some dirt and other junk from the grass. Then he started yelling at the top of his lungs: 'If you fill up my glass with beer, I'll guzzle the whole thing down in three seconds.' So Sharky's bought a whole quart of beer, filling up the rest of Full Hand's glass. Full Hand guzzled down the beer dirt junk as easily as if it was a Pepsi or Coke. Full Hand grinned real big and loudly exclaimed, 'That ain't nothin'.'

And ya know what else?" Lee asked. "Little kids, say two or three, sometimes wandered around the hot dog wagon while their daddies were in the tavern drinkin' away their lives," Lee dryly said.

Listening to all that crazy mess started my nerves popping like corn. At that very moment *I'd* sure have liked to pop that man of mine flat in the nose! "Look at what you're doin' to Lee," I carped to the hot dog man when he came home later on. My worn out eyes were glaring at Ralph, my mouth holding a heart-stopping scowl. But it didn't matter since he never listened to a word I said.

"By the way, Mom, Rick's tavern is now called Babby's, short for Barbara. Anyway, that's where you can call if ya ever need to reach us," Lee's voice softened. "Yeah, old Rick sold the place. I actually started drinking beer there with Dad when I was only fourteen," grimaced Lee, staring up nervously at the ceiling. "Yeah, and not only in *that* tavern but in *many* taverns. And all those times not one soul ever batted an eye, asking about my age."

Shuffling around in his chair, Lee relayed yet *another* tale. "One night a few months ago, a group of guys came out of Babby's Tavern," Lee began. "The whole lot of them were toting lawn chairs, fishing poles, sunglasses, a beer cooler, and of all things, a boom box. As usual, the traffic on 47th Street was heavy. Those silly guys lugged all their paraphernalia near the street when one of them started detouring all the buses, cars, and trucks, forcing the traffic to go around their little party. Those crazies actually opened up the sewer cover right in the middle of 47th, baiting their hooks so they could start fishing. They thought they were big shots, doing whatever they pleased. That continued for about ten minutes until the cops showed. Hurling all their junk into the paddy wagon, along went those goofs who wanted to go sewer fishing on 47th."

"Who would *do* something like that?" I quizzed Lee with upraised brows, the smell of hot dogs still fresh on his skin. Jiggling his head, Lee chewed on a crispy piece of my fried chicken. Pausing a moment to swallow, he continued his account.

"Mom, there's almost a new story every single night. One night, Sam's good friend takes another guy's bet whether or not he could crush up a shot glass inside his mouth and spit it back out again. As soon as the man slapped five bucks on the bar, Sam's friend gulped the shot glass straight down, stuffing the entire glass inside his mouth. Swallowing the whole shot glass mess, it broke and crunched right down his throat. The husky Pole was chewin' and chewin' until it all was just plain splinters. Leaving the bar with a huge smile on his face, the slivers and blood slid off the husky Pole's mouth. Taking a deep breath, he spat, blood and glass shards splattering everywhere. Yeah," Lee laughed. "Dad's best friend sure won that bet."

"Lee, those guys are so rough," I whined. Shivers ran down my back as I carried the dirty dishes to the sink; I was about ready to flip my lid. When Lee woke up in the morning, the poor kid didn't know if he was gettin' *off* the bus to go home, or gettin' *on* the bus in order to start a brand new day. Lee had been exposed to so much, so many incredibly rotten things. He had witnessed countless accidents and vulgar tavern fights, having seen more grit than I truly cared to think about. And Ralph still thought he was God's gift to the world—some king!

"You peasants use back door; I'm the King," Ralph sharply bellowed to Lee and I.

"You're no wretched king," I hollered to Ralph on more than one occasion. Sometimes that man lay in bed for days at a time without moving a single muscle. *Some king! King of fools, maybe.*

"I'm the King of 47th Street and the king of this castle, woman," Ralph belted back.

"You are just one big lunk," I replied, my jaw stiffened for effect. "That's exactly what you are. You're drivin' me batty, ya know that? And stop saying you're a king. Some folks think they're big shots when they're really not," I shot in return, my mouth opened wide enough to expose my missing tooth, the one my first husband knocked out in a terrible beating. All that brought me back to the day Lee and his dad returned home from working the factories and the streets. Suddenly Ralph asked Lee,

"Where are your keys, you big dummy?"

"The ignition switch on the Cushman was completely worn

out and my keys were too heavy," Lee sulked. "Guess they fell out somewhere," Lee answered honestly. My sad sack of a kid was staring at Ralph like an old miserable hound dog.

"That's it. Let's go," the hot dog man howled. So Ralph started struttin' around the house again, just like some 'ole king.

"Where are we goin'?" Lee questioned.

"We're goin' to get those keys back," countered Ralph, nearly causing poor Lee to fall down and faint.

So the two of them trekked out on foot; they had to backtrack, beginning at their corner on Seeley, pounding the pavement to Western Avenue, going past California, past Kedzie, past Pulaski, almost to Cicero. Block by block, mile after mile, there those two went looking for Lee's missing keys.

"Let's stop here," Ralph suddenly interrupted their madcap hike. Stopping at a bar where they were offering glasses of beer for ten cents apiece, Ralph's endless craving for beer overshadowed any problem with keys.

"We drank about a hundred glasses of beer that night," Lee steadily recalled. "That was a goooddd lesson for you, Kid Tiiidddy Eye," Ralph stuttered, calling our Lee by that new crazy name. "If you ever lose your keys again," Ralph's eyes narrowed like a fox. "If you ever lose them again, you're through."

And just like his father before him, Ralph meant it. Ralph's father was as hard as nails, but so was Sam—Ralph—Jerry, whatever that blasted man's name was. That incident, however, spiked Lee with images of what happened some years later. While drinking in a southern Illinois bar in East St. Louis, somehow Ralph and Lee became split up. Lee decided to walk home where we lived near Centerville. Barreling out the tavern door, three men dived on Lee like a pack of wolves. Hurling him into some nearby bushes, one of the guys stuck a .357 Magnum to Lee's temple, yelling like crazy in our son's ear.

"Give us your wallet! Give us your wallet!" they shouted, poor

Lee feeling the cold pistol against his warm skin. Lee, of course, handed over his wallet with $85.00 inside. "Give us everything else in your pockets," they ordered, the gun still plastered to sweet Lee's head. Forking over everything in all three of his pockets, the thugs suddenly heard Lee's keys rattle.

"Those are *my* keys and I can't give them to you," Lee told the muggers matter-of-factly, his eyes solid as a wrench.

Cocking the .357, at that moment one of those lousy guys warned, "If you don't give me them keys right now, I'm gonna blow your honkin' head right off!"

Lee's pulse did flips and flops, beating like a heavy rain. "You might as well do it right now," groveled Lee like a champ. "Because if I lose my keys again, my dad is gonna kill me anyway."

Uncocking his gun, "You one crazy honky," the mugger ripped. "You too crazy to kill." At that, Lee went straight home with his keys in tact, telling Ralph what happened.

"Good deal, kid," Ralph commended Lee. "We can always get some more dough, but you've got your keys. I'm happy with that, Kid Tidy Eye."

Lee was, by no means a saint, but there was something special about love, making people do things they would never think of doing. Love from God, could overcome a multitude of wrongs. Lee said with love—

"There's no such thing as time;
There's no such thing as strings;
There is no such thing as money or fame;
There is no condition that can stop true love;
There is no beginning; it has no end;
It is the greatest thing there is.
It overcomes any obstacle; time after time it wins;
Any evil will be erased because of it;
Without love, a person has nothing."

Cradling my head in my hands, I totally agreed: love *was* the key. Maybe *that was* why when Ralph demanded Lee fight for his keys, our Lee did so with all his might.

"Without *those keys* of love, you might as well be dead; it is the gold standard of life," Lee said, lifting his face into a wide smile. "The great 'I AM' is love. Love is why a person can thrive because, *without it there is nothing*," ended Lee, his eyes more somber than I had ever seen them.

Expertly driving that Cushman around those cramped city streets like a prizefighter, Lee constantly fought those roads and boulevards blanketed with soot, traffic, cursing, and haze. One day about ten o'clock in the morning as Lee was nearing the factories, an Illinois State Trooper suddenly pulled him over. Getting off the scooter, Lee yelled through the drone of choking cars, buses, and truck traffic. "What's the problem?"

"Get back to your vehicle," screeched the iron-faced Trooper, following Lee back to the scooter. "Let me see your Operator's License," the Trooper demanded. Presenting the license, "You don't have the correct license to drive this vehicle," he stated, perusing all the data.

"Where are *you* from?" Lee questioned the Trooper, politely enough.

"Pardon me?" the Trooper asked.

"Say, do you know who my dad is? Do you see all these factories right here?"

"Yes, of course I see them," the Trooper answered, peering at the square hills of glass, steel, and concrete.

Leafing through his wallet, Lee quickly yanked out a card his dad, Sam, the hot dog man, had given him. On that card was the name of the owner of all those factories.

"That man owns all this," Lee pointed to the card then spread his hands, gesturing toward the vast sea of factories. "And the police run all this jive. You dig?"

Mumbling a few choice words under his breathe, "You just keep your lights on when you're driving that thing," the Trooper snarled, pulling away from Lee like a bat out of hellfire. Nevertheless, Lee headed straight for the long ribbon of factories, offices, and industrial plants, making three important stops so he could turn out plenty of beans, what Sam often called money. Every day, you see, Ralph tested Lee like a schoolteacher and his student.

"How many beans did you pull in today, kid?" Ralph inquired.

His eyes lighting up like Christmas, Lee usually muttered, "Oh, about a bill or so." I supposed a bill meant about $100.00. Making all his stops on time, Lee waited a while at the A&P Produce factory. Afterward, he cut through the residential streets west of Pulaski. One summer morning as he was driving through the busy thoroughfares, Lee heard a guy yelling like mad through the wild maze of city traffic.

"Hey, hey. Dere's de guy, de guy from Damen," a man excitedly shouted. Stopping Lee in the middle of busy 47th Street near Pulaski, the immigrant Pole, (dressed in brown plaid polyester pants and a tee shirt), rushed toward Lee with an upraised hand. "Vait, vait." Twisting his head toward his yellow brick bungalow, "Hey Marta, Marta. Here's de guy from Damen. I treat you tonight; I git you tamale and hot dog. I git you terranger."

"Terranger?" Lee asked.

"Yeh, sausage," the starry-eyed Pole explained, his gold teeth glittering in the humid July sunlight. Hauling out his plastic change purse, the Pole couldn't wait to pay.

"Ninety cents," stated Lee.

Handing Lee a dollar, "You keep, you keep," the Pole insisted. Toting the big sack of meat and buns toward his bungalow, the Pole was ever so grateful. "Dank you, Samson. You kume back, okay?"

"I kume back whenever I git around these parts," Lee told the smiling Pole, his peanut-colored hair whipping around in the Chicago wind. Trying to squeeze the scooter back into the spitting maze of 47th Street traffic, Lee gazed at one of a hundred CTA buses that had cut him off since he started driving the scooter. His thoughts swirled to a few weeks earlier when the hot dog man was fuming because the bus was taking so long to reach their stop. Here's how Lee told it:

"That dirty rotten bus driver," Dad cursed. "Grumbling about how slow the bus was running, Sam had had it. Shuffling toward the rear exit, to the left was the red emergency pull cord. If the emergency cord was ever pulled, the whole cotton-pickin' bus would stop dead cold. At that stage of the game, I knew Sam would do just about anything. From the corner of my eye, I saw plain as day Sam yanking the red emergency cord. Instantly, the bus jerked to a forced halt."

"What'd ya do that for?" The familiar CTA driver yelled in shock at Sam.

"I wanna git off this miserable bus, that's why," Sam barked.

"Following Dad as he huffed down the grimy CTA steps," Lee sighed, "I guess Dad didn't want to wait one minute more, Mom."

The hot dog man was constantly bent on selling any new gadgets he had purchased on Maxwell Street. That husband of mine was a real hustler. He was such a hustler the Outfit wanted him—the Mafia. Thankfully, Sam said, "No thanks." Anyway, Sam bought some nice Van Heusen shirts to sell, along with hundreds of other items he stored inside his garage, as well as in the hot dog wagon.

"Sam even bought a huge Saint Bernard dog for just one buck," Lee divulged. But soon that giant of a dog devoured all Sam's stock, munching on the hot dogs like candy. I expect the dog disappeared after that. Suddenly, Lee stretched his cramped legs and yawned: *"Ma, I'm going to bed."*

LYNN

CHAPTER 21

Out of the Shadows

"July is my favorite month of the year," I said to Mother brightly on the telephone. My stomach still turned choppy, however, whenever I realized Sam was within earshot. On the delicate stillness of that summer day, I slugged through scores of thoughts. Attempting to make sense of my existence, how I longed to understand. Walking up the concrete stairs to our colonial frame house located in the far southwestern neighborhood called Ashburn, Ashburn got its name from a time when Chicago had dumped all its' coal ashes a few blocks to the west. Though loved by God as well as a good man, my soul often mimicked those strewn ashes—sooty remnants of a life I was still yearning to comprehend.

In 1977, at 21 years of age, I had been a Christian for nearly eight years, my surrender to God changing my life completely. Gone was my fear of hell. Gone was my fear of men. And gone were my penchant for pessimism, jealousy, and the ways of this world. It had all been replaced by peace, joy, and eternal hope. Since the heartbreak of moving away from my friends in Brighton Park, every time I got a few close friends, poof, they disappeared. First it was Gwen and the gang from Sawyer School. Next it was my Back of the Yards' pals and Mr. Wiles. Then worst of all came my school chums from Davis, all of them cruelly torn away. How I loved those Mexican kids—their warmth, their humor, their customs, their language, and their good common sense—so different from the harsh Eastern European girls saturating the Southwest Side. But like dust blown around the schoolyard on a scorching hot day, they were all gone, all because of Sam. Memories continually dripped through my veins like a cold autumn mist:

Not long after moving into our Brighton Park apartment in May, 1967, the girl across the hall from us was dressed with bottle black, teased hair, her fingernails painted in a chilling, frosted white. Sheila befriended me almost immediately, as I was brand new to the neighborhood.

"You're gonna want to get some boyfriends," Sheila smirked. Although I had just turned twelve, she was trying to lure me into sexual relationships with her high school boyfriends. Caking her eyes with *Maybelline* mascara, frosty lipstick was smeared all over her lips. At age thirteen, Sheila acted more like an adult than any girl I had ever known. And even on school nights she arrived home at a late hour, often meeting up with Sam.

"That girl is trouble, Virginia," Sam remarked the following day. "She strolled home the same time as me." Hurriedly finding new friends in Little Mexico a few blocks north of our school, Sheila's mother eventually suffered a fatal stroke and died. After Lee and I attended our first wake, Sheila and her older sister promptly moved away.

"My name Lupe," the elderly Mexican woman with puffy white hair kindly introduced herself to Mother and me. Filling the vacant flat across the hall, Lupe spoke in broken English. "I hid behind a wooden cart when Pancho Villa and his gang came into my pueblito," Lupe stated with large, adobe brown eyes. "Many others were kilt."

Since I was friendly with all the Mexican kids (who I truly envied because they eagerly practiced their culture) the pale-eyed, long-legged Lithuanian girls on my block were furious at my choice. Chasing me home from school like some hunted rat, they hoped like anything to smash me in pieces into the ground. One malty-skied afternoon, I hurdled the sidewalks as fast as a soaring squirrel, struggling to catch my breath. Dodging the lanky girls' twisted-face pursuit, my feet sprang toward St. Pancratius ("Pankracego" in Polish), on the corner of 40th and Sacramento. Though the Polish/Lithuanian church was located mere yards from our apartment, home seemed miles away. *Catholic churches were always open. If necessary, I could go in and pretend I was praying.* But instead of going inside the doors, I took cover in the shadows of the three cement archways framing the spotless corner church. Though my body was rattling like a storm window in the wind, I dared not suck in air. *I think I've lost them. Peeking from the shadows I prayed: Dear God, can I go home now?*

"You gettin' trashed?" someone asked me while I was just getting comfortable in the seventh grade at Davis School. "Getting trashed" was a Halloween custom which on Halloween Day, or Halloween Eve, most of the boys trashed and "smeared" the girls they liked with India ink. Coating girls' faces with squashed eggs and handfuls of assorted gunk, the boys used anything they could find to mush up inside several paper bags. They dubbed this practice, "getting trashed." Dipping my blonde head toward the ground as far as it would stretch, on Halloween afternoon I escaped as fast as I could from those boys, much the way I did the Lithuanians. My tennis-shoed feet sped home like supernatural lightning, my strides expanding unbelievably until I reached our front door. Often, gang members' black and green sweaters caused *"wedas"* like me to shudder, their baseball bats ready to beat whomever they pleased. Fights with knives, bats, and fists frequently broke out on Friday afternoons, racial tension hanging in the air between Mexican and Lithuanian, the Polish and Latino.

Hoping to straighten my long wavy hair with the new pink plastic hairbrush Mother had bought for me on Archer, I borrowed her *Aqua Net* hair spray to thoroughly coat my head. Hearing some commotion, Sam had wildly staggered through the front door. About a half hour before I left for school, Sam's bald glossy skull was littered with shards of protruding jagged glass and scattered knife nicks. My soul shivered as I peeked inside the bathroom.

"Uh, awh," moaned Sam, examining his head in the bathroom mirror.

"Hold still, Jerry," Mother scolded while her fingertips helped Sam pick out the jagged glass. "I'll never get into a fight with Puerto Ricans again; those punks carry knives. But I popped one in the head," Dad bragged. "Smacked that sucker in the noodle with my stick—all hollowed out and filled with lead. Left the silly dude lying on the tavern floor. They were all twisted; twisted sisters, they were."

"I sure hope they weren't any of *my* Latino friends' brothers, uncles, or fathers who got into that fight with Dad," I disclosed to Lee. "Yeah, I sure hope not." In order to break the monotony of Sam's antics, Mother took us to see the blockbuster movie, *Wait Until Dark,* with actress Audrey Hepburn. The Brighton Theatre had old-fashioned, red velvet curtains and a wide wooden stage once used for vaudeville acts. Trying to stay alive, I outran muggers and assorted drunks; I ignored guys' catcalls and dodged various gang members holed up in the poorly lit alleys strewn with cheap wine bottles, skimming all the ghostly corners of our neighborhood. When a killer was loose (having slaughtered seven student nurses near Chicago's Loop) everything in the city stopped. No one moved a muscle until the police captured the bleary-eyed madman, Richard Speck.

With my ears plastered to the exotic shrill refrains of, "The Green Tambourine" on my transistor radio (the one Sam bought each of us at Christmas), I was constantly trying to fit in with the rough bunch of kids in Brighton Park. One afternoon I nabbed a bottle of Sam's whiskey from the refrigerator; Sam was dead to the world while Mother shopped. But just as I started to slug down the bitter golden liquid, ready to put the glass against my pale lips, an invisible glass wall strangely surrounded me. Yes, it was actually a wall of glass I could actually touch and *feel*. The glass wall separated my entire body from the bottle. My mind and body were so stunned I rammed the bottle back into the refrigerator exactly where I found it. I would never attempt to take another drink of alcohol again—I got the point!

"I wish I could have friends over," I wished aloud out of sheer frustration. But I didn't want to embarrass Mother so I quickly dropped the issue. Daily, my mouth was hard as jawbreakers, and my teeth were tightly clenched. Terrified of having friends at the apartment because I never knew how Sam would be, his endless intimidation had become vicious. A few days later I scribbled in pencil on my dingy closet wall, "I wish Dad was dead. I wish *I* was dead." Quickly erasing the scrawl, my brain and heart still found it impossible to understand Sam and his bizarre antics. The only thing touching my heart even remotely when it came to Sam was what he did when passing any Catholic church, usually as he rode the CTA. Removing his hat, (whether formal or a simple cap), he looked at the particular church then gestured the sign of the cross. Many older women around the Southwest Side did the same while praying their rosaries—sparkling crystal beads, brilliant red beads, and dark, mostly black or dark brown beads for men. Since I had always been interested in spiritual things, Dad's practice spoke to my soul. And even though I despised my parents arguing about which was best, the Catholics or the Protestants, I saw some good things in each of them. But my Mexican friends made me laugh, calling me by the silly name, "Ya, Ya." I grew especially close to my classmate, Aurora, also known as Rory. Rory had a pretty mane of shiny black hair, and was one of nine siblings. The whole family lived in a second-floor apartment in Little Mexico.

"You like Mexican food?" Rory's mother eagerly questioned, her own silky dark hair flapping in the wind as she placed a spicy beef taco on my plate.

"Sure," I fibbed. With all my might I tried to digest the taco, smothered with salsa and scattered bits of *chiles*. Too shy to tell the truth, that was the very first time I had ever tasted Mexican food.

"You want water, *agua*? Water?"

Nodding, I guzzled it down hurriedly in an effort to cool my burning tongue.

"She's Swedish like us," Mother declared with a toothy grin. "Yes, Inga is a Swede. You wanna come with me tonight and help babysit her kids?" Mother asked with great pride. Always anxious to speak of her maternal grandmother, Hannah, my great-grandmother was a *Svenska Flicka* who came to America from Stockholm, Sweden. Settling first in Chicago, Hannah and her husband, Frank, eventually moved to Chicago Heights where Frank was a carpenter, building many of the frame houses in the suburban town. "Inga lives right near the church on Pershing Road," noted Mother. So Lee and I rode in Inga's car to her basement apartment, a welcome breather from another uncertain Saturday night with Sam. Inga was pretty and friendly as Mother, and she had an authentic Swedish accent. On Saturday night, *The Late, Late Show* was on Inga's console color television set. As time went on, every time we went to babysit Inga's two little girls, the same movie was on television—*The Inn of the Sixth Happiness*. The movie starred yet another Swede, the talented actress, Ingrid Bergman. The film was about a missionary in war-torn China, and I could never get its message out of my mind. Gladys Aylward, the missionary Miss Bergman played, would not allow anyone or anything stop her from going to China where she believed God had called her to minister, even though everyone told her the whole idea was impossible for a woman. Falling asleep on Inga's couch in the early morning hours, shortly before dawn we were awakened by, "cock-a-doodle-doos," penetrating the air.

"Here in the middle of the city, on the edge of Little Mexico there are roosters?" I questioned Mother in surprise, not knowing what to make of it. *Oh how I hated leaving this neighborhood I had grown to love.*

Shortly after moving to the Marquette Road house and the bombshell telephone call my parents received from Sam's sister Katrina, that amazing summer we all finally met. "There's no hot water in the whole house?" I questioned Mother with a stretched-out grimace, on our initial visit to meet Dad's mother, my Grandmother Louise.

"No, we've never had hot water in the house—tain't nothin,'" Sam quipped. His dancing eyes were scanning every nook and cranny of the sparsely furnished home, his boyhood home in Minnesota. Milling about room after room, it was if rough, tough Sam was a kid in a candy shop. Our trip to visit Sam's mother had left me in a dither. Riding ten hours to southern Minnesota from our Marquette Park house (part of which Sam helped drive even though he was without a proper driver's license) we carefully circled the serene streets around his boyhood home. Suddenly the six of us (Sam, Mother, Lee, Sam's driver, Joe from the Back of the Yards, his son, and me) settled our eyes on an elderly, grey-haired woman seated on the front porch swing. The mysterious house I had waited so very long to see was a green, two-story corner frame, not unlike our white frame home in Chicago. The air in that small town was so crystal clear I could barely believe that was the pretty city where my father, Sam, the hot dog man, grew up. With our hearts pounding all the way down to our toes, shivers overtook my whole body. Shaking like a leaf, my thoughts turned toward the woman, my only living grandparent and her husband, Albert, who died some months earlier. That was why Katrina, my Aunt Katrina, felt she could safely call her brother.

"Let's give them a moment," Joe kindly suggested as he drove up to the green frame. In the brilliant late afternoon light, Sam's brisk focus locked as solid steel onto the elderly woman, his mother. Trotting up the porch stairs as if still the teenager who had left home so many decades earlier, the old woman rose like the sun from her porch swing. Her mouth widening into a joyous smile, Louise's only son had finally come home. Hugging her tighter than I had ever seen anyone grab another person inside his arms, Sam didn't let go. Gazing around the rattletrap car filled with rough Back of the Yards' residents, hot tears dripped down all our cheeks. Even though those days I wasn't really talking very much at all to Dad, my heart was breaking into a thousand pieces. *What must it have been like to not see your own mother for nearly thirty years? Would that meeting change things?*

Kinking through my four years at Hubbard High School, I was learning, observing, and growing as I went along. I was *learning* about the world academically and carefully *observing* my mother's daily struggle with Sam. And I was *growing* continually in the things of the Lord, having found a small church near our house. Although Dad had happily reconciled with his mother, nothing else changed.

In time, we also met Aunt Katrina as well as her husband, our Uncle Brett, taking a trip with another friend from the Back of the Yards, south to St. Louis. In June of 1974, Lee and I had a double graduation. Lee graduated from Eberhart Elementary, and I from Hubbard High. But it was Mother's endless hardship, the constant onslaught of financial, mental, and emotional pain she endured with Sam, that was the real reason why I had not spoken to my father for nearly all of high school years. I barely spoke a word to him until the day I was married to Steve in 1976. That, in conjunction with a vile early morning incident when Sam toted home some of his "barflies," was just another on a long list of things that made me hopping mad.

"Come over here and sit on my lap," one of Sam's drinking buddies slurred his saucy words in my direction one morning before school. Spitting out his nasty enticement with soured whiskey breath, devilish flames flickered in the guy's blurry eyes. Sam's other pals were snickering like demons in the background of our small, tobacco-scented kitchen. A busy high school junior, my soul beat hard against their vulgar jabs. Grabbing my lunch from the refrigerator, I completely ignored the coarse man's comments. "Come on," the man goaded, patting his grimy thighs. Bending my head toward the guy's moldy face, I shot him the meanest glare I could rally. Grabbing my lunch bag, a tight knot gripped my throat. Feeling the mealy man's grin bristle the hairs on the back of my neck, my whole body raged. Even *Sam* was laughing! From that day forward I hid one of Mother's long butcher knives safely under my pillow, just in case.

"Think Lynn would ever use that knife on someone?" Lee quizzed Sam one day while they're working at the stand.

Coughing, then hurling spittle onto 47th's cracked sidewalk, "Sure she would, Lee," Sam replied matter-of-factly. "Yeah," Sam said peering into the misty distance. "Sure she would."

Then I began to wonder: *Would I?* And when Lee told Mother and me about an episode at the stand, it made me wonder even more.

"This friend of Sam's and his wife were fighting one night like cats and dogs," Lee recounted. Dad's friend had a broken beer bottle in his hand, holding the jagged edge up to his wife's neck. Sam pushed the two away from each other but the wife started yelling at Sam not to interfere. Boy, did Dad ever learn somethin' that night."

"What did Dad learn?" I asked.

"He learned to 'dummy up,' Lynn. Just be quiet."

I've also learned something else. And that is, if you think you've made it, *you might just be dead!*

Out of the Shadows
Part 2

Still, I wondered if God had given me the wrong father. Although many of my emotions and memories had been shut down while living with Sam, maybe I was supposed to eventually remember them.

"FIRE! Fire!" I had hollered to my family in mind-boggling fright, one morning before I was again off to school. On that crisp autumn day I was dressed in an embroidered peasant shirt and trendy bell-bottomed jeans. Upon reaching the first-floor landing of our house, acrid smoke greeted my nostrils. "Fire!" I screamed again to Mother, Lee, and ... and Sam. "There's a fire!" Frozen in my tracks, the panicked shriek awakened groggy-eyed Mother.

"Where? Where's the fire?" Mother woozily yelled.

At first, all I heard was hushed mumbling. But within seconds, Mother's form raced toward the kitchen. Her coily hair was flattened with tens of bobby pins and her slippered feet were skittish on the shag carpeting. Her eyes then completely ajar, Mother bolted like a firefighter straight through the gooey smoke.

"Oh the smoke!" she coughed. "So much smoke!" Pots and

pans started banging and clanking in the sink while the bed where Sam slept eerily creaked. My feet were still glued to the blue-green carpeting on the stair landing; I was scared to death to budge an inch. "Look at this blasted pot!" Mother scolded her snoring husband, Sam, stuck listlessly in bed following the last night's drinking binge. "You burned my poor pot to a crisp, you louse! That's what happened, Lynn," Mother yelled from the back of the house. Calling me into the kitchen, I viewed the charred remains firsthand. "Your father left hot dogs in that pot," she pointed to the sink in frustration and disgust. "And then he died to the world. Burned my poor pot to nothin'."

"Okay," I muttered, telling Mother a rickety good-bye. Walking to my friend's house a few blocks away, ever so slowly my pulsing heart evened out. I prayed no one noticed my knees and hands still shaking, thanks be to Sam. His persistent alcoholism had grown very annoying because he loved and worshipped beer, whiskey, and any sort of alcohol more than his own family—Mother, Lee, and me. No, he didn't even care if we all burned to death. Nonetheless, I was grateful because it could have been so much worse. Trotting quickly past the stately brick bungalows and the large old frame houses of our neighborhood, though my friend was chattering away about this and that, the morning's scene (not only the fire but of Sam lying naked while a picture of a smiling, haloed Mother Mary with last year's palm branches peered down at him) seared fresh as Nabisco's baking bread within my soul. How on earth would I ever get rid of a scene like *that*?

Ever since I could remember, a band of fear had encircled my life with my Sam. His roaring voice, his coarse scowl, and his bear-strong body all overtly relayed that giant could kill if he got heated enough. Closing my eyes, resentment snagged my inner parts. Images of a certain night, my most terrifying night in the Back of the Yards snatched my assorted thoughts. Dad and Mother had been harshly fighting; their screams and curse-filled jabs had escalated to the highest levels ever inside our apartment on 51st Street.

"*You* are a drunk, Jerry," Mother shrieked, trying to shake Sam from his sickening addiction, confronting him head-on.

"Hey! Hey," Sam screamed to Mother in return, his bleary eyes dark with venom. Flooded to the gills with whiskey and beer, a cold chill abruptly bathed the apartment. In the suddenness of a bitter north wind, Sam suddenly removed his shiny silver gun from his crumpled bag. Pointing the weapon straight at Mother, I was standing some feet behind her, at the threshold of my bedroom door. Dressed in a thin, short nightgown, my eyes stung with unbearable dread. In the shadowy background, my two bony knees knocked together uncontrollably. Stepping into the smoky light, my thumping heart steadily prayed: *No God, no. Please don't take Mother.*

"Put that away, Jerry," Mother meekly whispered. So just as fast as it all began, the horror was over. Once again Sam was snickering, muttering vile curses next to the greasy kitchen stove. Breathing a huge sigh of relief, I was completely sure my father was capable of killing because Sam often boasted of times when, "this chump," or "that sucker," attempted to move his hand near the wagon's coveted moneybox.

"If you even *try* to steal that money I'll shot you right between the eyeballs," Sam bragged, recalling how he would "put the fear of God" into any potential thief.

"Eh, you wouldn't do that, Sammy, would you?" the guy tested Sam with a blubbery snicker.

Pulling out his silver revolver, Sam expertly twirled the gun barrel. Without hesitation, the shiny gun was pointed straight in the direction of the guy's head.

"That stupid punk took off in a flash," Sam blew his own horn in truck-size pride. "Yeah. I'd shoot that sucker and keep on pedaling hot dogs. Fool chump. No difference. No matter."

The moment that bear of a man appeared in the doorway, the second his eyes unhinged, and the minute Sam's soul immersed any space, the juices inside my stomach dived then plummeted like a falling rock. Gurgling like steaming sewage, fear, though I despised it, habitually ruled my life. The fear of stray dogs caused me to shudder. The fear of bad storms ripped at my soul. And often I *feared* men. I was terrified to speak since Sam would no doubt condemn my thoughts. Much more at ease by simply remaining silent, worry and panic nearly overwhelmed me. But even worse, after moving into our Marquette Park house, from time to time Dad stumbled upstairs into my bedroom. In the early morning hours while I was fast asleep, Sam's burning alcoholic breath threatened my whole existence, exhaling fire like a dragon. Snuggling up to my fourteen-year-old cheek as I laid mute and motionless in my twin bed, Sam planted a sloppy kiss on my forehead while I pretended to be asleep.

Oh God, please don't let him … My night-gowned body as taut as a belt, after mumbling a few words Sam staggered away into the pre-dawn din. Exhaling a lengthy mouthful of air, I gratefully listened as Sam's heavy footsteps quaked like stone boulders down the carpeted staircase: *The knife was still under my pillow.*

"I can't say a single word to him because all Dad wants to do is argue," I repeatedly complained to Mother. She, more than anyone, was painfully aware how impossible it was to deal with Sam. "So what's the use of saying anything to him at all? It's pointless," I sharply reasoned. Agreeing with my feelings, I realized our dear Mother had stuck by Sam through thick and thin. Yes, Mother had intimately known alcoholism, neglect, betrayal, verbal abuse, intimidation, and recurring financial hardship.

"I can't take it anymore," Mother sobbed one day with fat long tears running down her sweet face. Suddenly, I saw Mother praying, praying for a miracle the three of us might make it yet another day. Keeping the family together only because of Lee and

I, Mother's sorrow was relentless. And although Lee was held hostage within Sam's powerful grip, I was not. After marrying at age nineteen, my witty husband, Steve, taught me how to laugh and joke, demonstrating firsthand how to enjoy life. I finally had peace with God and tranquility at home; it was a new and refreshing existence as I had finally stepped out of the shadows.

Prior to our 1976 spring wedding, Steve lovingly urged, "You need to reconcile with your dad before we get married, Lynn. You need to forgive. It's better for our marriage if you did." Pondering Steve's words, my mind was in turmoil. *How could I ever forgive Sam for all that he had done?* Then, like a sunshiny ray peeking through molten thunderclouds, my heart traveled to five years earlier, to our first visit to Minnesota. I squinted and remembered the first day we met Dad's mother, my Grandmother Louise, the summer we discovered Sam's name was really Ralph. Not Sam, not Gus, but *Ralph*! Not Polachek but Polaieck. Keeping Dad's bedroom perfectly in tact since the day he had unexpectedly left home at age fourteen, Louise had saved his scrapbook, many of his school pictures from Divine Rosary School, his baseball glove, and even the canvas bag from his paper route, all sitting innate in Dad's second-floor bedroom. When the tough-as-nails hot dog man took his first look inside his old room, tears leaked down his permanently sunburned face. Like one of those prickly turtles rising up for air in Marquette Park's lagoon, it was on that day I too rose up for air. Suddenly, real understanding surfaced from deep within my soul. Compassionate understanding of Sam/ Ralph, was set in motion.

Imagining life in the cold formal house of my grandparents, what would *I* have done if *I* had been hurled into the mean streets of this world, thrown into a vicious den of wolves, as was Dad? I was abruptly juxtaposed with my own father, Sam, the same man who had spent hundreds, probably thousands of dollars on drink when our family had had so many needs. Sam, the same man greatly celebrated by hundreds in the Back of the Yards. Suddenly I viewed my father with very different eyes. But, *could I truly forgive him?*

And I also quietly worried about Lee since Lee was strictly under Sam's control, gripped inside his intimidating spell. Constructing a cardboard room in our damp basement, Lee installed a backlight in his crazy private room, decorating it with tin foil and neon pictures. Spending good times there with his friend, Larry, and other kids from the neighborhood, he stayed true to our parents' wishes. Refraining from all kinds of pretty girls he would have desperately loved to date, one day when Lee was selling hot dogs, the distinct smell of diesel fuel increased steadily around the wagon. A huge, 300-pound man gruffly hollered toward Lee.

"Hey, hey; let's go, bud," the huge man snapped. "Where's my four Polish and two tamales?"

Shocked to the core, "Man, I'm sorry," apologized Lee, fixing the man's order in one Chicago minute flat.

"I never saw anyone make food so fast," the big guy's eyes locked onto Lee's swift-working hands. "And here I thought it was going to be quite a long deal, making up my big order."

"I guess I was day dreaming for a minute," Lee admitted.

"Yeah, and you're probably tipsy from those stinkin' diesel fumes," Lee's customer noted, eagerly chomping his portion of the order. "That smell would kill anyone."

After Lee relays *that* story, it briskly led to another one. One night when Sam and Lee were busily working the stand, just as they thought they were ready to pack up and call it a night, another mob of customers showed up wanting to place an order. Turning up their Coleman lantern full blast, father and son took special care of every customer, always giving their clients the best food possible. Holding a tire-size grin Sam proudly bragged, "I'll *never* serve any food I wouldn't eat myself. Yeah!" Lee firmly believed the same. Finally calling it a night, "Hey, Lee," Sam briskly called. "Take those extra onions over there and sell 'em to the lady running the joint about four blocks down. Beat it, kid," ordered Sam, no questions asked.

Totally exhausted, Lee had little to drink that night but water. Nearing 2:30 a.m., Lee had been awake since six that morning. So, selling onions to some character down the line was about the last thing any sane person would ever want to do. Nonetheless, walking inside the bar about four blocks away from the stand, the owner lady beamed at the sight of sweet Lee.

"Hiya, Samson. What's ya got there to peddle?"

"Look at these beauties," Lee paraded the golden onions before the lady's clever eyes. His own eyelids were sagging as his dusty feet trudged like weighty bricks across the wood-slated floor. "See, I got Spanish onions."

"How much ya need?" the owner lady asked.

"Two bucks."

No holes barred, the tavern lady handed Lee two crisp one-dollar bills. Both of them were pleased as punch with their early morning transaction. The interesting thing about that particular tavern was the owner lady always had a fan blowing in the opposite direction of her customers. The whizzing fan was on her side of the bar at all times. Whenever her half-soused patrons slapped their money on top of the bar, the fan sucked their money right underneath it. The lady's feet were always dancing, kicking the money as close to the underbelly of the bar as she could. Actually, she was a very nice person, and her bar sure made a ton of cash.

Returning to Sam's garage, "I peddled all the Spanish onions, Dad," Lee speedily reported.

"Good deal, kid," Sam replied with a crooked smile. Placing a spare board securely between the garage door amidst numerous steel padlocks, the two finally traipsed home to grab a couple hours of sleep before the sun rose over Lake Michigan, signaling another new day. Much like the Archer Avenue Express, Lee's life was non-stop—no complaining, no monkey business, no pifflin' around. Selling scores of hot dogs and tamales every night in front of the large two-story, corner frame apartment building on 47th Street, on occasion the cops made drug busts right in front of Sam's stand. Young girls pinched, punched, and scratched each other's skin like lionesses, pulling each other's hair, and swearing up a storm. Across the alley, the guys battled with their fists. Taking a drag on his cigar, Sam peered at the weedy ground and exhaled.

"Excuse me, Miss," Sam addressed the brawling females. "I don't want to step on your hair, but I just need an inch to get in the cooler for some pop. You're good," shuffled Sam across the sidewalk, the syrupy scent of beer mingling with the ever-present traffic exhaust, cigarette smoke, cigar vapors, and wafting hot dog steam. Swigging sweet wine and slurping from clear whiskey bottles bought at Babby's, folks trickled coins into Sam's palms as he handed them their "dogs," his ears plastered to the classical strains of the Chicago Symphony Orchestra. The compositions beamed lazily into the abrasive air from a two-dollar, AM transistor Sam bought years ago on Maxwell Street. Located on 16th and Halsted in the heart of Chicago's West Side, the Maxwell Street market offered outdoor stalls selling wares of produce, a mix of clothes, a conglomeration of tools, and everything from A to Z with few questions asked. Named after Dr. Philip Maxwell, the noisy street was originally a simple plank road. "Now *that* is real music," Sam crowed, nodding his gleaming head to the crowd.

"Running a business on 47th Street was certainly no picnic," Lee sourly groaned. "One night a woman called for a cab and the wide yellow car just sat on the street for an entire hour," Lee pointed out.

"Don't worry," the woman told the driver. "Just keep the meter running," she ordered. "Idling her time away in Babby's, she drank like a fish while her taxi tab went sky high. Every so often," Lee continued, "The Good Humor Man stopped his truck in the middle of busy 47th, shooting the breeze with King Sammy as if those two guys owned the whole blasted block. Scores of black folks hopped off the dull, green and white city buses, gettin' in line to buy Sam's red hots. By the time they got back on the bus going east, half their dogs were chomped to the nub."

Cocking one brow, Lee flexed his right arm. "And then there was Little Jackie," Lee resumed. "Little Jackie had skin as chocolate as Sam's creamy Fudgecicles, and he also loved Maxwell Street. The five-foot-two fellow, (his mouth void of teeth save two or three) was a resident of the CHA—Chicago Housing Authority, known as "the projects." Sashaying off the 47th Street bus, Little Jackie lugged all sorts of things to Sam's stand, odds and ends he hoped to sell.

"Hiya, Sammy," Little Jackie hailed, a full-size smile shot straight toward Sam. Tucked inside his ankle-length coat, Little Jackie had stashed away various sizes of wristwatches, pocketknives, key chains, wallets, and a wide variety of pens. After several minutes of bartering with the King of 47th Street, Little Jackie took his profits directly into Babby's. Getting thoroughly trashed, he jived and boogied with any woman available. After a few hours in Babby's, a taxicab stopped in the middle of 47th Street, right in front of the tavern. Little Jackie's better half soberly lumbered out of a bulky, yellow cab.

"Whatcha doin' in there, Jackie?" Little Jackie's brawny-armed wife hollered toward Babby's. Her question thundered through the air even before her chunky form veered across the cracked path of city sidewalk. Without batting a single eyelash, Little Jackie's wife ordered the cab driver, "Wait there, I be right back." With a wobble that wouldn't quit, roaring a few choice curse words, the woman grabbed Little Jackie by the collar. "I say, what's ya doin' in here Jackie? You comin' home right now. Letz go."

Scooting Little Jackie's five-foot-two body all the way back into the waiting cab, "I guess Little Jackie's had his fun for the night.

That's the end of that," Sam quipped to Lee, the two chuckling like hens at the hilarious fuss.

"I hate that stupid car!" a regular customer of Sam's shrieked at the top of his lungs one night that summer. Spewing a block-long string of profanity, the guy had staggered wildly out of Babby's. Parked near the bus stop, he plopped down in the driver's side of his car. Starting the engine, the guy floored the pedal to the ground until the car essentially blew her top. KABOOM! Grabbing his keys, he stumbled into the street, ripping the car key off his key ring. Flinging the key like a baseball straight at the car's door, he strolled casually back across Seeley, heading toward Babby's. Aiming a quick wink at Sam and Lee, the guy yelled toward the stand,

"Hey guys, you want something to drink? Sox are winnin' 5 to 2, bottom of the 7th," he happily reported. Forgetting all about his blown-up engine just a few feet away, it was time to get another drink.

"Say Marco, how ya doin'? Ya wanna go to Bridgeport? Let's go to Ronny's in Bridgeport," Sam directed a few weeks later to his good friend, Marco, on a slow afternoon at the stand. "The kid will take care of the wagon." Yanking up his pants at the waistline, Sam copped a ride with Marco in order to go to Ronny's since the hot dog man had amassed a pocketful of tickets. Those parking tickets (the Back of the Yards' folks keenly recognized), when given to Sam, would eventually be fixed. Sam, you see, liked to take very good care of his friends.

One evening in the late summer of 1976, Mother mentioned how Lee and Sam had smartly remade new boxes for hot dogs in their two Cushman wagons. After a period of thunderstorms, Sam gave Lee another gripping command. And when Sam gave a command, you had no other option but to obey. "Get in the wagon, kid," Sam demanded. Riding next to the jittery propane tank, the whole shebang bounced up and down like a beach ball on a Lake Michigan wave. Settling inside the greasy garage, that night Lee and Sam would not be going home. Wrapping himself in some old coats and rags to stave off the cold, Lee fell asleep in Sam's garage, sleeping straight up in the parked Cushman, next to the remade box. The whole thing reminded Lee of all the times when he was real young when Sam flopped down on the upholstered couch and said, "Lee, get in your hole." Dutifully, Lee positioned his body in back of Sam's sweaty back, where the two stuck were together like pigs in a pen.

"Wake up, Gus," Sam called the next morning to Lee. "We're taking the bus to the West Side because it is raining like mad. We sure as Mother Mary can't sell today. We're goin' to Maxwell Street." Clutching his trademark-crumpled bag, no one but God knew what exactly was inside Sam's mysterious paper sack because it varied from day to day. Typically, the crumpled brown bag carried all kinds of stuff to sell. It didn't matter if the paper was wet and crinkly as long as it didn't get a hole. When the paper finally did give way, Sam got a new paper grocery bag and folded it up to carry around. One object we *always* knew was inside the crumbled bag was Sam's trusty .38 Huscavarna, oiled up and ready to pop if necessary. On one chilly night, Sam was coming home late. Walking down our alley on Marquette Road, some kid crept out of the shadows. The crazy kid started yelling wildly toward Sam, the kid's lips quivering in the soggy city air.

"Hey old man, give me all your money," the kid screamed. At that noise, Sam turned around on his heels like a dime.

Pulling out his oiled up handgun from his crumbled paper sack, "Okay," Sam replied. "I can't give you any money, but would you like a piece of *this* baby?" Sam asked, sporting his familiar smirk. Brandishing his shiny .38, he aimed the gun straight toward the kid's shocked jaws. In Chicago, you see, lots of people carried guns.

Used solely for protection, those weapons were crucial. Darting off like greased lightning, Sam was never bothered in our dark, deserted alley again.

On yet another summer night, Sam and Lee were peddling hot dogs as usual at the stand. When Sam peered into Lee's beat-out eyes, he felt sorry for my little brother for once in his frenzied life. Knowing the poor kid was dead worn-out, "Your great-grandfather was a king, Lee Boy; *you* are a blue blood," Sam disclosed the bizarre revelation to Lee. Lee's shoulders were drooped, and he had absolutely no idea what Sam was talking about. Not until years later, when it was discovered our great grandfather was of the Bavarian monarchy did Lee and I understand Sam's comment. "You peasants! You peasants use the back door! I'm a king!" Sam habitually barked. All along, Sam knew the truth, but for some reason, he never let on.

But believe it or not, many Chicago politicians had fathers who drank with Sam. Yep, all kinds of city councilmen, precinct captains, and ward bosses—their parents or grandparents had once eaten at Sam's hot dog stand, or dined in Sam's Snack Shop. Some of them knew Sam from somewhere in the Loop, and others knew him from the bowling alleys and restaurants he had worked throughout the city. Magnetic Sam even drank with famous Cubs' catcher Gabby Hartnett, the two getting along fabulously on the city's North Side, Sam's favorite part of the Windy City. Catching many years for the great pitcher, Dizzy Dean, Gabby's fingers were painfully bent, he had gently confided to Sam. Like an ancient king who *was* his nation, it was as if Sam *was* The Back of the Yards, one in the same.

Almost nightly, Sam and Lee were on 47th and Kedzie at three a.m., waiting for the bus to go home. The CTA, of course, ran much slower at that time of the morning. One early morning, Sam blurted out his frustration.

"Kid, I'm tired of this noise; I'm gonna hail a cab." Naturally,

Lee thought Sam meant a taxicab. With incredulous eyes, Lee watched as a blue-and-white cop car pulled up to the near empty street. Striding like a warhorse into the busy road, Sam stopped the cop car as if hailing a cab.

"Where to, Sammy?" the cop inquired.

"West Marquette Road," Sam requested. Handing the cop anywhere from two to five dollars, the cop summoned his radio, then informed Dad,

"Sam, there will be a car ready for you soon."

"How good that warm cop car felt with those nice soft cushions, the new car smell, that great smooth ride," Lee fondly recalled the nice ride home. But the following night, father and son were back riding on the old rocky bus, the poor man's limousine.

"She was a wonderful woman," Louise's long-time caretaker, Mrs. Blaire Sands conveyed to Sam by telephone a few days before his birthday. Unexpectedly, Sam's mother, our only grandmother, was found dead on November 2, 1976. Her husband, Albert, had passed away five years earlier in July of 1971. Speaking in broken English, Louise's spirit was always sweet. Following Louise's death, one afternoon in 1977 Lee was finishing his stops on Chicago's rain-slicked roads. Upon returning to the garage on 47th Street, Lee saw our skinny Aunt Katrina; she was standing at Sam's hot dog stand. By Thanksgiving, Lee, Dad, and Mother were preparing to move from Chicago to a town just outside East St. Louis, Illinois, right next door to Katrina. Scattered memories flooded my mind as my family of origin planned to move. It seemed like yesterday Lee and I were at our local dentist, Dr. Steinberg's office on the second floor of a huge brick building near the corner of 63rd and Kedzie.

"That will be five dollars for Lee's three cavities," Dr. Steinberg told Mother. Thumbing through her change purse, Mother metered out four one-dollar bills and some change, always trying to make due. How I would miss Lee and Mother. Oh the hardship, as well as the fun, the three of us had.

"It's like we've moved from the fire into the frying pan, Lynn," Lee excitedly exclaimed from their new house in southern Illinois. "The temperature here reaches 107 degrees in the shade," Lee quipped. But Mother had confessed how she had been praying they might move from the many bad influences on Lee's life.

I too was happy Lee would be better off. Maybe *he had* finally made it—or had he? How could he, *living with a man like Sam?*

CHAPTER 22

Samson's Day

Although Sam, Lee, and Mother had sold their Marquette Park house and moved to southern Illinois, the hot dog man and his son returned to Chicago when the new selling season started again in spring. Though known to his family as Ralph, to Chicago, Dad was forever known as Sam—Sam, the hot dog man—Big Sammy of 47th Street, King of 47th Street. As bad as my relationship once was with Dad, my own trial didn't seem to compare to what Lee experienced on a daily basis, particularly during the heavy selling season. Waking up at 6 a.m., Lee and Sam washed and ate their usual gargantuan breakfast of anything they could lay their thick hands upon.

"Those two eat like thrashers," Mother frequently complained with an upraised brow. "I know because I used to help Gram and Mother make breakfast for the field thrashers out in the country."

Constantly passing a dilapidated hotel on the corner of Kedzie and 47th Street, "Goin' Strong 'til Dawn," was the hotel's famous motto. Fitted with seedy, red garish doors, its windows were shabby and irregular. Equally battered women were dressed in rib-hugging mini-skirts as decades of ghosts wafted around the medieval-like ruins.

Arriving in the Back of the Yards by eight, Sam unlocked the myriad of padlocks securing his relish-scented garage. As Sam drove his scooter to buy hot dogs, Polish, and tamales at the factory near 47th and Washtenaw, Lee purchased a 50-pound block of ice at the icehouse. Returning to the garage to chop onions, clean the wagon, and empty the steam box of grease, Lee performed general maintenance on the scooter. When Sam returned from his shopping trip, Lee dutifully rinsed his scooter, loading both vehicles with sodas and other supplies. Leaving for the factories at 9:15, (since after all, it took 45 minutes to travel five miles fully gassed up), the scooters moved a whopping 23 mph—top speed.

"Ready, letz go," Sam playfully quipped to Lee, waving him off like a racecar driver, his chunky brown cigar lit and fuming.

"You had to steer the wagon real carefully through the traffic maze because big semis would cut you off," Lee detailed the normal scenario. "Cars honked like crazy and the rough South Siders loved to curse and swear. 'Get that miserable thing off the road,' they yelled as if I was nothin' but chump change," Lee said with a swallow.

By 10 a.m., Lee had made his first stop at Sears Distribution. The Sears' workers were allowed only a fifteen-minute break so Lee hustled like a Hawthorne racehorse, getting every order to perfection. Making his next stop at the jar factory, he worked the next factory and the next building, and then the next sprawling office complex. By 11:30, Lee was really sailing, selling hot dogs, Polish sausages, tamales, and soda to the mammoth lunch crowd, swollen into the hundreds. When high noon overtook the city, the kid had to be in three places at once. He had no choice because when the lunch bell sounded, it was off to the races—finish one factory, move to the next at 12:07, and work the third at 12:15. Howling their orders in Lee's once genteel face, my little brother learned to joke and enjoy it, shooting the breeze with this guy and that, exactly as Sam had taught him. He carefully treated every customer like a king. The next stop was at 12:30; the last was at one. From 10 a.m. until 1—thirteen factory stops in all, plus a few stragglers on the side.

"When all the factory stops were finished, I headed back to 47th and Seeley," Lee recounted. Grabbing a hot, juicy beef sandwich and gurgling down big pitchers of cool water at a local eatery, Lee met up with Sam at the garage. Chopping mounds of Spanish onions, Lee used a genuine stockyard knife, cutting and slicing like a pro. After cleaning the wagons, they settled on their corner around 6 p.m., just in time for the dinner crowd. From seven o'clock all the way until Babby's Tavern closed at two a.m., people slobbered on poor Lee. Kissing him on the cheeks, the same drunks wanted to start arguments with sweet Samson depending on their alcohol intake.

A Jewish guy named, "Brains," visited the hot dog wagon on a hot night that summer, and then he headed straight into Babby's. Brains always sported a toothpick inside his mouth. Around eleven that night, Brains took a bet for a sawbuck. He then told the whole crowd in Babby's,

"If someone can get rid of this toothpick from my mouth," Brains boasted pointing to the spiky toothpick, "I'll give you this sawbuck."

Lee was relaxing with a few beers, having worked like a dog all day and night. Bumping hard into one of Sam's best friends named Large Leo, the toothpick tumbled out of Brain's mouth in two seconds flat. "Here ya go, pal," Brains said, slappin' ten dollars on the bar. Rushing to his house east of Ashland Avenue, Large Leo forgot to grab the sawbuck. After fifteen minutes, there came Leo.

"Hey," hollered Large Leo. "I was just gettin' into bed and I remembered my ten bucks. Grabbing the sawbuck, Leo was dressed in his bathrobe and house slippers. "Guess I'll have a few shots," Large Leo grinned, "long as I'm here."

"There went Leo's sawbuck," Sam chortled along with Lee, the two laughing like hyenas at the colorful characters of the Back of the Yards.

"Remember the Gypsy family living on 47th Street?" I questioned Lee.

"Yeah sure," Lee nodded his head with a half smile.

We had watched the mysterious Gypsies who lived the Back of the Yards with curiosity, particularly when we lived on 51st Street. About a half block from Sam's stand lived a whole clan of Gypsies. Lugging a full-length sofa in front of their storefront, the Gypsy parents of a four-year-old girl constantly sent their little daughter into Babby's to buy a measly ten-cent bag of chips. Cute as a button, the silky-haired little girl hopped up onto a bar stool as she'd been instructed. The kid blabbered as fast as the dickens so she could nab the customers' money with her roving, nimble fingers. Skipping out of the tavern, the girl headed home with the cold hard cash. Hiding inside their house, the Gypsies then laid low, disappearing completely from their sidewalk sofa. Returning about midnight, they bought beer and hot dogs with the little girl's profits. The Gypsy clan did that about three times a week, trying not to get people too annoyed at their cheap ploy.

"How come you Gypsies steal?" Sam asked the old Gypsy lady straight out. The bottom hem of her wrinkled cotton skirt was twisted around her stocky ankles, similar to that of a smooth winding snake.

"Dat is vat God put us on this earth fer, to steal," the old Gypsy woman coolly stated to Sam, holding a half-baked smirk. "And if you tell a soul 'bout it, I will put da evil eye on you."

The Gypsy woman, you see, had a chain around her neck bearing a medallion with an eyeball smack in the center of it. The springing eyeball followed you whenever the Gypsy woman turned or moved. Squeezing her arms snug around Sam's waist one summer night, he instantly wiggled away from the woman's creepy death grip.

"She's a sharp one," Sam observed. Lodging his hands securely inside his pockets, Sam safeguarded his billfold whenever Gypsy woman was on the scene. He sure wasn't fallin' for that trick.

"Lock up, kid," Sam directed Lee, the two heaving their scooters inside the greasy garage after another long night of selling. Three old padlocks firmly secured the back door; four locks were placed tightly on the overhead. Burglaries were commonplace all over the neighborhood but nothing, and no one, ever bothered Sam's garage.

"The city's got a new law, Sammy," a county health inspector advised Sam some days later. "They're crackin' down on hot dog vendors ya know," the cheery-eyed inspector warned.

"Nize day," Sam retorted with a thin smile.

"Listen Sam, you gotta have running water on all food-operating vehicles and food stands. That's the new law."

"I got plenty of water, see," Sam huffed. With cigar smoke encircling the heath inspector in miniature clouds, Sam always carried a full gallon pickle jar stowed conveniently inside the wagon. The jar was filled to the gills with water. Bringing the jug atop the wagon, Sam opened the lid. With one hand he held the jug by the lip, pouring out the water with his other hand. "See, now *that* is running water." Inhaling a deep drag on his El Producto cigar, Sam shook hands with the health inspector. A crisp twenty-dollar bill was snuggled between their two clasped hands. Grinning as wide as Michigan Avenue, "How's the family?" Sam then quipped, after several minutes of shooting the breeze.

"Fine. They're all fine. Good deal," the health inspector waved. "See you in six months, Sammy."

Gazing over at Lee, "You see, kid," Sam exhaled. "Now *that's* business. Business in Chicago."

For a time, Lee was simply burned out. Sam's son had witnessed things most people throughout their entire lives would never believe could happen in the United States, or in fact, the whole world. Squinting against the murky smog, Sam realized Lee was young and sensitive to the raw harshness of inner city street life, a ruthlessness Lee couldn't begin to understand.

"Cheer up, Lee Boy," Sam burst in an unusually sparkly tone. "Better days are comin.' And you'll be rewarded in heaven," Sam added. In due course, Lee understood why Sam had treated him so roughly, showing him plenty of hardness so Lee could eventually learn how to experience the difficult things of life.

"Do you know when I was two years old living in Minnesota I spilled over an entire ten-pound flour crock?" Sam asked Lee one night during a slight lull in the action. Lee's ears perked up since Sam rarely talked of his childhood. Sam then continued. "Yeah, all that flour was scattered over the floor. Your grandmother spanked me and then I cried," Sam said, recalling the story with a teeny glint in his eyes. Leaning over the wagon's edge, Sam ended with a warning. "Son, if you don't listen, you'll have to suffer. That's what my mother taught me and she was right on the money." And Lee sure listened to Sam with wide-opened ears . . .

At the end of the hot dog season in October of 1977, Lee, Larry, and their friend, Doug from Marquette Park went for a ride in Lee's 1969 Ford LTD, the car Aunt Katrina bought so Lee and Sam could get around. Driving around the upscale Beverly neighborhood near the southern suburb where our Aunt Adelyn and her family once lived, the boys steered through curvy Longwood Drive and 111th Street. Whenever Larry and Lee got together, they constantly laughed their tails off, joking about everything and anything. It was God's Holy Spirit who joined Larry and Lee in the first place, since years later Larry and Lee still stayed in touch. Of course, God was Lee's number one Friend; then came Lee's wife, Sherrie, then me, his big sister. But Larry was that *one friend* Sam talked about years earlier. Though their lives would be very different, they were also very similar. Lee never wanted anything from Larry except his friendship and love. In turn, Larry never asked Lee for anything but the same. But those good old days were about to end because it would be back to selling hot dogs and tamales, soon enough.

Renting a flophouse above a tavern near 47th and Damen, one hazy summer night, Lee invited Larry and Doug to stay with he and Sam in their rented room. Although they had a blast, when Larry woke up, he rubbed his eyes and moaned.

"Oh dear Lord, Lee. How can you possibly stand living in such a filthy place as this? This place is worse than living in a doghouse. I've got to get out of here and go home and take a shower," Larry groaned.

Little did Larry realize, however, to Lee, a place like that was akin to the Taj Mahal. On countless days Lee had fallen asleep in Sam's freezing garage, wrapped in some stinking rags. Sometimes he'd be nestled on the cold cement garage floor, or even in some toilet at a neighborhood gas station. But just like Sam, Lee had learned to adapt *whenever*, and *wherever*, he must. That was the way it always was for Lee, Mother, and me, learning to adapt to Sam's unpredictable moods and his endless mind-games of control.

"Tech," Sam often blurted out. "I use Tech on people."

"Tech?" Lee curiously questioned.

"Yeah; playin' with their minds. I like playing with people's minds," Sam grinned.

In 1970's Chicago, there was a huge deal going on the CTA in order to draw more Sunday business. On Sundays, riders could get what was called a "Super Transfer." For a mere seventy cents you could ride the bus all day long. In the winter, Sam took Lee all over the city on the Sunday "Super Transfer." Whenever Sam met someone he knew, he instantly started talking their "lingo," speaking the exact dialect to any person—black, white, rich, poor,

Irish, German, Jewish, Italian, Democrat or Republican. Sam, somehow, knew any kind of culture, any kind of demeanor, any type of individual, and any nationality.

"It was an amazing thing to watch," observed Lee, steeped in deep thought. "If you hadn't seen it with your own eyes you might have never believed it. Sam knew a little German, a little Polish, a little Hebrew, some Italiano, and a little chatter from the hood, chewin' the fat in almost any language spoken in Chicago," Lee considered, pondering Sam's game.

"Hey Sammy," a lanky black man from the South Side housing projects happily approached the stand. "I'm goin' up to the "Green" (Cabrini Green) fer a party, Sammy. Need 'bout half dozen dogs. Yeah, yer my man."

"Yeah. Here ya go, man," Sam rapped back. "You gonna have fun at the Greeeeen."

And though I was happily married and free from Sam, I could not forget how often he would simply disappear. Frequently gone for two or three days at a crack, (cutting out particularly on long holiday weekends), though it gave us all a break from his growling alcoholism, inwardly I often reasoned: *Did Dad have another family? When Dad was all dressed up, smelling of cologne and smacking his Wrigley's gum with the green wrapping, he must have had a place to stay. Didn't Mother know what was going on?*

When Sam would finally return home on late Sunday night or early Monday morning after two or three days being away, Mother's lips would curl as she gave him the business.

"Why don't you stay outta the gutter, you louse? You're playin' like a kid all the time," Mother yelled as loudly as possible. "Are you ever gonna grow up?"

"Play, play, play," Sam mocked. "Grow up, grow up," he echoed, totally ignoring the cruel problem at hand.

But the knotted noose Sam had held over my life limped away when I married Steve. That noose was booted even further into the past when Dad and the family moved to downstate Illinois. Despite the fact I had suffered through deep times of torment, an ending had finally arrived. Endings, however, were merely "Grand Openings" to a new beginning.

When the pressure of Sam's chaotic life suddenly vanished after decades of confusing pain, in due course it was my key challenge to understand their eternal purpose—*piece by tiny piece.*

PART FOUR

Top Shape

LEE

CHAPTER 23

Ain't Good No More

"I miss Lynn," I mentioned to Mother while we were getting settled in our new home.

"Me too," agreed Mom.

Leaving Lynn and Steve behind in Chicago, Dad, Mother, and I had made a new start in southern Illinois in 1977. But everything had been different in our house since Lynn had married Steve. The move downstate was surely my very own, "Grand Opening." Born in Chicago's Sacred Cross Hospital, I had never lived in any other place so I was pretty keyed up about moving. On the way to our new house, (a block house my Uncle Brett was fixing up), my stomach was poisoned by a spoiled hamburger I had eaten in Illinois' capital city, Springfield.

"I hope that wasn't a bad sign of things to come," I gloomily remarked. Settling in the house next door to my aunt and uncle, Aunt Katrina could not have been any nicer. Reedy and jittery, often staring into the distance as if stuck in another land, Dad's big sister had a heart of gold. Being such a caring person, she had bought my 1969 Ford LTD. With some money I had saved from selling with Dad, I bought the lot next door. Purchasing a mobile home to put on it, I rented out the mobile for income. At age eighteen, I then bought my first house, hoping to rent that structure too.

Secretly, we all had hoped Sam would somehow be transformed since living next door to his long-lost sister. But I personally knew Sam, Chicago's hot dog man, better than anyone else in the world, including his own wife. My gut feeling was Sam was as tough as iron—nothing and no one would *ever* change him. Not even his sister. Nonetheless, I kept going, buying another mobile home, and renting that one too. I also purchased several old cars, restoring them to ultimately sell. Buying and selling, selling and buying. How proud Sam was of all my labors, and how happy I was too, living the good life in our new environment. They say you can't buy love, and that was true enough. But you *sure could* work real hard. Yes, you could work hard enough to make someone proud of you, especially when it was your own father. On the down side, the fact was Mother and Dad were not getting along at all. If truth be told, my parents were growing wider apart than the Mississippi River.

"Her name is Sherrie," Mother informed Lynn by telephone. On June 8, 1982, I met a beautiful girl named Sherrie Marie. A cute blonde and great cook, Sherrie was sandwiched between an older and younger sister. A native of nearby Belleville, Sherrie's family had lived in the area for several generations. For the first time in my entire life, another person, that sweet young girl named Sherrie, threatened the intimate bond between Sam and me. I had begun spending precious time with Sherrie instead of him. In time, however, Sam realized Sherrie was indeed the girl for me. She was my true love—*the* girl I had been waiting for all my life. Just a few months before meeting Sherrie, however, I had taken Dad and Mother on a wonderful trip out west. We had mainly visited the beautiful Grand Canyon, Mother's lifelong dream. And since I had made *Mother's* dream come true, I guess God was fulfilling mine.

Of course, it had been terribly hard to hear Mother's words all those years ago about staying away from girls. But I had to finally admit that she was right.

And of course, it was also very hard to go through all I went through with Sam. But I again had to admit, he too was right.

For me, Mother was my anchor; Dad was my ship. I had sailed with my father Sam to all sorts of colorful ports while Mother consoled me when those curling waves almost sank me down to the bottom of the sea. Since living downstate, Sam had made a huge, one-acre garden on our property, canning tomatoes, cucumbers, and pickles. I guess he would always be in the food business, one way or the other. One of my main jobs was to keep the tenants happy as well as constantly cutting our couple acres of lawn with the power mower.

"I gotta be careful to dodge all sorts of slithering snakes slinking around the grounds," I said to Lynn. "This area is so hot and humid; it's a real southern climate."

"Be careful, Lee," Lynn always warned. One day I was in the garage when I heard the dogs outside barking wildly. Peering square into the face of a huge, gigantic black cat, its oblong eyes almost pierced a hole straight through my heart. Backing up slowly, my feet tiptoed carefully inside the house.

"Mom! Dad! Sherrie! There's a black panther out there!" I wheezed, my heart thumping in fear.

"Lee, have you been drinking?" The family giggled. But the following day, over our local radio station, the newscaster reported a black panther was indeed spotted on the outskirts of East St. Louis. The large cat was following the giant bluffs across from our property, chomping up any pet getting in its way. The family wasn't laughing anymore.

"All that's left of those poor folks' pets were their bones and the chains," the newscaster glumly reported. Thankfully, my own dogs had not been any of its victims. The following winter, I got rid of one of the mobile homes because the pipes had totally frozen. But by that point Mother was so fed up with Sam (unable to get out and about as freely as she did in the city), she moved into the mobile home next door.

"Your father has hit my last raw nerve," Mother groaned in pure frustration, her eyes bloodshot and bleary. "I wish he would just cease and desist! Why doesn't he mind his "P's" and "Q's and quit agitating me to pieces?" Sam, (as I had rightly figured) did not change whatsoever; it was just more smoke and mirrors. Holding her forehead inside her sweet hands, Mother's hands were wrinkled and cracked from years of washing dishes, sorting clothes, making meals, cleaning windows, and scrubbing floors. In reaction to Mother's move, and after I bought our main house from Dad, the hot dog man started missing Chicago more than anything. We had returned to Chicago to sell during the past two years of 1978 and '79, and Sam had even traveled to Brighton Park to see the new Polish Pope, Pope John Paul II in October 1979. Pressed into the gigantic crowd of Poles waiting to get a peek at the Pope, what a thrill it was for Sam.

"I was three feet from the Pope! Three feet!" Sam boasted to anyone who would listen. Watching the popular pontiff travel down Archer Avenue on the way to an outdoor Mass at Five Holy Martyrs Church in Brighton Park, "three feet," Sam once again stressed, his eyes gleaming as the brightest star in the midnight sky.

So as the trees budded anew in spring, Dad yearned to live yet again as Sam—Sam, the hot dog man. Traveling back Chicago that spring, Sam eagerly tried selling hot dogs in the Back of the Yards just one more time, for one more season.

"Dad," I pleaded, "I love you with all my heart. Please stay here with Sherrie and me," I begged. Nonetheless, Sam desperately missed the Back of the Yards, clamoring after the occupation he had known and loved for twenty-five years. In his heart of hearts Sam desperately sought the people he adored, and systematically understood, folks who loved and understood the hot dog man in return. Frankly, all three of us deeply missed our hometown. So in the spring of 1980, on the day Sam left for Chicago, it was pouring rain. It continued raining for eleven days straight. On the twelfth day, our telephone rang.

"Lee, Chicago ain't good no more," Sam heaved with a heavy, sorrowful sigh. "Ain't good for sellin'," he emphasized, his familiar breath labored but firm. "Lee, come get me." Suddenly, my heart was filled with joy. The very next day I got into my two-seater Fiat and I was in Chicago by noon. Grabbing some hot dogs, Polish, and tamales at the wholesale house, we slowly passed the famous Hylander's Ice Cream plant. By nightfall, we were back home downstate. The next day it was sunny, and so was Sam; so was I. For a while, Sam was nice. But in no time he was back at it, being his old self again. Then, one night Sherrie's eyes were dripping with tears. Her face was painted in utter frustration.

"Lee, I can't live with that guy anymore. Your Dad is just way too mean."

"Well Sherrie," I began, praying for help. "The tenants just moved out of the green house I own, about a half block away from our main house. Why don't you and Mother stay there?" I offered. "I'll stay here with Dad. Think that would work?"

So there I went, back and forth, trying with all my might to make everyone in my family happy. My plan seemed to work, for a while. Mother was peace-filled and happy. And so were Sherrie and Dad. Sherrie and I went out almost every night, often taking Mother, seeing movies and eating at nice restaurants. Likewise, I took Sam wherever *he* wanted to go. I spent plenty of time with him watching television shows like *Sanford and Son*. Then I went to the green house and watched *Miami Vice, Cheers*, and other television shows with Sherrie and Mother. Much like trying to manage the maze of harried Chicago traffic, I traveled frantically between the two houses. With that unique way of life, Sherrie and I did not marry since Sam still hadn't believed she was good enough for me. But no matter what happened, Mother always forgave. And I always obeyed my father.

"Whew," I sighed, wiping my brow. Working like a dog as I was buying and selling, and caring for my property, I once again proved to Sam my worth as a hustler. I continued keeping my family together; I desperately did not want to lose any one of them. On many days I laid on my bed thinking about the old days in Chicago. I fondly envisioned the last hot dog I helped Sam sell in 1980. Since 1955, Sam had faithfully sold in Clearing, South Chicago, parts of Englewood, Bridgeport, and of course, the Back of the Yards. With a knot threatening to strangle my throat, I sadly recalled the day someone stole our beloved dog, Gwen, (then thirteen years old), out of our backyard in Marquette Park. Lynn had an idea who had taken her, but nonetheless, it hurt us all. And I laughed deep in my belly thinking of the great times I experienced at Hubbard High, and the crazy fun Larry and I had in Marquette Park. I then reflected on one particular night we were selling hot dogs at the stand. There were no customers at the time so Sam began preaching to the smoky air like a high-flying preacher:

"You must ask and it will be given to you, seek and you will find," Sam's mouth opened in stark confidence. At that time, I was totally unaware that expression was written in the Bible. Staring toward the ceiling, I plainly visualized the push rod of the old Coleman lantern we had used for light, the lantern growing brighter and brighter against the glossy night sky of the Back of the Yards. One night on the way home from the stand, Sam suddenly pointed toward a newly built gas station near the corner of 55th.

"Old George used to have a furniture place on that very spot at 55th and Pulaski. I knew old Georgie," Sam revealed with a telling grin. "He was a Southwest Side bootlegger. Yeah, a gangster like Capone. Part of the gang." Now *my* mouth was ajar, never knowing what Sam would say next, or whom he would suddenly call an old friend. And nothing, and I mean nothing, ever bothered him. "The Man upstairs will take care of the bizness," Sam stated more times than I could count. Some nights later, a man from the projects made a bet he could run his hand through one of Sam's scooter windows. Shoving his hand right through the glass, "pull your hand out slowly," Sam warned the gassed-up guy. But that character didn't listen and part of his hand got caught on the jagged glass, hitting a vein.

"Oh no!" the girls in the crowd yelled. "Whatcha gonna do, Sam? Do something, Sam," they screamed in panic.

"I ain't gonna do nothin'," Sam answered. "Got no time to monkey with that."

"Oh Sammy!" Minutes later someone had called an ambulance, and there came the cops, speeding down 47th Street. All those "good times."

One special memory of my Grandmother Louise flatly emerged inside my tottering mind. I thought back to the day I was shooting my BB gun haphazardly at some birds in Grandma Louise's backyard. "Here iz sum bread," said Grandma one day while we were visiting her in Minnesota. "*Feed* the birds, don't hurt them," she instructed, her lips expanding in a tender smile.

Fooling around with the gun on another occasion while visiting Minnesota, I aimed at a bird and shot. Careening down from the tree, I watched as the innocent bird gave up its life. Crying my eyes out, I made a solemn promise: "God, I will never shoot another bird again in my lifetime." And so I never did. That bird gave up its poor life for my fun. That day I learned a big lesson—killing was wrong. And this truth never left me.

As the years passed, one night while Dad and I were having a few beers in East St. Louis, one of my friends from the hood decided to come to the house to see me. Drinking some brews together, my friend said, "Lee, I'll be right back."

Earlier we had been discussing guns, since at the time I had owned a few guns. Returning on his tractor, the guy started lugging out a few automatic machine guns. Like a crazy fool, I set up some targets and shot that machine gun straight through a metal sign with a block of wood stuck behind it. My gun was banging the metal sign so many times the barrel was sizzling hot. Firing like an idiot, I got my thirty aught six, and shot that thing too. Without any warning, a local cop abruptly appeared in my backyard. Shouting at the top of his lungs toward my friend and I, "Hiya fellows," he shouted. How ya all doin' tonight?"

"Fine," we sheepishly replied.

"Do you have any other guns?" the cop singled me out with his inquiry.

"I sure do, buddy," I said, handing him all my guns. Flinging every one of our guns into the police car's trunk, the cop hauled my buddy and I into the backseat of his car, the two of us under arrest. Locked up in separate cells, stinking excrement floated down a nearby trough of the jail. There were no cots in this jail, just stiff steel bunks. I could not think of anything to do so I started singing Christian songs. The jailers instantly grabbed my shoelaces so I didn't hang myself. Oddly, they forgot to check my pockets. That was exactly where my trusty pocketknife was always stashed. Every one of these beat-up bunks had gang signs and satanic emblems carved into the thin metal. Finding a free spot not yet been carved into, I boldly notched in big letters: JESUS LOVES YOU.

I was held inside that moldy cell until Dad and Mother obtained a hundred dollars for my bail. Quickly retaining a lawyer, in one minute flat my case was dismissed. But they kept all the guns and my money. That was the last time I would ever shoot a gun. In fact, one time I come across a gun I forgot I had. Tearing it apart with my bare hands, I later learned you could powerfully command

Satan out of a person who was trying to kill you instead of shooting them with a weapon. After becoming a Christian, I did that very thing while playing basketball with a guy twice my size.

"You *fouled* me," the guy on the court grumbled.

"No, I *didn't* foul you," I determinedly answered.

Staring at me with tornado-like eyes, the guy eerily warned, "I'm gonna punch you out, then I'm gonna kill you."

"I command Satan out of you in the name of Jesus!" I murmured under my breath.

"*What* did you say?" The guy yelled.

"I command Satan out of you in the name of Jesus!" I shouted back. Soon, I was nearly screaming at the top of my lungs. At that point, the big basketball player started running away, blurting all kinds of crazy things into the air. When I conveyed that story in an Iowa food store named, "Econo," a man I had never met suddenly piped up.

"I know that guy's story is true," stated the man in this grocery store. "It's true because I saw it with my own eyes."

I never in my life saw that guy from Econo. Maybe he was some sort of angel, I really didn't know. Not long after this wild incident with the police, Uncle Brett and Aunt Katrina unexpectedly purchased a house in Belleville since our area was getting bad. Before we knew it, they had moved away. Oddly enough, the door was opened for *us* to move. So Dad and I began our search. Traveling first to Stillwater, Minnesota, we hunted out our old friend, Hank. Promptly locating Hank's house, we visited the same place where we camped in 1968. Having bought an older home on some riverfront property, Hank told us he paid a full $48,000 for the entire property.

"The reason it was so high," smiling Hank reasoned, "was because in 1985, Minneapolis grew so large people started to commute from Stillwater to Minneapolis." Unlike when we were there in '68, Stillwater had expanded quite substantially. And since

Hank truly adored fishing, while in Stillwater we devoured some of the finest smoked salmon on earth. But that lovely location was not to be our new home. From Minnesota, Sam and I trekked all over the state, ending up in a campground in Tama, Iowa.

"I used to set pins in bowling alleys in Oskaloosa and Ottumwa, Iowa," Sam fondly recalled. Visiting Council Bluffs, the houses were cheap but the town didn't have the right feel. It was the same with several other Iowa towns. Camping in Iowa's south central region, we stopped in Ottumwa, a clean, quiet, hilly town decorated with a beautiful park.

Founded in 1797, the serene hills and green fields surrounding East St. Louis had been medicine to our souls. But since Katrina and Uncle Brett had sold their house next door and moved away— oh how things constantly changed!

Nevertheless, there was something attracting us to the scenic city of Ottumwa, Iowa, located on the Des Moines River. The three of us were desperately seeking peace, quiet, and happiness. We sure hoped to find it in Ottumwa's humble people, its tree-lined streets, and its modest homes. Maybe that town was it; *maybe*.

CHAPTER 24

Now You're Talkin'

"No, *thank* you," Sherrie confessed as we toured pretty Green Bay, Wisconsin. We were scouting that city out as another possible new home, but the temperature had registered forty degrees that morning, in the middle of July! While passing through Chicago on our way home, I took Sherrie up to the Sears Tower sky deck; how amazed she was at the view from the 103rd floor. Traveling home in my one-hundred-dollar, 1950's Studebaker, Sherrie, Mother, and I then returned to Tama, Iowa. Camping there overnight, we headed to Ottumwa, seeking out a realtor for a listing of homes. Exploring all sorts of houses, Sherrie and I settled on one.

"Oh, that house is gonna cost way too much," I cynically commented. Shifting my feet from side to side, my tattered pants and shirt whooshed against my perspiring body.

"Well, let's just see," Sherrie countered, brightening my mood.

Discovering the house listed at $7,900.00, I remarked in the surprise of my life, "What?! Well, let's have a look inside."

When the realtor took us inside the house, without hesitation Sherrie firmly agreed. "Lee, this is the house."

Examining the roof and the basement of the two-story,

bark-colored frame home, I made an offer to the realtor for seven thousand even.

"I'll call you as soon as I know if the owner will accept your offer," the realtor said. "How is your credit?"

At that stark moment, considering all I had ever been through with my father, Sam, (all those days and nights of selling dogs, tamales, and Polish sausage in the rain, heat, fog, and cold) one thing he always stressed was paying with cash:

"Cash is king, Lee Boy," Sam continually voiced.

"I'm going to pay cash," I disclosed, her face as cheerful as an August rosebush. In no time at all, the realtor telephoned back.

"They'll take the seven thousand," she happily declared.

Obtaining a cashier's check for the transaction, Sam and I traveled to Ottumwa with the camper. On October 29th, 1987, we took possession of the house, paid in full. Returning to East St. Louis we said good-bye to Uncle Brett and Aunt Katrina, traveling back and forth until everything was sold. In a few months, we were in Ottumwa for good. Known as, "The City of Bridges," Ottumwa was located in Wapello County, Iowa, split in half by the Des Moines River. For an entire decade, living in Iowa was like heaven. On our home's second floor, Sherrie and I had our own bedroom next to Mother's room while Dad had his private quarters downstairs. Together yet apart, that seemed to be the best way for Mother and Sam to coexist, the ultimate love-hate relationship.

"Lee, you sure have cheap property taxes," Lynn exclaimed to me over the telephone one night, comparing her Illinois' tax bill to Iowa's relatively lower cost of living. By that time, Steve and Lynn were busily raising their family, living in suburban Chicago.

"Mother, Dad, and Sherrie and I split all the bills in our new house," I told Lynn. "So things are working out really well." Scouring hundreds of garage sales in the summer months for antiques to buy and sell, Sam and I attended several auctions around Wapello County. Additionally, I had also started a small lawn care business. Even though I was not making that much money, I was thrilled my family was content under one roof. From time to time, Mother and Sam squabbled, but by then I figured that was how they got their juices going, so to speak. I, for one, was grateful each one of my precious parents had their own little corner to take a break and regroup, enjoying their retirement years and well-deserved rest.

"Wanna barbecue tonight?" I questioned Dad one warm summer afternoon. His large garden at the right side of the house was flourishing, brimming with plump tomatoes, crisp cucumbers, onions, and fragrant dill for canning. Sam was often called "Pops," and unless he was sleeping he constantly wore a dark beige fedora, the cigar-fragranced hat framing his nearly baldhead from morning till night.

"Yeah, I'm hungry," Dad readily agreed, having turned sixty-four in November 1988. Dad and I attended the Catholic church each Sunday, while Mother faithfully went to the Methodist church on Church Street, several blocks away. There was very little crime in Ottumwa. No, we only had some jaywalking and public intoxication, akin to the character, Otis, on *The Andy Griffith Show*. Blessed with air clean as crystal, the sky was sapphire blue. Our local grocery store sold the finest meats in the country's heartland since Ottumwa was famous for its various meatpacking houses and corporations. Oddly enough, many of those same corporations had originally been located in Chicago's, Back of the Yards. And Ottumwa's supermarket workers always took their customers' shopping carts into the parking lot for them, politely loading groceries inside your car's trunk. God had given us a wonderful gift, living in such a tranquil place especially after all those years of gut-wrenching stress.

Seated in our backyard at the picnic table, Sam and I guzzled beer after beer as we chatted about how good God had been to us. "Isn't God good?" I regularly asked Sam.

Nodding, the two of us blabbered on for hours. During the first eight years we were in Ottumwa, Dad and I had dumped about 150 tons of gravel on our driveway, maintaining the property the best I possibly could.

"Everything is in top shape," Sam quipped, his cataract-plagued eyes gazing at the poured grey gravel. As his sight scrutinized my latest work, Dad's approval was still so very vital. Although the *house* was in top shape, *I* paraded around Ottumwa like a homeless bum. My pants were in shreds because I never bought a stitch of new clothing, never. Only receiving clothes at Christmas from Sherrie and Mother, I carefully saved every penny. If I bought anything at all, it was not for my own personal pleasure but solely for the purpose of resale, in order to make a profit. That seemed to be my mission in life: buy low and sell high.

"Wake up and smell the coffee," Sam still barked, one of his all-time favorite sayings. Often addressing Mother with that silly catchphrase, by the mid-1990's, Jerry, Gus, Sam, Ralph, "Pops," had finally mellowed with time.

"Come down to the basement," I called to Dad one wintry day in 1995. "I want to show you something," I added. My heart walloped hard against my chest as Sam followed me down the musty, but well-built basement stairs. Handing Sam my bankbook, chills raced through my blood. With fourteen thousand dollars in the bankbook, near where Dad and I stood were two metal safes. Each safe overflowed with money. Spending hours chiseling out a hole in the basement wall about thirteen inches deep, a 1920's safety deposit box I had found at a garage sale was ready for my use. Mixing slushy cement with water and plaster, I carried over some paint and a brand new roll of large, clear plastic tape and plastic wrap. Fetching Dad a cigar and a beer, I proudly rested wads of hundreds, fifties, and twenty-dollar bills in the presence of King Sam. The whole stack was nearly a foot high.

"Dad," I addressed him in all seriousness as if he was our nation's president. "You told me when I was six years old to save my money. Remember?" As I displayed the big pile of money, in addition to a five-thousand-dollar IRA, Dad's mouth blossomed into a full-blown beam. Knowing my life had vividly merged into that one dramatic moment, in order to please my father I had done my level best to fully obey. Squishing down all the money, I bound the pile of bills tightly with the clear plastic wrap. Taping the bundle firmly, I scribbled on the plastic with a marker: $35,000.00. Stuffing it into the steel box, there was so much money it could barely all fit. Locking the box with an old, long key, I placed it snugly inside the cold basement wall. Carefully arranging screening around the box, I then cemented it securely inside the wall. Sitting and gabbing in the basement, Sam and I drank beer as the gritty cement dried. Placing yet more screening inside the cement for added protection, I plastered over the top until it mimicked the stucco wall. After gulping down another beer, I painted the top of it with the same paint I used to coat the basement walls. My job was finally complete.

"Now you're talkin'," squealed Sam with joy as if I'd discovered a cure for some fatal disease. "Yeah, you finally got some smarts."

Smarts? Though I was totally electrified by Dad's verbal acceptance, climbing up the stairs from the dingy basement my forehead suddenly crumpled. My brain did twists as I realized some of that plastered-in money came from the two-cent pop bottles I had picked up in Marquette Park, walking eight full blocks in order to get thirty-two cents. Some of that money stemmed from the first twenty-five-cent pocketknife I sold at school when I was only six years old. And some of the money came from the times when Dad gave me an allowance. While all the other kids in the lunchroom were eating hot meals on a very cold day, I would be munching on broken pretzels I had paid a nickel apiece to the lunch lady. Some of that money also came from the many times

I would go without food I could have bought when I was really hungry. And some of the money came from the cold streets I would deliberately walk because I hadn't wanted to shell out change for a bus. And some of that money came from the many, many times I had sold bubble gum to the kids at school for a penny. *All that money. All that pain.*

Nevertheless, all that suffering was worth every minute because my father, Chicago's famous hot dog man, was proud of me on that great night in our Iowa basement in the winter of 1995. The New Year of 1996 arrived with great optimism, especially for Sherrie and me. When summer arrived, Dad and I were yet again enjoying another delicious cookout. When Dad went into the house to use the bathroom, my eyes were suddenly impressed to look up at the billowy clouds. Scanning down to the wood trim on the house, I started to think. For some reason since the start of that year, I had begun reading the Bible daily. Turning the crisp pages of Scripture, its words started to gently turn my own heart.

"Lee, are you reading the *Bible*?" Mother curiously inquired, noticing I had been spending hours quietly alone in my bedroom.

"Yes Mom, I am."

Peering intently at the house's tan trim while Sam was still in the house, I unexpectedly expressed some unusual words from the depths of my heart:

"God, whatever you want to do to me on this earth, do it, God. I want to go to heaven and I want *you* to be happy with me."

At the mute, heartfelt expression, my soul felt as if I was floating in another place. The summer of 1996 quickly moved into 1997. On New Year's Eve, an auctioneer friend and his wife came to the house to celebrate. During our joyous celebration I did not realize everything in my life was about to change. Yet, back on that summer's day when I happened to stare up at the tan house trim, I could sense something was "in the air." At the time, I thought it was the house trim talking to me, but actually it was God. The

Holy Spirit had been preparing me, just like Sam had prepared me for different events that would unfold in my life. Yes, God was preparing me, just as Mother had lovingly prepared me …

"How can you live with all this rag bag furniture?" Mother asked me with a baffled gaze at the start of the New Year. Pondering Mother's strange question, I suddenly began to see her point. "You should at least get a new couch," she remarked. Almost instantly, I started spending money for the first time in my life. Freely buying some nice rugs, new pictures, new drapes, and a couch, remarkably, everything was brand new in the downstairs portion of the house. I even bought beautiful new doors. Mother really wanted it, so I redid everything especially for her. Sam certainly didn't care about the furnishings; he was saturated in his own world. And while Sherrie liked the new furniture, it didn't really matter to her one way or the other. It was all for Mother, and she was thrilled to pieces I had finally made our house look nice. That January I began to realize idle money was worse than a flea-bitten dog, way worse. At least the fleas were doing something! Then, out of the blue, Mother complained her side was hurting terribly. It was a deep, slicing pain.

"I think I need to see a chiropractor for my back," she moaned, softly massaging the lower edge of her body. Mother's treatment at the chiropractor, however, was of little help. As a result, she decided to go to the nearby clinic. Reaching for the ringing telephone, I listened to Mother's quivery voice at the opposite end: "Lee, they've found a tumor on my liver." The second I heard those awful words, time eerily stood still. "They're going to run some tests," Mother warily added. We went to the hospital daily, and by February our dear Mother had hospice nurses assisting her every move. Lynn and her family traveled to Iowa to visit Mother, and I could tell Lynn's oldest child, (Mother's first granddaughter), was pretty torn up about the desperate illness of her only living grandmother.

Lynn stayed as strong as possible, but she too was hurting badly. Meanwhile, Sam was in denial.

"Ouch," I yelled one afternoon while tending to Mother. My foot was swollen, throbbing like anything. I soon discovered my foot was broken. Lying down on Mother's bed just like I did when I was a little boy, "Jesus will take care of everything, Mom," I tried to encourage. Shifting around on the bed, I hoped to get comfortable. After returning home, while the two of us were watching television in her room one day, Mother sat halfway up. With her mouth slightly ajar, she whispered into the sterile air,

"Lee, I don't feel like I am going to die." Mother sighed. Hugging her as tightly as I could, she asked if I might rub her back. My fingers gently massaged the area near her liver; I was doing everything possible to ease her pain. For as long as I could remember, Mother had given me unconditional love. I deeply desired to give that love back to her in return. "I want to go back to the hospital," she requested suddenly with a pale, puckered brow.

"Okay," I agreed. Immediately, I helped Mom get settled inside the city's main hospital.

"I struggled so much in my early life," Mother weakly began to recall bits from her shattered past. "So when I met your father," she continued, using all the strength she could muster. "When I met your father, I asked God if He would give me *another* boy and girl to replace the two I had lost. 'I will dedicate them to you,' I solemnly promised. And that is what I did."

And sure enough, that was exactly what had happened. Lynn and I had been dedicated to God many years before our births. It had all begun to make, *perfect sense.*

CHAPTER 25

I Sure Miss Virge

"She will die on Sunday." Hearing that jarring word of warning, I darted up straight as a needle in the bed where I lay opposite Mother. By some strange circumstance, two angels had invoked those telling words inside my soul. Showing me exactly what would happen following Mother's death, I dreamed I was seated on a leather couch while two men from a funeral home soberly spoke. Upon awakening, I blurted out with sweat pouring down my armpits: "Sherrie! Sherrie! Mom is going to die on Sunday." And that was how it happened, exactly the way the angels had shown me. Standing near Mother's bed, I uttered for one last time out of a million previous times, "Mom, I love you."

"I love you too, Lee," she whispered with locked eyes, her breathing having grown gradual and thin. "I can see my whole body," she suddenly expressed in a bleary fog, an otherworldly air encompassing the entire room. "I can smell clover, like the clover fields from the farm, the sweetest clover I ever … " Mother trailed off in strange sigh, her words fading, her life on earth nearing its end.

The next day, the nurses relayed whenever Mother was in pain I could push a button to relieve it through strong medicines invading her system. Yet, whenever I pushed that button, I felt I was pushing Mother closer to eternity. Lengthy shadows crept over my face as the following morning I awoke with a sudden twinge. On that Sunday morning, I pressed the button then curled my arms tightly around Mother. At two o'clock in the afternoon on March 9, 1997, Sam's loyal, faithful, and believing wife, and our tender, long-suffering Mother, Virginia "Virgie" Mae Polachek, died peacefully in my arms.

"I could feel her spirit leave her body, Sherrie," I expressed the words breathlessly. "Her scent, her love, and her spirit are gone," I edged. Tears generously soaked our eyes as Sherrie and I stared at the ceiling. Mournfully, we waved "good-bye" to Mother. "Bye, bye, Mom," Sherrie and I bid her farewell through the shower of tears washing our faces. "She was the sweetest, softest, most tender person I've ever met, the exact opposite of hard-nosed Sam," I told Sherrie amidst my sobs.

"Do you want to stay here with her?" one of the nurses asked.

"No, she's gone. She's gone now," I replied. In moments, I was seated on a leather couch and two funeral men came to speak with me, precisely as the angels foretold. "Mom has died," I informed Dad when we finally arrived home, my eyes having turned blood-shot and watery. Before me was Sam, King of 47th Street, the man who had lost the only woman with enough spiritual fortitude to endure his lifetime of addiction, intimidation, and pain. His stiff mouth instantly paled from the news,

"No lie?" Sam questioned in disbelief.

"She's gone," I tearfully admitted.

For the first several hours, Sam was in silent denial of Mother's death. Later on, he freely admitted the loss. "Man, I sure miss Virge," Dad moaned in sheer agony. *I* could hardly believe it either. When everyone was against me, Mother was there. When I was sick, *she* was right there. Nursing me back to health, there were so many times she came to my aid. When I was confused, beaten, and worn-out, Mother was always there, supernaturally equipped with a cheer-filled word.

Worrying over everything I ever did, Mother always knew how I felt inside. Helping anyone whoever came across her path, Mother despised when people took advantage of others. Sobbing over any stray dog haphazardly wandering into the street, her compassion was renowned, particularly toward battered women as well as the tiniest creature created by God. Lynn and I could have never wished for a better Mother. And Sam was sure blessed to have Virginia as a wife because without Virginia, Sam would have died many times over. Even though they argued constantly, deep down, Virginia and Sam possessed an unusual love strangely unable to be broken. It was a relationship divinely instituted by the Lord God. Sure, I took care of Mother when she was sick, but she cared for anyone who entered her presence, (especially the outcasts and underdogs), giving them unconditional love, with no strings attached.

My Worst and My Best Day — *It was the night of Mother's funeral, March 12, 1997. At seven o'clock, I trudged up to my bedroom. My heart was torn into a billion, tear-stained pieces. The pain of Mother's death, her stark departure seemed unbearable. I loved Mom so very much and she loved me so much in return. Her love was gone, vanished like a brilliant autumn leaf in the bitter wind. Even then, I could still hear Mother's heartening phrase: 'Lee, don't worry. Everything will work out.' But it didn't work out. Giving up all hope I desperately prayed:*

Dear Lord God, I don't want what this
world has to offer. I can't take
it anymore. Dear Lord Jesus, I am a sinner.
I believe, You, Jesus Christ,
died on the cross for my sins and You,
Jesus, rose from the dead. Please

forgive my sins, Jesus. Come into my heart,
Jesus. Save me, Jesus. Amen.

Suddenly, I felt an inexplicable peace. It was the strongest love I'd ever felt. I knew what love was, but that kind of love was totally different. The entire world of pain, suffering, and sin had been lifted from my chest. I could fly! I could fly! So much joy welled inside my heart I hollered, IT'S JESUS! IT'S JESUS! Jesus saved me and I was so happy I couldn't contain the love. Jumping up and down, the carpeted wooden floor beneath me creaked and softly swayed. I realized I wasn't going to die the death of eternal hell. No, I was going to live forever. At age 36, on the night of March 12, 1997, at seven o'clock at night, in my second-floor bedroom in Ottumwa, Iowa, my worst day was miraculously transformed into my best day.

Opening my eyes the next morning, I felt altogether different.

"Wow! I was free at last! The truth, I had discovered, plainly created hope, hope where none had ever existed before. Dad, Sherrie, and I were attending the Catholic church across from our house, going to Mass each and every Sunday. The church's young priest, Father Ted, came to visit me, recalling how torn up I was at Mother's funeral service at the Methodist church where she had faithfully attended.

Walking inside our front door, Father Ted questioned me with an uneasy frown, "How are you doing, Lee?"

"I'm feeling great," I replied with a spongy smile. Eyeing me as if I had flipped my lid, the four of us held hands and prayed. On the telephone later that night, I explained to Father Ted how Jesus saved me on the night of Mother's funeral. Telling me he too was saved, Father Ted remarked how blessed I was to have had such a beautiful experience with the Lord. Eventually, I continued working as hard as usual. But my heart was not in my work as it had once been. Months later, on September 14, 1997, I woke up at 5 a.m. Beforehand, I had completely restored a van, making the vehicle look almost as good as new. That morning, the van was ready to be sold to a young couple.

Give them the van, I heard the Holy Spirit of God distinctly relay.

"*I will,*" came my quick reply. As soon as I uttered those words, I was filled with the Holy Spirit, speaking in a heavenly language, unable to stop laughing. I wanted to yell to the world — "JESUS IS REAL; THE HOLY SPIRIT IS ALIVE!"

That entire day I went around laughing and giggling in the lightness of my freedom from the heaviness of sin. When the young couple placed $2,400.00 in front of me for the price of the van, I gave the money right back to them, signing over the title and charging them only one dollar. The van, however, had only one key so I returned their dollar saying, "Here's your dollar back for a new key." Thrilled, I, of course, possessed even greater happiness than the young couple since my soul was filled with carloads of joy. That was only the beginning of my release from the insatiable greed that continually ruled my young life.

For seven months, God taught me a variety of lessons. Pouring thoughts, ideas, and concepts deep into my soul, I was like a cactus being watered in the middle of a desert. Writing seven books, I read the Bible so much I wore out two of them in no time. I laughed, I cried, I drew pictures of Jesus, and I wrote spiritual poems. I talked to God and He talked to me. And I gave away money to Christian ministries, and even more money to the poor. One day I opened my basement safe, and I finally confessed the truth to Sherrie,

"There is $35,000 down here, Sherrie," I calmly admitted. "I have hidden it all behind this wall."

"Lee, you've got to be kidding," Sherrie shrieked, her mouth falling wide open as our back door. Putting the money into a CD account, we gave some of it away as the Lord led. My conversion was so extreme, I witnessed to everyone from basketball players to people on the street. I eagerly visited 7,000 houses on our city's south side, bringing them the Good News of Jesus Christ. Meanwhile, as my first book was being published, every time it returned from the publisher, I found another major error.

"The more I learn about God and the Bible," I told Lynn by phone, "the less I actually know." Visiting practically every church in our town, I followed so many doctrines I became totally confused. For a grueling ten-day stretch, all I did was write and read the Bible, barely eating, and not even taking a bath. Thousands of papers littered my bedroom floor until one stray paper finally read: "It is done now and Jesus loves you." Eventually, all my money was used up except for my $5,500.00 CD. On our anniversary, with the last $150.00 I owned, I purchased a ring for Sherrie, and we were finally married on April 16, 1997.

Cupping my cheeks inside my two palms, one night at the beginning of 1998, I realized we are nearly penniless. Seated at our wood kitchen table, Sam suddenly urged, "Lee, get a job in a factory."

"Okay," I instantly agreed with Dad, as usual. That is what I did, always obeying my father without question. Many people were saved in the factory where I worked for well over a year. On the other hand, the factory was also a terribly dangerous place. It was so dangerous, I was badly injured by the blades of a machine slicing off one of my fingers. After experiencing horrifying nightmares from the incident, I was ultimately sent home for good. Suffering the effects of nerve damage and severe PTSD, I found myself disabled, and on constant medication. "I never thought something like this could happen to me," I told Sherrie months later. As the seasons passed, I began holding church services inside my home, and several people were healed, saved, and delivered. But in my home church, I preached the same way most modern preachers preached. It soon became impossible to deny the fact I was genuinely disabled. *Maybe God had a specific reason for it. Just maybe.*

"Send the papers for me to cancel the book," I finally directed the publisher. And although the publisher talked about the potential money we might generate, I recognized the book I had worked on for so long was nothing but a lie. For the next seven years, Sherrie and I cared exclusively for Sam. Watching over him ever since the onset of the Alzheimer's disease that was stealing away his body and his once, razor-sharp mind, the dreadful disease began to pull the plug on Sam's life.

"I wish I didn't have this old-timer's," Sam often complained with a fractured frown. Frail and thin, Dad wandered the house, unaware of the day, month, who the president is, or even the current year. Chicago's Sam was nowhere to be found, a mere shell of the hot dog man, "The King of 47th Street." After months of debilitation and a brief hospital stay, we restlessly brought Dad home. Without warning, on a crisp autumn night in 2003, the father I had known and loved all my life, Ralph, "Sam, the Hot Dog Man" Polachek had passed away.

Ralph—Minnesota kid, football player, fourteen-year-old castaway

Jerry—Chicago hustler, tough jerry-rigging man of a thousand streets

Gus—South Side businessman, friend of the Jews as well as the Greeks

Sam—"Nize day" Back of the Yards' jiver, fierce-working husband and father, King of 47th Street

Gone. Sam had died of natural causes.

"I can't believe Dad is gone," I moaned to Sherrie repeatedly.

"Neither can I," Sherrie shook her head. "Neither can I."

Decades of torment slowly drained from my shoulders as I sat on a chair and thought. Though my mind was muddled with grief, there were two things I desperately needed to learn—how to *live*, and how to *die*. My father, Sam Polachek, taught me these two vital things, in his own special way. My insides quivered as I realized God alone had placed us on this earth. And when He alone says we had accomplished our mission, only then was it time to make our final exit. Many people, for instance, have jumped off San Francisco's Golden Gate Bridge and then cried, "Oh no, I made a mistake." Somehow, through God's mercy, they have lived to tell about it. Honestly, the truth of *all* truths was that people might have planned all kinds of things, but the Lord's will would always be accomplished.

"I doubt anyone has ever experienced as many jobs as our father," I said one night to Lynn, pondering Sam's life in wonder.

Starting out selling newspapers as a boy in Minnesota, then working in bowling alleys and taverns as a young man, after hopping train after train, Dad routinely worked in the coal and lead mines of the West. Shifting eastward, he worked, "The Roxy Bowl" in New York's Bowery, Buffalo's "Main Street Bowl," Cincinnati's "Hog Head Joe's," the "Roger Bowl" in St. Louis, and Milwaukee's "Billy Sixty Bowl," named after Wisconsin legend William Soechting. While laboring in produce companies and factories of all types, he often worked at the largest corn refining plant in the world.

"That plant had the biggest rats on earth," Sam remarked, demonstrating their enormous size with his huge hands. "Those suckers were big as dogs."

Sam once worked with a guy who owned a semi-truck, the guy stopping in the middle of any street so he could pick up stray hubcaps. While working at a lumberyard near 47th and Hoyne, Sam once delivered a single piece of plywood to a Lake Shore Drive high-rise, hauling it up the elevator, a few blocks from the Magnificent Mile. Making money as a cement man in construction, he especially loved working the railroads, about fifty railroad companies in all. Regularly maintaining the train tracks, Sam moved the heavy railroad ties, and he checked the spike rails as well as the switch cars. Often cooking in the train galleys, Sam worked any job besides being a train engineer. Doing some roofing with his old pals, Sam had worked at General Foods and Yellow Freight. He did painting from time to time, and once worked for our uncle's moving company. While visiting the Pioche, Nevada lead mines in 1982 where he had worked during World War II, Sam was thrilled to learn it had become an actual gold mine. From doing light hauling with a step van, to setting up at flea markets and working hundreds of garage sales in Iowa with Lee, though Sam drank heavily since having his first beer at age ten, he never had a headache until the last three months of his life. Although Sam was never prone to headaches, ironically Virginia was often plagued with severe migraines though never taking a drop of alcohol since the moment Lee and I were conceived. An iconic card player, (especially Poker) as well as a pool hustler in just about every tavern he set foot, Sam loved to charm "half-twisted" men with his pinball expertise, the poor cads wondering what had happened the moment Sammy got a hold of them.

Our father, "Sam, the Hot Dog Man," was often a package of grating irritation. But more often than not, he was a package of intense intimidation, and jaw-dropping honesty.

For most of his chaotic life, Sam lived in a brutal emotional storm. However, whenever anyone asked how he was feeling, Sam always replied, with his cigar meandering from side to side within his broad, rugged mouth,

"I'm in Top Shape. Yeah. Top Shape."

During his final year, though Sam's mental state had greatly declined, he may not have known it, but our father continued to be in, *"Top Shape."*

EPILOGUE—LYNN

Along the shoreline of a serene lake near my home, perched on a sturdy limb across the turquoise water sat a regal, snowy white heron. Locking my sight onto the large graceful bird, back and forth its head incessantly rotated. The elegant ivory heron diligently studied the soothing waves, searching the water for prospective prey. Watching the huge bird's detailed observation of not only the water but also my own human form, it was as if the stately bird mimicked much of my life with Sam. I could not get the question out of my mind: *Did God give me the wrong father?*

Smoothing my hair in the light lake breeze, I had realized early on my father was curiously complex, deeply troubled, and always "on the run." Whenever he *was* around, fear, roaring criticism, intimidation, and addiction surrounded him like a hovering cloud but what was the purpose? The moment I decided to forgive, that act of mercy opened the pathway toward *understanding* God's plan. Sam's harsh life in a strange way had become a gift, a hidden blessing still being unraveled. Just as Lee believed Sam was hard on him so he would be prepared for the tougher things of life, likewise, Dad's intimidating manner, his grueling alcoholism, and his frequent absences had taught *me* many lessons, having directed me into the loving arms of my heavenly Father.

At age thirteen I gave my heart, soul, body, and mind to Jesus

Christ. Some months later, while visiting Sam's childhood home when I was fourteen years old, the initial onset of my understanding began.

As an adult, my relationship with Sam had finally grown agreeable yet many mysteries remained. One morning, following Dad's death, God had led me to search one of those mysteries. Recalling how frequently Sam had spoken of his royal lineage proudly sputtering,

"I am king of this castle and you are the peasants," Dad customarily boasted on more times than I could count. Stalwartly he added, "I am a king."

Divinely guided to an old atlas on royal European genealogy, I quickly leafed through the musty pages to the German House of Bavaria, since I had discovered Sam was of German descent. A particular dynasty caught my eye. That dynasty was one of the royal families ousted the same era Dad had always claimed his father, Albert, had arrived in America following the World War I revolution. Amazed at a photograph of Bavaria's King Lietpold I had discovered in our local library, the king's resemblance to Sam was so strong it was as if my own father was staring at me from the grave! That king, along with prior Bavarian kings, and all the way back to Otto the Great, every royal portrait held some overt physical characteristic of Sam.

Studying the fractured relationship between these kings and their sons, I began to compare their family traits to the characteristics of my own family of origin. From the family's sterile remoteness, as well as the lack of emotion common to palace life, to their affection for cigars and Bavarian beer, to their strict adherence to Catholicism, their bizarre peculiarities, to their stifled then overwhelming anger, including stomping their feet as well as their intimidating pride, and to the immorality frequent to many monarchies, repeatedly I was awed.

Then, in a remarkable turn of events in my exhaustive search, on the very night of Dad's death God gave me a trio of astounding dreams.

In my first dream, I plainly saw a particular castle, the family home of a Bavarian king. The roof of that castle was on fire, dark smoke heavily billowing into the sky. I interpreted the dream to portray the various generational transferences of that lineage being burnt away. My second dream depicted a nineteenth-century monarch standing at the foot of this same castle. The king had twisted a thin wire against a man's throat, ruthlessly strangling him. I thought back to some of Sam's callous attitudes, as well as my own elementary school incident when a little boy had tried to strangle me. And my third dream involved a father with three children, two girls and a boy. That father was not very concerned about his children's welfare, caring more about his own life and personal comforts. The dream demonstrated my own father, Sam, never had a proper fatherly example to follow; he had done the best he could. Understanding and mercy overwhelmed my soul.

With that vital information, I mercifully began to understand, and forgive, much of my father's behaviors, attitudes, and oddities, realizing they were formed outside of himself, bearing in mind it was all for a purpose. Whenever confronted with intimidation of any sort, *because of Sam* I was equipped with extraordinary understanding, accustomed to dealing with one of the greatest intimidators the world had ever seen. Secondly, change was Sam's trademark: *changing* cities, *changing* jobs, *changing* situations, and *changing* names. But *because of Sam*, I could change at a moment's notice. Lastly, *because of Sam*, I possessed a knack for relating to different cultures and groups—just like Sam.

During the uneasy days following Sam's death, I began to think about his eternal home: *Is Dad truly in heaven?* Astonishingly, God gave me yet another dramatic dream. Slim and in his mid-thirties, in that wonderful dream Sam was standing in a brilliantly white room, holding a big pile of clothes. Looking straight into my eyes, Sam confidently exclaimed, "I don't need these old clothes anymore, Lynn," Dad said. "No, I've got new ones," he stated with stark assurance.

When awakening from the dream, I was overwhelmed with peace, confident my father was indeed in heaven, having accomplished *all* the Lord had created him to do. That dream had confirmed every situation that happened to Dad, Mother, Lee, and I occurred for an expressed purpose. Through untold suffering, as well as moments of fun, joy, and reflection, it was all His design.

Portraying himself as a Chicago tough guy, (and he truly was) few ever had the nerve to mess with Sam. Amazingly, the tough hustler, the father I knew and strived with all my might to understand, actually kept his first love's diary right up until his dying day.

But because of Sam's intimidation and alcoholism, as a child I often thought I must have gotten the wrong father. In reality, even though there appeared to be much bad in my life with Sam, God had meant it *all* for the good. Principally, since Sam was an expert intimidator, I was instantly able to identify the spirit of intimidators who crossed my path. And because of Sam's relentless alcoholism, I was free from destructive addictions since I had witnessed their devastation firsthand.

Yes, by the grace of God, He had given me the perfect father, the exact one I exactly needed. He had given the right father all along.

SAM'S 25 TOP SAYINGS

1. "Nize Day!"
2. "Never Fear, Sammy's Here!"
3. Holding up a hot dog, Sam says to an adoring crowd: "All dressed and ready to eat; someone take a picture. Come on, come on. Take a picture of this baby, she's beeeautiful!"
4. "$10-Sawski; $20-Double Sawski; $5-Fin; $1/$100-One Bean; 50 Cents-Four Bits"
5. "Dey saw you comin' a mile away, you chumpo."
6. "That sucker thought he was gonna catch me-Huh!"
7. "You can catch a thief, but it's almost impossible to catch a liar."
8. "Don't put off today what you can put off tomorrow."
9. "Good shoes make a man."
10. "Don't slouch your shoulders back straight!"
11. "My name's Sammy. Sammy, the Hot Dog King. King of 47th Street."
12. "Eat hearty; it may your last!"
13. "He who hesitates is lost."
14. "Back of the Yards—good peoples."
15. "God takes care of drunks and fools."
16. "If ya move any slower, you'll stop altogether."
17. "Watch out for the quiet ones-they're always thinkin'."

18. "I was three feet from the Pope—Gimme anoder shot of *Zabrooska*, will ya?"
19. "Ain't no one can git ahead of me."
20. "Never point a gun at no one unless you're gonna shoot that sucker!"
21. "There ain't nothin' worse than waitin'."
22. "What's a matter by you, you deef?"
23. "A dull knife will cut you faster than a sharp one."
24. "Always be prepared, like a Boy Scout."
25. "Goodbye Charlie. That's all she wrote!"